the CRIMSON gods

CHRIS M CHRISTIAN

the
CRIMSON
gods

The Crimson Gods

ISBN: 978-1-7373430-2-8 (Paperback)
ISBN: 978-1-7373430-1-1 (Hardcover)
ISBN: 978-1-7373430-0-4 (eBook)
ISBN: 978-1-7373430-3-5 (Audiobook)

Library of Congress Control Number: 2021911984

Illustrations: Ertaç Altınöz
Cover Design: Damonza
Map Design by Kellerica Maps
Formatting: Enchanted Ink Publishing
Editing: Enchanted Ink Publishing, Lambda Editing, Angela Traficante, Amanda Rutter

Printed by Lochmoor Productions LLC / SmokeScreen Press in the United States of America.

First printing edition 2021.

Lochmoor Productions LLC
PO Box 1011
Kannapolis, NC 28083

WWW.CHRISMCHRISTIAN.COM

SmokeScreen press

For Kamdyn.
What do we do when we fall down?

Prologue

The change was abrupt. Merek had never seen such fog. It loomed ahead as if the gods had poured a thick cloud upon the earth. It seemed a living thing, twisting slowly, devouring itself. The Order of Preceptors had not written much of this place, but whispers of its past were steeped in mystery and legend, among darker tales. This "giant's breath," as some called it, made those tales seem more believable.

"What are we doing here again?" Mitchel, his apprentice, asked from the back of his horse.

"You know damn well why we are here," said Merek.

"No, why are *we* here?"

"We volunteered, remember?"

"*You* volunteered."

Merek looked over to him. "Mitch, you've always wanted to go on these wanderings as much as I have. We get to travel and meet interesting people. In return, we simply have to report back the condition of roads and any specifics worth noting to the council."

Mitch rolled his eyes. "And sleep on the ground most nights."

"Is there some other reason you would rather be home? Do the stories of this place scare you?"

Mitch did not respond.

"Is it my sister?" Merek prodded.

"Why would you say that?"

"I see the way you look at her."

Mitch looked to the isle ahead. "Ashaya? Nonsense."

Merek smiled as Mitch's cheeks turned a rosy red.

Mitch glanced away. "Let's take a look so we can go home and report."

"No, Mitch, *you* go home. Tell them we made it," said Merek.

"I was only japing. Mostly." Confusion crept into Mitch's tone. "Go home? Now?"

"Yes." Merek climbed off his destrier and patted his neck. Shadow seemed uneasy here, nickering at him. Merek removed the leather band from his long silver-blond ponytail. His scalp ached from the constant pull.

Mitch brushed the hair from his eyes. "What is there to report? Looks to be just another isle. Why would you stay here alone?"

"The council is likely already arriving in Wolfpine. Go report to them. Small isle or not, I want to have a proper look," Merek said, staring across the water.

"An isle where people go missing!" Mitch pointed out.

"So the 'ceptors say."

"And the fisherman!"

"Do you believe every story your mother told you while putting you to bed?"

"Fine." Mitchel had that look on his face. He had been Merek's apprentice long enough to know there was no point in arguing. "What will you do?"

"I will find a way across on the morrow and have a look around. It should only take two days, three at most."

Mitch stood quietly for a moment. "I do not like this place."

"Why? Is it this place, or what you have *heard* of this place?"

"Both. And it smells like shit." Mitchel turned to him. "Are you sure?"

"Yes. Go. I will be fine." They both turned toward the snapping of a dead tree limb in the wood behind them. "I think."

They both chuckled. Merek noticed a subtle tension around Mitch's grey eyes. "Go on, you will be fine. Besides, we managed to stay out of trouble on the way here by keeping near the coast. You can take the Middle Sea to Capeton and be home within two days if the winds are favorable." Merek lifted the short skirt of his black, boiled-leather armor and dug out a sack of coins, tossing it to Mitchel. He caught it clumsily, almost falling from his horse. The sack clinked as he pulled it from the air.

"Alright. But for the record, this is not my idea. I will tell your family—"

"I will tell them myself. I will not be far behind you."

Mitchel mounted his horse and turned back toward the wood. "Are you—"

Merek could not help but smile. "Dammit, Mitch!"

"I just wanted to be sure. I will see you in a few days."

Merek watched him vanish into the wood and turned back toward the isle. Shadow turned to him, nudging Merek's shoulder with his muzzle. "Do not look at me like that. He needs to know that I will not always be by his side."

Before the fog stood hundreds of trees, blackened and gnarled, with their limbs twisting downward. Their bark resembled charred parchment, each tree reaching toward the earth with a hundred scorched arms, weeping in their corruption. *Mitch was right.* The air smelled of decay but with a tinge of sweetness riding the breeze. There existed a vast difference between what he looked upon across the water and where he stood now.

Merek stretched his arms out to his sides and looked up, enjoying the sun's warmth on his face. Small waves rippled before him, and the song of leafhoppers echoed behind. Merek sighed deeply, closing his eyes, savoring the last drop of sunlight. He turned back to make camp in a wooded area a few hundred yards behind him, where the strange ruins lay.

His journey had begun many fortnights ago, although he had lost exact count of the days. He was leagues from his home in Vaegomar and had no boat to get to the isle. *Perhaps there is a bridge of some kind. If not, I may have to swim.*

"Shadow, do you thirst, boy?" He led his horse to the small brook snaking through the trees near the clearing. He found a small pool where the water settled. Hundreds of blood-red lotus flowers stabbed at the surface. Shadow followed willingly, nickering and flicking his tail. Because he was a large horse with skin as dark as coal, most thought his name was due to his coloring, but he had taken to Merek as a foal and followed him around the training yards when he was put under saddle. His twin sister, Ashaya, had always been jealous as she had wanted him to ride for herself.

As dusk took hold and the blue moon's light began to shine on him through the towering pines, Shadow almost seemed to have a dark purple hue. His black mane ruffled in the cool breeze, the trees whispering around them. Although they had taken the easternmost route with sparse wood, he had felt some relief from the days prior, spent in the Bloody Sands and its unforgiving sun. They had left the last proper inn four or five days before, somewhere in Ethorya, along with their last decent meal and feather bed. *That barn in Thurel did not count.*

Merek approached the ruins—what appeared to be a short stone wall. The stone was blood-red splotched with white quartz. He squatted down and ran his fingers over its surface, noticing the remaining stones to be almost molded together. He had never seen this type of work from any stonemason in Wolfpine. The overgrown stone path seemed to lead back to the isle.

Shadow snorted again, and Merek knew what he wanted. "Are you in need of assistance?" he asked the horse as if he would reply. He spied a broken sapling laid over the wall with black sap oozing from its break like a festering wound. *That would be a good place to air out his saddle.* The ride had been long, and they both needed a proper bath.

He removed the saddle and readjusted the caparison on the horse's back, taking a moment to stop and look around. He had spent a lot of time alone in the wilds of Vaegomar, but an uneasy feeling came over him as the sky grew darker. Something fluttered in the pit of his stomach. The breeze seemed to whisper his name. Shadow still nickered at him as he looked around the darkening wood. He patted the horse reassuringly. "Oh, well. I did tell Mitch to go home. I suppose it is just us."

As Merek wandered through the pine, gathering kindling, he thought of his siblings. He had spent many nights with Ashaya and his older half-brother, Sirich, in the wilds of Vaegomar. They had always enjoyed camping, hunting, and hawking, longing to get out of the confines of their keep. He had seen little of Aahsgoth but yearned to see more, which is why he had asked to take this ranging.

Merek's stomach growled with hunger as the light faded. He had already taken stones from the brook and built a fire ring. He added his kindling and pulled a worn piece of flint from his dirt-stained saddlebag. With just a few strokes from his dagger, a large spark leapt from the blade, and budding flames quickly danced to life, engulfing the dried pine needles and kindling. Sirich would have jested with him about building such a large fire. His half-brother seemed to enjoy the darkness. This was more to keep the bloodthirsty pinflies away, and to hopefully cook supper. He would check his snares shortly, but first he reached for his bedroll and laid it out next to the fire to warm. It was old and worn doeskin, but it would have to suffice.

The darkness deepened around him. *I should not have sent Mitch back.* Merek enjoyed his company, but he had promised his family that he would send word. *Dammit, I should have stopped at Marshwood to send a corvid.*

Merek removed his armor and frayed, tattered half-cloak from his shoulder. He stood and walked over to a young ash tree and hung the garment over a low-hanging limb as if to display it to any passersby. Like his armor, it was dyed black with his house sigil, a red glyph of the sun, emblazoned on the lower portion of the cloak almost as wide as the cloth itself. The red glyph was a simple circle surrounded by eight points. It always reminded him of a wind rose on one of the many maps he had seen back home in his father's study. He finally removed his bracers. His forearms were blistered and raw where the edges of the leather had bitten into his skin through his undershirt. He left his undershirt on as the cold thickened around him.

His stomach again reminded him to go check the snares he had set. He had not been here long, but the red moon now peeked out from behind the larger blue moon as if it had been in hiding. It had been a few hours. Hopefully a rabbit or perhaps a small doe had snagged itself, or it would be salt beef again this night—further depleting his rations. He stood and felt the sting of a pinfly and grunted as he swatted his neck, leaving a splotch of blood in its place. *Bastards.*

He leaned his head back and rolled his eyes. "Gods!" he cursed. "Shit for supper." As he checked his last snare, he adjusted the small hemp noose and hoped for a good meal to break his fast come the morning star. As he headed toward the flickering light of his campfire, the shadows danced among the trees, and he thought he heard a faint voice through the light breeze. *Perhaps it was just leaves rustling or whispers of the wind.*

But then he heard it again. This time, he was sure he was not alone.

"Who goes there?"

"My lord?" said a high-pitched voice as it drew closer.

"Who are you?" Merek replied.

"My name is Ivan, good sir. I'm sorry for startling you, my lord. I have been traveling north and saw your fire."

As the boy approached the light, Merek could see he was no more than ten or twelve, although it was hard to tell with the shadows tangling with the trees. He had no facial hair and shoulder-length dark hair. He was a commoner, judging by his sun-faded and tattered linen tunic, dusty brown breeches made of coarse wool, and lack of shoes. He had a small linen pack hanging over his shoulder, a long walking stick in his left hand, and a short blade with a silver handle sheathed in leather on his hip. A small wool bandage was tied around his wrist.

"Are you alone, boy?" Merek asked, looking around. He picked up his sword from beside the bedroll.

"Yes, my lord, as I said—"

"Please, call me Merek. No need for such formality here."

The boy nodded. "I just saw your banner there, my lor... eh, Sir Merek."

"Sir?" Merek smiled. "Are you from the east?"

"You are from a noble house—unless that is not your sigil?"

"It is," Merek nodded. "What do you know of noble houses of Vaegomar?"

"Vaegomar? Is that in the north?"

"Yes, the northernmost kingdom, although we have no king. Where are you from, Ivan? Why would you be here alone?" Merek did not notice anything unusual other than this young boy in his camp. He turned back and sat down beside the fire.

"I am from High Rock, a village on the Rainy Isles, as far south as south goes. My father sent me to buy cotton."

"What does your father do?"

The boy hesitated. "He makes candles."

"The son of a candlemaker, this far north on foot? What do you know of this strange place?"

"The isle? Father says it's haunted."

So, others hear the same tales. "Do you not have merchants in High Rock, Ivan? Certainly, there are many on the coast."

"Yes, my lor... sir. We did, but he died a while ago. We haven't seen any traders since."

"You are welcome to share my fire," offered Merek. "I only have salt beef for supper, though. A bow and well-placed arrow would have saved the day."

"Thank you, sir, but I'd better keep going. I travel by night to avoid the heat."

"Are you sure?" Merek asked. "A young boy traveling alone at night without a sword is not safe, and that dagger will not do you much good. There is no shortage of wolves, and sand-people still raid travelers from here to Ethorya."

"Yes, I'll be alright. Have you passed a village or market lately?"

"Water's Edge, three days north in Thurel, is a small trading village. You will find your cotton there if you stay on Marcus' Pass."

"Who is Marcus?" Ivan asked.

Merek laughed as he grabbed his small pouch of salt beef. He handed the boy a piece and bit a chunk from his own. He spoke as he chewed, "The last so-called king of this region, Marcus the Fourth, for whom the old road is named. Well, as much as you can call it a road. More like an overgrown path."

"I see." The boy seemed puzzled. "So... are you a prince or something?"

Merek looked down, smiling. "I used to be."

"I've never met a prince before." Ivan stood. "Thank you, sir. I'll be on my way."

"Leaving so soon?"

"Yes. My father is waiting for me."

"Fair enough." Merek picked up his waterskin, took a drink, and offered it to the boy.

"No, thank you. I don't drink wine."

Merek laughed. "It is only water." He shoved it toward the boy. "Take it. I have another, and plenty of water here to refill it."

The boy hesitantly took the skin and a drink. "Thank you for your kindness. May the Elder give you a blessed night." The boy bowed and turned toward the darkness.

"Be well, Ivan," Merek replied as he walked over to a tree

to relieve himself. He watched the boy disappear through the trees.

Merek pulled his second waterskin from the saddle bag and filled it in the stream. The leaf hoppers had grown louder, and their song filled the night around him. Shadow stirred uneasily. Merek heard another song through the blanket of chirping. "Wolves. They are not near us, and they wouldn't approach a fire." He patted his horse on the back. "Get some shut-eye. We have to ride at dawn to meet this mystery ahead."

Merek sat down on his bedroll, which was now warm to the touch. He took off his boots and laid them near the fire, adding additional logs for a few more hours of warmth. He pulled the saddlebag over and slid it under his head, lying back and studying the sky. Embers from his fire raced toward the peaks of the pine trees, resplendent against a sea of stars. The moons, now high in the sky, stared back at him as he closed his eyes.

As Merek took a deep breath and tried to relax, he thought more of this place. Something hung in the air here that seemed oddly familiar to him. Legends of the Crescent Isle were abundant, likely from tales of haunted ruins, wraiths, witches, and mages. Merek wanted to see for himself. Galen had told him of one such tale where people would offer their children to so-called night demons. They were probably fairytales, from the imaginations of singers and storytellers, but it did intrigue him.

Wolves still howled in the distance. Shadow snorted again, but Merek ignored it as the crackling of the fire had finally put him at ease. He missed his love, Elya. He longed to feel her warmth tonight, to hear her voice. He thought of her soft lips, her long black hair tickling the small of her back. The curve of her hips and buttocks, her smooth skin, the way her tongue showed between her teeth when she smiled. Arousal filled him as his thoughts wove into a dream. He faded into sleep with a slight grin as she straddled him. He held her hips as she rode him slowly, looking into his eyes, moaning in pleasure.

One moment, he felt her warmth—then he felt the pain. It struck like lightning. Merek opened his eyes and inhaled loudly. He looked down to see his hands sticky with blood, grasping at a silver handle buried in his chest. His lifeblood dyed his undershirt black around the blade and quickly expanded outward, raging fire now coursing through his veins.

Merek rolled over to try and stand. A hazy darkness marred his field of vision. He was on his elbow, trying to reach forward as his other hand found only dirt. He could not push himself up, his strength leaving him. He lifted his chin to glimpse bare feet in front of him. Merek tried to speak, tried to breathe. He managed a gurgled "Wha… Why?" Blood filled his throat; he spat and tried to breathe once more. As he fell on his back, the stars all seemed to merge into one.

Then darkness.

"I told you, my lord," said a muffled voice. "I told you I'd found him."

The wolves continued to howl, and the fire in Merek's veins went cold.

Chapter One

Ashaya

In the crisp morning air, a star still shone above the inner towers of the castle, and the market was alive with movement. Ashaya wore a smile, walking among the vendors outside the walls of Wolfpine. The smells of smoked fish from Capeton, fresh fruits from Ashbourne, and exotic wines from the Bronze Isles filled the air. Vendors swarmed to and fro, preparing and displaying their wares. Colorful ribbons, banners, and tents stretched out endlessly. The small trade town of Old Tree stood in the shadow of Wolfpine, and although it was as big as any castle in Aahsgoth, Ashaya loved the freedom she felt when not surrounded by stone walls, never-ending halls, and cramped courtyards.

"*Gisnagrah geme, gaifam don grahgis. Vandondru gis nagrah gon talun. Gon unurveh untaimer uged van drumegon!*" a woman shouted as Ashaya approached.

Which Gods this time? Ashaya thought. She stopped for a moment. She did not recognize the language, but she had understood it. *How?* "Perhaps it was the Old Tongue?" she mumbled. Galen had taught her the Old Tongue years ago, but she did not remember it sounding so foreign.

The woman stood on the back of a wagon half-filled with garlic and onions on the main square where Peddler Alley met Flat Road, wearing a ragged black robe with a stitched red-dragon pattern. Her braided black hair whipped around as she turned her head. A small crowd stood before her. Some listened, some barked back at her.

"Fuck off, witch!" a man yelled.

"You!" shouted the woman. Ashaya locked eyes with the priestess. The strange woman's gaze cut through her. Ashaya looked away, pulled her hood tight to her face, and quickly made her way past the growing crowd.

Ashaya did not think much of gods since they had never seemed to listen to her prayers as a child. There had been more and more broods of holy men and priestesses in town as of late. This woman had the same tattoo on her wrist as the last one, a fortnight past. *A star... or flower, perhaps?* Ashaya continued to hold her hood close to her face.

Her handmaiden, Clara, had laid out another velvet dress—this time a maroon red with a matching corset. She did not like how they restricted her breathing with the laces so tight. She never understood why a dress so pretty and well-made should be worn only to be dragged through the mud. She enjoyed dressing prettily at times, but ultimately preferred comfort. As usual, she had left it on her vanity and opted for a brown soft-leather tunic over a grey cotton undershirt and matching overskirt. As always, she had her sheathed wolf-bone dagger in her dark leather girdle, her longbow over one shoulder, and black riding boots. She was sure she would hear about it from Clara at supper.

Clara had been Ashaya's handmaiden for as long as she could remember, and she sometimes felt bad for making her job difficult. Ashaya *did* wear the emerald-green hooded half-cape anytime she was in town, to lessen the advances she received. Her long silver-blonde hair and emerald-green eyes otherwise stood out in the crowd. She often got propositioned as if she were some common brothel wench. At times, however, she enjoyed the attention.

When she was younger, boys would jape her, calling her "Fat Ash," but her brothers would always chase them off with wooden training swords. They were still protective of her, although she could handle herself. She had never enjoyed sewing, dancing, and all the other things that were expected of her. Instead, she had always preferred sword play with her brothers, and she had especially taken a liking to the bow and arrow.

"Ash!" called a voice through the surrounding song of commerce. Ashaya knew that voice. She turned to see Mitchel, her brother's apprentice. "Slow down! Where are you going?" he asked.

Why did I ever lay with him? She rolled her eyes but put on a smile before she turned. "That's none of your concern. Why do you care?" she teased.

"At least let me walk with you."

"No, leave me be." Ashaya kept walking. She could not keep her teasing up any longer. A part of her was pleased to see him, so she turned and hugged him. *Did I miss him?* He pulled back to kiss her, but she awkwardly kissed him on the cheek first.

"How went Merek's ranging?" she asked.

"He hasn't returned. He sent me back here to inform

your father and the council that he had arrived and would ride back within a fortnight."

"You left him *alone* in the Bloody Sands?"

"Well, yes. He is a capable warrior, and there should be nothing there to worry about but perhaps the wolves—"

"And sand raiders!" she interrupted.

"We were getting close to the Crescent Isle, and there were no castles to send a corvid, only the occasional village or farmhouse once out of Ethorya. Besides, is there a war going on I am unaware of?"

Ashaya tightened her lips. *Mitch was right.* The last time she had sparred with Merek, he had disarmed her after only a few strikes, even though she had bested many of the fighters she'd trained with. They had grown up training in the courtyards of Wolfpine. She had followed Sirich around like a shadow since he was older, already a sword in his hand before she could lift one. She had always preferred the bow and had earned a new nickname in town, "Ash the Arrow," when she had finally bested her brothers on the range.

He will be fine. Merek liked solitude in the wood on occasion.

"Ash, you never answered. Where are you walking?" Mitch prodded.

"I'm going to practice."

"But you have many a range in the yards."

"There are no rabbits in the yards at Wolfpine, at least not already boiling. I am riding into the Smoking Wood. What better way to practice than to hunt?"

"You have cooks for that."

"I'll catch my own supper tonight. Walk with me back to the stables if you wish, but first I want fruit."

Ashaya stopped at the first fruit vendor she saw and dug into her knapsack looking for her coin. She found the leather coin sack and bit down on the knot to loosen it. She dumped a few coins onto the table, the sun gleaming off the pile.

"How much?" Instead of digging for coppers she picked up a coin which the sun must have warmed; it felt hot in her hand as if held to a candle. She handed the woman the silver piece for a few pomegranates although the price was only a copper each. The vendor thanked her three times over, putting her hands together and bowing. The woman cut one open that she had picked. The taste was bittersweet, as it had not fully ripened yet.

Mitch watched her bite into the fruit. "Ash, you have—"

"I know," she interrupted. The dark red juice running from the corner of her mouth tickled her chin. She wiped it away with her sleeve.

She thanked the woman as they turned back toward the gates of Wolfpine, heading for the stables that stood just inside the outer wall. Ashaya walked quickly as Mitch tried to keep up, awkwardly shuffling to avoid bumping into anyone. As they reached the open gates, four house guards parted like opening double doors, two on each side.

"Lady Ashaya," one of the guards said as they all bowed their heads.

"Please, Goran, I am no lady," she said teasingly, with the hint of a smile. The guard's face turned turnip red. "How fares your mother?" she asked.

"She's well, my lady."

"I will visit her soon. Maybe I'll take her some rabbits for a stew," she responded as Mitch followed her through the gates. The other guards were still snickering as they passed. Her house guards were mostly young men from families whom she had known growing up. As they got older and moved into formal roles, she made a point of speaking to everyone when she could. She did not fully understand why things had to be different now. A few years earlier, no one worried about such formalities and titles.

"I will be back before dusk falls." Ashaya nodded toward the stable boy.

"Ash, I wanted to come with you. While Merek is away, I thought we could…"

"We can speak another time. Perhaps tonight?" Ashaya said. Mitch nodded, a glimmer of hope in his eyes.

"May Dyanial of the Thirteen bless your hunt." His voice trailed off as he looked down.

"Thank you, Mitch." She rubbed her eyes and put on a smile.

The stable boy led over Acorn—a chestnut-brown stallion with a white blaze along his muzzle. He was equipped with a brown leather hunting saddle and matching reins. The stable boy had remembered this time to attach her arrow quiver to the right side of the saddle. She traded her longbow for a shorter hunting bow. "He has fresh shoes, my lady," said the boy as he held the reins. Ashaya climbed onto the horse's back.

"Thank you, Walter." Ashaya looked down to Mitch. "Join me for supper in the great hall?" she asked, unsure. Mitch took a few steps back. She snapped the reins lightly and rode toward the gate. She looked back to see Mitch watching her ride beyond the outer wall.

Ashaya brought Acorn to a trot as she came out of the wood on the northern side of Wolfpine. It was her favorite part of the castle. The morning mist hung over the outer walls, and the sun shone bright on the queen's tower. It was the tallest of the castle, and it always made her think of her mother. *What was she like?* Ashaya would wonder from time to time. She halted her horse and stared at the tower for a moment. The wider tower and more elaborate stonework almost glowed in the sun, and the other towers seemed to fade away. She looked down to the giant twisted oak tree by the riverbed below. She would sneak out here as a child after dusk when the moonlight would almost silhouette the towers. The bats would always accompany her, casting about for their prey. She would cross the broken bridge and climb down to the old river to catch fireflies in a basket and bring them to Sirich. Merek never cared, but Sirich would at least pretend to like the gift.

Ashaya kept moving and found her way to the Highland Trail. She turned left to ride north. The road led all the way from the Icy Shore to the head of the Crystal River in the Highland Mountains to the southwest. She had taken this road hundreds of times, along with her brothers, as they traveled on adventures through the Smoking Wood to Dragon Point. It had not rained in a fortnight, so the road was dry. Every step the horse took, a small cloud of dust would fill the air behind her, leaving a ghostly trail.

Riding was one of her favorite pastimes. Ashaya could ride alone for hours. The smells of the wood, the wind in her hair, the songs of birds—they gave her time to think. She thought of Mitch and the look in his eyes when she left him at the south gate. He had followed her around since he had arrived in Wolfpine. *Persistent.*

"And he *is* handsome and treats me well," she mumbled to the empty wood. She had always been torn about him. Her father had spoken of her eventually marrying Robert Thorne, a young lord, son of a council member. Mitch's father was a council member as well, but her father did not seem to like

Lord Promen. She was not sure he would approve of Mitch, so they had kept their rendezvous a secret, even from her brothers.

He had been taken on as Merek's retainer, destined to someday be dubbed a warrior for the loyal service of his house. Although she did not see why all those customs need affect her. *Why should I be required to marry anyone?* Marriage, liege lords, oaths of fealty, councils, kings—it was all too complicated for her taste. In some ways, she was glad her father was no longer king. She wouldn't have to pretend to be a princess.

Ashaya continued north, avoiding low-hanging branches. Her thoughts drifted to last night. This morning before breaking her fast and heading to the market, she had awoken from dreams of flying, along with other strange imaginings. She had seen an immense and ancient oak tree split by a lightning bolt of red flames that shot down from a stormy sky. Half of the tree turned white as it fell. It never hit the earth, transforming instead into a four-legged beast and running toward the mountains in the background. The other half of the great oak turned black with bright orange flashes of fiery embers consuming it until it faded. Only ash hit the ground, the remaining stump blackened. She then found herself lying on the ground, staring at a sea of stars. The stars had fallen one by one, streaking across the sky until it was one blinding, bright-white light. It was so overwhelming she felt she could not breathe. She saw herself struggling to pull on something, but she could not remember clearly. *Whatever it was, I was hesitating.* Her mind was foggy now, only vaguely recalling that she had awoken sweating and breathless.

Most nights, she slept soundly. Clara had always japed about how hard it was getting her out of her featherbed. Ash was not one to rise at dawn, no matter how much the roosters persisted. At times, when she was young, her father would come into her chambers to wake her, kissing her on the forehead and asking if she had gotten enough beauty sleep. Only recently did her dreams seem so strange.

"This is usually a good spot," she told her horse as she came upon a thicket not too far from the road. Plenty of trees, shrubs, and game trails. She tied Acorn off to an oak sapling and pulled an apple from her saddlebag to feed him. She patted him on his neck as she removed the quiver from the saddle and looped it over her right shoulder, setting off deeper into the forest.

Ashaya knew this wood well. She held her hunting bow in her left hand, pulled an arrow from over her right shoulder, and nocked it. She had carved this set herself from a freshly downed hickory tree in the garden at Wolfpine, fallen during a storm the year before. It was shorter than her longbow, but the recurve at either end made the arrow come out quicker for a short bow, perfect for horseback or hunting. She had Gavin teach her; he had been a smith and fletcher before becoming the quartermaster of Wolfpine. She had stained it a dark cherry red, wrapped it with a black leather grip, and added a wolf-bone arrow rest. She had a bundle of cottonwood arrows she had fletched herself. There was no shortage of feathers from the many quails, magpies, and ravens kept in the aviary.

She walked slowly and observed her surroundings. Sunlight flickered through the canopy of pines, firs, and cottonwoods above. Bright green moss had overtaken the stones below. Birds whistled around her, and a stream trickled nearby. The sun warmed her face each time she passed through an opening where the light could reach. Immersed in the beauty around her, she came to a clearing and a small game trail. She knelt and rubbed her fingers in the soil. It was damp.

Still a fresh trail. Surely she would find something here. She stood and slowly followed the trail, keeping her eyes focused and feet steady on the slick, moss-covered soil. She moved as silently as a shadow, one footfall at a time.

There it stood.

A large brown jackrabbit on its hind legs chewing intently and on high alert. Ashaya's heart raced despite having done this a hundred times before. She slowly moved into position and took aim. The light dimmed as a cloud blocked the sun, but she did not take her eyes away. She leaned her head over to line her eye up with the arrow and slowly drew the string back. She took a deep breath and exhaled slowly and quietly.

Ashaya was so focused that she seemed to see a red aura around the animal. Her heartbeat thudded in her ears. The jackrabbit looked right at her but did not move. She loosed the arrow. The rabbit jumped once and fell beside a rooster fern, green with red tips. "All too easy," she mumbled as she put the bow over her shoulder and walked toward her prize.

As she approached, a blur of black and white came from behind a tree next to her kill. A short scream managed to escape her throat as she lunged backward, falling to one knee. The low growl made the hair stand up on her neck. She regained her balance and turned back toward the sound. She quickly nocked another arrow, studying her surroundings, her hands trembling and her breath quick. It was gone. She saw nothing but the branch of a sapling waving at her.

"What in the…" she said. *A wolf? A feral dog?* She looked around. The silence of the trees and the sapling mocked her. She remembered her rabbit. All that remained was a small splattering of blood on the fern and moss where it had lain. Despite her growing anger, she started to giggle.

"Shit! A damn dog took my supper. The old goddess mocks me!" At the least, it would be a funny story to tell when she returned home. She had never seen anything but small grey wolves in this region. *A black bear perhaps? No... it would have eaten the rabbit where it lay.*

Ashaya decided it was time to go home. She continued to snicker. Sirich and her father would be amused, at least. Perhaps she would settle for whatever the cooks prepared tonight and dine with Mitch after all.

As she hiked back toward her horse, she suddenly recalled another part of the dream she'd had. *That's it.* She had been pulling on the string of a bow, but it would not budge. *Or I was hesitating.* What she was aiming for was still hazy in her mind.

Ashaya put her quiver back on the saddle, untied Acorn, and mounted the horse. As she turned to head south, all she could think about was her father and brothers laughing when she told them of the monster that had stolen her supper. Looking back once more, she shook her head with a grin. She steered the horse toward home as it began to rain.

Chapter Two

Sirich

The sun burned.

Sirich slowly peeled his eyes open, meeting the rays of light pushing through his chamber windows. Dust particles swirled in the narrow sunbeams. His quarters seemed brighter than usual. He sat up in his featherbed, taking a moment to shake off the grogginess. He did not remember leaving the window ajar, and the cold bite of the room chilled him. He recalled dreaming. He could not remember the details, only that he had awoken to see the moonlight many times throughout the night.

As he tried harder to remember, he noticed the taste of steel in his mouth and rubbed his finger on the inside edge of his lower lip. His finger was stained crimson red. *I must have bitten my lip while sleeping.*

Sirich leaned over to pick up the book he had been reading before sleep finally took him. A tome about the ancient oddities of Aahsgoth. The worn, brown leather-bound book was dusty and faded. He could not make out the name of the 'ceptor who had written it. He had always enjoyed history, living through every era of time though the pages of a book. He had recently been exploring the so-called Age of Gods. Wolfpine had an immense library, only second to the Library of Ashbourne, where the preceptors lived. He wondered what it would be like to come across some of these creatures—if they had ever existed. He had read of dragons, bloodkin, and other tales of magick and sorcery over the years. If magick was real, it had died long ago.

He laid the book down on his bedside table, next to what was left of last night's candle. A lump of wax was all that remained. The melting candle had snaked over the edge of the oak table, white drippings frozen in time. A few drops had reached the floor, adding another layer on top of the many from previous nights. He stood to stretch and ran his fingers through his midnight-black hair, looking for his brush. It was nowhere to be found, so he grabbed a leather strap, got out what tangles he could, and pulled it up into a ponytail that reached his shoulder blades. It would have to do.

Sirich saw that Clara had filled his wash basin, although the water was now cold. He leaned down and rinsed his face. The water soothed his burning eyes, the stinging subsiding, at least for now. He grabbed the white linen towel hanging below the mirror and patted his face, shadowed with stubble. *A shave would be nice*, he thought. *I will ask Tommen after supper.*

He had slept in his breeches again, so he walked back and sat on the edge of his featherbed and pulled on his black leather riding boots, still dusty from yesterday's ride to the brothel at the crossroads. He stood and snatched the white cotton undershirt from the bed where he had left it last night. As he slid it over his head, a slight grin came to his face as a woman's scent filled his chamber. His head emerged, spotting Elya at his door out of the corner of his eye. "You move like a shadow, but I could smell your sweet perfume."

She smiled as she entered the room and closed the door behind her. "That's quite the nose you have, my lord, but I'm not wearing any," she said, studying him as he pulled his shirt down to his waist.

She wore a simple grey cotton dress with white stitching that formed a floral pattern below her neck, some of her long black hair pulled up into a silk knot of braids as the rest flowed over her shoulder. Her olive skin glistened in the sunlight. Her inviting brown eyes met his.

"It's like you were cut from the very stone you stand on." She stepped toward him. "Your blue eyes seem... brighter." She bit her bottom lip.

He grabbed her, pulling her close and kissing her deeply.

"You did not come to me last night," he said as they took a breath.

"Did you miss me, my lord?" She stood on her toes and lightly kissed his neck, sliding her hands under his shirt and caressing his chest, her fingers exploring every inch of him. She slowly sank to her knees and untied his breeches to reveal his manhood. She looked up into his eyes as she started to stroke him. He leaned his head back and exhaled deeply as she took him in her mouth. She slid one hand around to his buttocks and pulled him closer. After a few moments, he could not resist any longer.

Sirich pulled her up almost violently, spinning her around and pushing her against the wall as he positioned himself behind her. He swept her hair aside and nibbled at her neck, pulling her dress up and over her hips. Both were breathing heavily now. She closed her eyes and uttered heavy sighs as if she were whispering to the wall. He sank to taste her. His hands squeezed her buttocks, and she exhaled deeply in pleasure as he explored her with his tongue.

A moment later, he stood quickly and held himself, the other hand on her shoulder. He entered her slowly, enjoying the sight of her gripping the stone wall with her hand, her entrance already warm and wet with ecstasy. His hands slid back up to her hips as he began to thrust slowly. After a few moments, the intensity grew. She arched her back and moaned, sneaking a glance back to look at him with piercing, smoldering eyes. For a moment, he worried someone would enter, but the fear was fleeting. She whimpered to the rhythm of their bodies driving together faster and faster, her buttocks beginning to glisten with the sweat that had pooled in the small of her back.

She must have felt him grow larger inside her. "Yes, yes, yes!" she repeated in a breathy whisper, trying to stay quiet. He exploded inside her, grunting with each lunge as she peaked with him in unison. She reached back and pulled his face close to hers, both of them gasping for air. Sweat rolled from his brow as she rotated her pelvis and hips against his. She stopped their rhythm before pulling away and lowering her dress.

"We shouldn't keep doing this, my lord," she managed to say in a whispery exhale.

"And why not?" he replied, catching his breath, finding his tunic once again.

"If my lord father finds out, he'll—"

"Do nothing," Sirich interrupted. "My father is his liege lord. What could he do?"

"My father sits on the council," she replied. "And I'm promised to someone else."

"Your father should be grateful. You are not some common kitchen wench, are you?" He raised his eyebrows and tightened his lips. "Perhaps we could marry."

"You would marry me?" she asked. "Do you think they would allow it?"

"If you are lucky," he teased. "I *could* ask my father. The council meets today."

"Your father wants you to attend."

"Me?" Sirich said in surprise. "The council meeting?"

"Indeed. Perhaps he wants you to take his seat one day?"

"I suppose. Maybe I will sleep better there." They giggled like children as he tied his breeches once again and she adjusted her dress.

Elya gave him one last kiss on the cheek before she walked past him toward the door. "Enjoy your meeting."

"I do not think I should go. This council makes no sense. I—"

She turned to him and put her hands on his chest, then buttoned his tunic. "Do what your father wants. Go to his meeting."

"I suppose. Will I see you tonight?"

"If you are lucky," she responded with a devilish grin on her face and left his chambers.

Sirich wiped the sweat from his forehead and took a deep breath. He felt he could go back to sleep for a century. He needed to break his fast, although it was likely noon, feeling feverish and racked with hunger pains.

He turned and pulled the rusty iron handle to open the door and found Clara standing there with her fist in the air. "Damn, you startled me!"

"Apologies, my lord, but your father wants to see you. I brought your—"

"Yes, yes, I will see him after I have a shit!" he said, stomping past her.

"Yes, of course, my…"

Her voice faded behind him.

Sirich walked from the privy beside his chambers through the grey stone halls of the old keep, heading toward his father's study in the old king's tower. The stone in the old keep had grown dark over the centuries. Compared to the outer walls, it looked a different castle. The tops of the inner towers were now jagged where stone had broken loose and fallen ages ago. The southwest tower they called "Rockfall" after a small stone had fallen and hit Merek in the head when they were young. Luckily, it had only left a scar on his forehead.

In the hallways, water stains pointed downward, resembling black daggers stabbing the floor. There were few windows here, so candles had to burn constantly. Rusted iron sconces were placed about every ten footfalls, and the dim light flickered, shadows dancing on the stone as he passed. This part of the castle remained damp, and in some areas, moss grew out of cracks in the stone, green fingers reaching toward any glimmer of sunlight from open chamber doors. Occasionally, it was cleared by servants, but it always returned. He came to the north tower, where he took the winding staircase that descended into darkness. The heavy oak door creaked as he pulled it open to reveal the great hall before him.

He stood in the light once more. He had always felt nostalgic here, with his house banner draped on the front wall over the great hearth. This was where his ancestors had ruled, planned battles, and shared meat and mead with noble houses and allies. Servants scrubbed the long wooden tables that filled the room. His grandfather had been the last true king before his own father changed Aahsgoth forever. Now the banners of nine noble houses hung on the walls between the tall, stained windows on each side of the hall, leaving room for more. A rainbow of colors filled the room.

He walked between the stone columns toward the front table, slightly elevated where the high lords of old had sat. At times, the tables were moved for mummers' plays, singers, and tricksters. He glanced at the banners and their rune sigils as he passed. The lightning bolt of House Thorne, the odd skull-like glyph of House Cherne. His favorite was the glyph of House Lucian. He was not sure why. It resembled a droplet of water, perhaps blood. So much history was unknown, even to those who bore the sigils.

He came to the table and walked around behind the old stone chair—as most called it—where his grandfather had once sat, the chair his father had surrendered. He rubbed his hand across the back, feeling the crevices around the stone-carved sun that would rise above the head of anyone who sat there. If the entire castle fell, surely this would stand.

"Not much of a throne, aye?" a voice echoed from the back of the hall.

"No, but it's perfect," Sirich responded with a grin. "Are you following me, sister?"

Ashaya grabbed him, stood on her toes, and kissed his cheek. "Good morning, brother. Or should I say afternoon?"

"Yes, my lord father," he muttered teasingly. "I'll hear it soon enough. I'm off to see him soon. Eat with me." He gestured to a servant. "I'll have four boiled eggs, honeyed toast, and a plate of bacon burned black."

"Ale as usual, my lord?" the girl asked.

"Yes, and hurry it up. I am starving."

"Thank you, Daria," Ashaya said as she sat down at the table. "Please forgive my brother. He was just born yesterday and has no manners."

"Yes, my lady," the girl chuckled, nodding her head and leaving for the kitchens.

"I was born a prince," he mumbled.

"Yes, brother, you were, but you have to let that go. Now you are just an asshole." She smiled.

Sirich heard the clang of pots and utensils when Daria opened the door. "Are they not supposed to serve us?" he asked.

"Yes, but they are not slaves!" Ashaya insisted. Sirich rolled his eyes, walking around the table to take a seat across from her.

Their father walked in from the double doors. "There you are." William walked over, put his hands on Ashaya's shoulders, and kissed her head. "My lovely daughter, how are you today?"

Ashaya covered her father's hand with her own. "I'm fine, Father. Are you looking forward to the days of meetings?"

William shook his head. "So happy I just may burst!"

Daria returned with ale and sat it on the table.

William poured himself a cup of ale and drank. "Sirich, come to my office when you are done. I want you—"

"So I hear. I will, Father."

"Good. I'll see you shortly. I love you both. And Ashaya, keep watch over him. Make sure he gets to me," he said, laughing as he walked away.

"I shall, father," she said with a snicker. Sirich rolled his eyes.

Ashaya looked back to Sirich and lowered her voice. "So, who is she?"

Sirich widened his eyes and took a long pause. "Who is who? I do not—"

"Then are you wearing perfume now?" she asked with a grin. Sirich did not say a word. "So, you did have a good morning," she mocked. "Is it Galen's newest apprentice?"

Sirich frowned. "Who?"

"Nivara. She likes you, you know."

"How do you know?"

"I see the way she looks at you."

A smile came to his face. "Now that I think of it, she *is* pretty, and has nice—" Ashaya smacked his arm and he stopped short. "Perhaps I will go visit her." His grin grew wider.

"Stop it!" Ashaya looked around.

"So, I hear you lost your supper last night?"

Ashaya looked puzzled. "How did you—"

"These walls speak, you know," he interrupted with a smile.

"Whom did I speak to when I returned? Only Mitch. Certainly, he wouldn't mention it."

"No, Mitchel loves you too much. Do not worry, I have my sources."

Ash rolled her eyes. "How did you hear?"

"I told you these walls speak," he said smiling. "Besides he's followed you around like a wounded dog since his father sent him here."

Ashaya took a drink. "Anyway, I wanted to tell you myself."

"You can tell me later. The old man will be pissed already

by my delay." Daria returned with a pewter plate of bacon and eggs and picked up the remaining ale. "Leave the flagon," he said, prompting Ashaya to kick him under the table with angry eyes. "Please," he added as the girl nodded and left them.

"I can tell you now," Ash insisted. "Father can wait. It's not just the theft of my supper. You know the Smoking Wood better than anyone—have you ever seen anything other than small grey wolves in that forest?"

"No, but your thief was likely just a bear," he said dismissively.

"This was no bear. It was too quick. Besides, it would have eaten where it stood." Her hands cupped her chin.

"Perhaps it was a lycan that stole your rabbit. A dire wolf. A large bat. Why does this matter, anyway?" He smirked as he reached for his cup.

"A bat? Are you mad? You think Aethial, the supposed goddess of the skies, sent a bat to take my rabbit?" Ashaya laughed before her face went stern again. "I'm not interested in fairytales. And if any remain, dire wolves live somewhere in the west. As funny as it is now, it was strange. I felt like I was being watched the whole time." Ash looked to be thinking while he devoured his food. "Perhaps it was just a wild dog?"

Sirich spoke as he chewed. "More than likely," he said as he finished all but one piece of his bacon and washed it down with ale. He put the last piece in his pocket.

Ash remained puzzled but started to smile as she finished her cup. "Oh well, that's what cooks are for, I suppose," she said.

"You see, you do think like me! We're the same, you and I." Sirich smiled and poured them both another cup of ale and drank it down before standing and wiping his mouth with his sleeve. "Don't worry about it, Ash. You were frightened and didn't get a good look. I must go hear Father's moaning. I will see you after the council meeting?"

"*You* are attending the council meeting?"

"I suppose I am. Father mentioned it yesterday while you were getting robbed of your supper."

"Perhaps he wants you to see more of Aahsgoth. All you have seen as of late are the backs of asses and eyelids."

Sirich could not disagree. Although his father had called him a night owl since he was a boy, he had not been himself lately, and today felt even worse.

"Most of the lords have arrived," she added. "Don't make any more of a fool of yourself than you already are."

"The council meetings will last a fortnight. I have plenty of time to make a fool of myself, dear sister." He walked around the table to her, took her by the shoulders, and leaned down to kiss the top of her head before turning toward the doors behind the hearth that led to the inner courtyard.

"Mitch has returned, you know. No word from Merek as of yet," she called, standing.

"I'm sure he's well. Merek likely found a brothel he likes in Ethorya and has fallen in love. You know how he follows your ladies around like a lost puppy," he yelled back as he opened the double doors to the yard.

Sirich winced as he walked into the light of the yard, a light breeze cooling his face. Autumn was close, and the courtyard was busy with movement. He took in the sights, from the men chopping wood to be burned throughout winter to the women washing and hanging out clothing to dry.

It was mostly house retainers who worked in the inner courtyards. People fed goats and hogs in their pens; children ran by laughing as they made a game of chasing chickens. He passed mothers with babes at their breasts and house guards at their posts bored and watching it all themselves. Smoke from the many fires filled the air, and young boys practiced hitting their targets. The song of the smiths' hammers rang out, forging new tools and weapons.

I need to see Gavin to acquire a new sword. His was worn from practice, although hitting nothing but straw men. He sometimes secretly longed for a proper battle. Recently, there had been only small skirmishes that needed intervention. Mostly small houses fighting over land, and some militant religious groups fighting for their gods. But no real battles, no adventure, nothing to help him emerge as hero like the songs.

He made his way through the crowd, occasionally nodding at people who made eye contact. Some still nodded or bowed. As he approached the tower, he knelt to pet the little brown mutt that always came up to him. He pulled out the piece of bacon and held it out. "Here, boy, your favorite." The dog's ears perked. He came closer then stopped, baring his teeth and growling. "Come here. What is your problem?" The dog yelped and ran back into the crowd.

That is odd, he has never...

Sirich finally approached the king's tower after what seemed like an eternity. Suddenly, he could hear all the sounds in the yard at once. Laughter echoed, the smiths' hammers clanked, the fires crackled, so loud in his head at once. He covered his ears as the noise overwhelmed him. The world spun around him, and he almost lost his footing, but at the last second, a guard grabbed his arm and steadied him. The chaos in his ears and dizziness subsided after a moment. He could hear what sounded like his own heartbeat.

The guard let go. "You alright, my lord?"

"Yes, I am fine," Sirich replied, unsure. The guard stepped back beside the door as Sirich stumbled forward.

The two guards nodded. They opened the heavy oak doors, looking at each other in confusion as he passed.

He climbed the spiral stairs, identical to those in the north tower, up to the third level. He paused momentarily, realizing he was slightly out of breath. His ears still rang slightly, and now his gut hurt again as if he had not just eaten. For a moment, he felt nauseated and clutched his stomach, a slight sweat breaking out on his forehead.

Perhaps I am dying, he thought as he walked toward the black-stained double doors of his father's study. He knocked on the door briefly and entered the room. *If my lord father doesn't kill me first.*

Chapter Three

William

William sat behind his desk, stroking his silver-white beard, lost in thought. He ran a hand through his matching hair, cut short and receding from his forehead. He was a man of fifty and had written as many letters in the last fortnight. He dipped his quill into the pewter inkwell and resumed writing. The creak of the doors to his study drew his attention.

"You don't look well, son," he said, barely raising his eyes to meet Sirich's gaze.

"I have not slept well, Father. I just…"

"You look like you have seen a shade, the color your face has gone. Sleep is all you *do* lately. Go see the damn 'ceptor," William snapped back.

"I will," Sirich replied, rubbing his eyes. William signed

his name and sprinkled pounce on the letter. He turned in his chair and blew the powder off before rolling up the parchment. He poured black sealing wax on the seal and stamped the sun glyph of his house. While it dried, he leaned over and blew out the candle under the wax melting pot. "We are at a crossroads, son. I need you today."

"Wouldn't this all be much easier if you were to simply take back your crown? I do not understand."

"Understand what? That you cannot be king?" William raised his deep, scratchy voice, nearing a shout. "There have been kings since the dawn of time, when the Elder saw fit to put us here in his image, and it's done nothing but spill blood!"

Sirich was quick to respond. "Coming from the last king of Aahsgoth, who earned the nickname 'Killiam' while spilling blood!"

William's face flushed with anger. "Yes, I have, and for what? A golden hat? People do not need to be led like cattle! People should lead themselves! Why is this so hard to grasp?" William was almost fully leaning over his desk, his knuckles pressing into the sturdy oak.

"People want to be led. They do not care who it is, or about the affairs of high lords and what they do in their castles," Sirich responded. "Bringing other lords into the fray only complicates things."

"People want to be left alone and they certainly care when some lord decides he wants a damned golden hat for himself, burns their lands, and carries their sons off to war to get it! Most never return." William paused to take a breath. "I'm trying to change Aahsgoth so that it lives for eternity, and I need you to understand that, son." His voice had softened.

Sirich looked to be in deep thought, stroking his chin. "What did my mother think of this?"

William leaned back in his chair as he sighed deeply. "Sit down."

Sirich nodded and sat before him in the noisy oak chair.

"Your mother never had the chance to tell me what she thought," William said softly.

"So, she was the last queen," Sirich replied, almost whispering.

"When I took another wife, she left after I told her my plans to abdicate my crown. I waited years for her to return before I convened the beginnings of a council. Perhaps she did not like the idea of being the last queen either," William responded in a defeated tone. They both sat in silence for a moment.

"What was she like? I only have vague memories of her."

"Odd… You have never asked about her." William took a deep breath and sighed, his hazel eyes starting to glisten. "I loved Val more than life itself. She was beautiful and wise. She had an old soul about her, a knowledge of things unlike I have ever known. She must have read every book in Ashbourne." A smile came to his lips as he thought of her. "Long black hair, eyes like stars. When she told me she was with child, I knew I had to act, to protect my children and their children after them." William paused for a moment. "When a man has children, he could not be happier or more fearful. The world takes on a new meaning. Only, that day was bittersweet. The wet nurse put a babe in my arms and said my wife had gone against Galen's orders.

"I walked the castle and rode the city grounds looking for her. I came back here to find only this."

William stood and walked over to a shelf of dusty books. He reached for the top shelf, peeling a black book out of its place. From the hole in the shelf, he pulled a small roll of paper, walked back over, and sat on the edge of his desk. He slid the paper toward his son. "I do not know what it reads. Years ago, I had one of Galen's assistants look to see if he knew this tongue. He found nothing."

Sirich took the ragged parchment, the strange rune-like symbols written in faded red ink. "So, what does it say?" Sirich asked. Hope glimmered in his eyes.

"To this day, I do not know." They both sat in silence. "Enough. We can discuss this another time. The council is here. I want you to attend."

Sirich held the note and lightly caressed the ink with his thumb. He placed the letter back on the old desk. "So I hear. What can I add to this?"

"Just pay attention, and if you feel the need to speak, then do so. I want you to learn of our process as we continue to learn ourselves. I know you were born a prince, but a good king puts his people first, not his own vanity and a damned title." William stood and handed two sealed letters to Sirich. "Take these to one of the 'ceptors, and I will see you in the hall. Tell the new girl... What is her name?"

"Nivara?" Sirich reminded him.

"Yes, her. Have her send this to Jon Horsman in Springfell. My old friend Gerald Dustyn has died." William paused. "He was the last of his line, no sons, and a daughter lost by marriage. We must invite one of his longest standing bannermen to Wolfpine. One by corvid, the other by rider, so as to make sure some random archer doesn't impede our progress."

Sirich looked puzzled. "Why Springfell?" Sirich asked as he walked toward the door. "You have the council here."

"We need a bigger council."

"I do not understand, Father. How many do you need?"

"Enough to represent all of Aahsgoth." William grinned

and put his hand on Sirich's shoulder. "And go see Galen, son," he said sternly, closing the door behind Sirich.

William entered the great hall and saw that some of the other lords awaited him. He walked the semicircle of tables to greet them where they gathered. They murmured to themselves, several conversations being had at once. The great hall was alive with movement. Serving girls brought wine, young boys helped remove cloaks, and candle fire danced on wicks while the house guard watched at each entrance.

William had chosen a black, button-down tunic with an intricate diamond pattern of golden thread. It wrapped around to the back where the threading formed the Blacksun glyph. It was a little tighter around his midsection than he remembered. His matching breeches, tucked in his boots, were loose and made a swooshing sound with each step. Will inquisitively greeted each lord, the men grabbing each other's forearms as was the customary greeting.

William saw Heath Promen approaching. *Oh gods.*

"Will! You look well," said the man with a broad smile.

"You're too kind, my lord. How fares your family?"

"We are doing well. I'm joyed to see my children again since they have been here in Wolfpine for over a year. You northerners are rubbing off on my daughter! That tongue of hers will be the death of me." He turned and walked with William. "And how fare your sons and daughter?"

Will nodded and forced a smile. "Well, my lord, as far as I know. Merek hasn't returned from his ranging."

"I'm sure he's enjoying the women of Ethorya," Heath replied, a smirk spreading across his black-bearded face.

"Perhaps, but he should have returned before this meeting."

"I can't say I blame the boy. I have spent many a night there. The Ethoryans are very... hospitable," Heath replied with a hand on William's shoulder.

"Yes, and we need a member of the Gazi here to represent Ethorya."

"Who do you have in mind?"

"An old friend."

William made his rounds to the other lords. He did not enjoy formalities, but this meeting had to go smoothly. This was the ninth council meeting in as many years, and it had grown.

He made his way to the center table. "My lords, shall we begin?" William said, raising his voice as he hit a fork against a pewter cup.

Silence filled the room as the ring of the cup echoed throughout the hall. The men shuffled around the tables and took their seats facing each other. William walked past his old chair and sat at the center table with Atohi Cherne and Osmond Thorne.

"Thank you, my lords, for travelling to Wolfpine once again," William began. "We have many days of discussion ahead of us. I would like to address our newer members and remind others that over a decade ago, I was your king. I now sit among you as an equal. I abdicated my crown and that damned chair." He motioned to the old stone seat behind him.

Heath Promen was the first to stand and respond. "But you are now self-appointed overlord of this council. Is that not the same thing?"

"That's what *I* told him," boomed a voice from the back of the hall.

William looked up as Sirich walked toward the council, eyeing him sternly. "Pardon my son's tardiness, my lords. I have asked him to attend this meeting, if it pleases you. He needs to take an interest in the way of things in Aahsgoth."

Sirich came to a stop and bowed to the council. He then walked backwards to take a seat at another table near the back of the hall. He picked up a cup of wine from a serving girl's tray as she passed. "As I said, I would agree, Lord Promen, but this is important to my father and the realm. I fully support my father and would like to understand my future role here."

"Of course," Gabe Aethon of Eagle's Nest chimed in.

"Please, do continue, my lords," Sirich proclaimed as he sat. William smiled, pride swelling in him. He was glad to know Sirich was maturing.

William continued his original thought without any more hesitation. "I understand that concern, but as you know, my lords, you have an equal say here. As council overlord, I am but a tie breaker if need be. And your regions also need to know this, as well as what we are working toward." William paced, his heavy footsteps echoing in the hall. "I would like to first ask the council to consider bringing Marcus Lucian into the fold. We need him to stabilize Old Lucian and reclaim his homeland."

"The same homeland where you killed his father during the last rebellion? When Marcus was but a boy?" Heath Promen asked with a sneer. The other lords looked among each other, surprised.

"That was a different time. I harbor no ill will toward the boy," William said. "He had no say in what his late father did. Besides, he is a man grown and should sit on this council. As of now, that region is lawless." The lords all mumbled among themselves. "We have many matters to discuss, we do not have to decide now." William sat down and looked over at Sirich with a smile.

As the council continued to speak on matters of law, finance, and war, William noticed even the lords among him likely did not grasp his full intentions. The more words that were spoken, the less wine remained, and he sensed a misunderstanding. William intervened to bring the topic of discussion back to governance itself. "My lords, you all speak as if you will sit here forever, or your sons after you, deciding these things for commoners. At some point, the people will decide who sits here, regardless of name."

William looked at Sirich and motioned. "Take my own son. Although likely, he may *not* have a future role on this council." Sirich looked up hesitantly.

"You mean commoners could replace noble houses and have a say in the affairs of Aahsgoth?" replied Lord Cherne. His forehead wrinkled in confusion.

"Yes," William replied sternly. "It may be next year or a decade from now, but our goal is to put a proper system in place and then hand it over to them, I don't want you to simply rule them, I want you to *represent* them. What gives us the right to—"

"Lord Blacksun!" came a muffled shout from the back of the hall.

"Let him in," William ordered. The two guards let the rider pass. He entered the hall, wearing the yellow and blue colors of House Bore of the Highlands. He was gasping for breath and muddy from the road.

Heath Promen stood. "What is it, boy? Spit it out."

"Forgive me, my lords, I rode as fast as I could," the young man panted.

"Bring him water." William motioned to a serving girl. "Catch your breath and tell us what ails you." The rider took the cup from the girl, spilling half of it before he drank it down as if he had never tasted anything sweeter.

The boy's lip started to quiver. "Your Grace, a corvid that was meant for Wolfpine came to us in Greenhill. Something has happened down south in Alarya, I think. The entire village of Valton has been killed, Your Grace. Slaughtered!"

Shock painted the faces of everyone who had heard. For a moment, silence held the room. William stood angrily.

Lord Promen walked toward the rider. He looked back at William then turned to the boy. "What do you mean? I passed there a fortnight ago on the way here. It's only a few leagues from Mudstone."

The boy tried to find the words. "They are gone, my lord. My sister lived there…" His voice trailed off as he dropped to his knees and tried to gather himself.

Heath Promen stood beside the young man. "I will leave at once. Have your 'ceptor send a corvid to Mudstone. They are to send a hundred men to find out what happened and bring the perpetrators to justice!" he said, his voice growing louder. "It was likely one of the mountain clans. Savages!"

William walked around to the center of the room. "Wait. We need to answer this crime united. Send your men, Heath, but we shall all send troops. All of our colors shall march together to restore the peace." The bloodlust of war called to William. He raised his hand. "All who agree to this, raise your right hand."

The councilmen looked at each other and all raised their hands.

Heath Promen spoke. "It's on my lands. I will gladly lead our troops."

"No!" shouted a commanding voice at the back of the room. Sirich helped the whimpering boy to his feet, squared his shoulders, and stared at his father. "I will."

Chapter Four

Galen

Galen was all but done with his duties for the day and prepared to settle into the warmth of his featherbed. A man of sixty-two years, he had served House Blacksun of Wolfpine for the last two decades. He sat on the edge of his featherbed and sighed deeply, rubbing his hands through what was left of the short white hair on the back and sides of his otherwise bald head. The men had called him "Galen Horseshoe" when they were children; they did it now from time to time, even William.

He had grown tired as the years passed. He rubbed at his burning eyes as if to wipe the sting away. A long day it had been—too many trips up and down the stairs, to and from the aviary to send William's many letters to the lords of Aahsgoth and receive their replies. *Those damn stairs.*

A long first day of the council meeting did not help, although he had one of his apprentices help to scribe the events. He had received the honor of Master Preceptor some thirty years earlier and had served Wolfpine the last twenty-five.

The cold room made him think of Ashbourne and the warm climate of the Greenlands. Galen tried to visit his son there once a year. Wolfpine had been his home since he had requested to serve William after helping to restore the library. It had reminded him of reading about the so-called "Plight of Ashbourne" centuries before. Besides, Ashbourne was almost a thousand leagues away, and it seemed to get further every year as the journey became harder to bear, despite travel by boat across the Middle Sea making it much faster.

As the light dimmed within his chamber, he walked over to the hearth and added a log to the fire. Goosebumps rose on his arms as he closed his windows for the night. He emptied the many pockets of his heavy black robe and changed into his white cotton bed gown. He had almost forgotten the small flask of elderberry extract that had fallen to the floor. The seal had not broken, but he added a bit more wax to the opening of the bottle to be sure before setting it on the dusty shelf behind his desk with the countless other potions, crystals, herbs, and poisons.

Galen prepared to write in his journal as he did every night. It was his custom, but more importantly, the duty of all preceptors to record the daily events of the respective families they served. The Order of Preceptors documented everything, and copies were sent to the great library, one of the few remaining ancient wonders of Aahsgoth.

As he dipped his quill into the inkwell and started to write his account of the day, a knock on his door interrupted him before the first word had dried.

"Come!" he called.

"Galen, may I have a moment?" asked a pale looking Sirich, poking his head in the door.

"You don't look well, boy. Sit." Galen motioned toward a bench beside his desk. Sirich sat reluctantly. "What ails you, Siri? I can see you need sleep, as do I. The dark circles under your eyes are almost as bad as mine," Galen said with the hint of a smile.

"I do not know. I have felt... strange all day. Earlier, I almost collapsed in the yard. Everything was so loud, and all at once. I could hear what seemed to be my own heartbeat in my ears. Even now, I hear it, although very faint."

"Collapsed?" Galen felt Sirich's head. "Anything else?"

"My belly hurts like I have not eaten, and I feel weak. I must ride south, as you know. We leave on the morrow. I have to prove to Father that I want to help his cause, but I don't want to pass out while on horseback."

Galen could see the frustration on his face and smiled. "Your father is a good man, trying to do good things. You know, House Serwyn descended from a long line of scholars, teachers, healers, and—some say—mages and sorcerers. Your family have always been kings, but Will is the first to act so boldly. Of your forefathers, some were good men, while others... not so much, according to the histories. But your father is the first to try something of this magnitude. There are a few councils in the Eastern Kingdoms that rule together over their subjects, but to my knowledge, they are no more than kings agreeing to share power. The people are still their subjects all the same. William is trying to go well beyond that."

"I suppose. It just does not seem fair. I am trying—"

"I know you were born a prince. I brought you and your brother and sister into this world, so it brings me joy that you understand what he does. Ambitious it is, but it must be done." Galen patted Sirich on the head as he stood and smiled.

Sirich jerked his head away. "Just give me something to sleep, old man," he said with a grin.

"That I can do, but first let me have a look at you."

Galen held Sirich's head still and looked in his ears. He felt his neck and looked in his eyes for a moment. "Your eyes are lighter than they used to be, and you smell of ale. Lean back a bit." He pushed on Sirich's belly. "Does that hurt?"

"Not at the moment. It seems to come and go."

"I don't think you are dying. Let us start with a good night's rest. It can do wonders by itself. As for the other symptoms, it could be any number of things. A gut worm perhaps, with maybe an infection of the ears. Although a strange combination. Have you been swimming in the twins again?"

"Not for a fortnight at least. It is becoming too cold," Sirich replied. Galen walked back over and felt his forehead.

"You have a light fever. An infection is likely," he said, walking back to his shelves and shuffling through the many glass bottles. "Here," he muttered, returning to Sirich. "Take two to three drops on your tongue or in a cup of wine."

"What is this?" Sirich asked, studying the green liquid.

"Oil of hemlock. You do not remember?" Galen asked, raising his brow. "Occasionally, as a child, I gave you and your siblings a drop when you refused to sleep." Galen paused to reminisce. "They looked up to you then as they do now. What you did, they followed. Ashaya was practically your shadow."

Sirich smiled back at him. "Thank you, Lord Horseshoe."

"More like a full moon now," Galen responded, patting him on the shoulder. "Only a few drops now. More than that, and it becomes poisonous. Come back first thing in the morning before you depart. I will consult Tommen at daybreak."

Sirich stood as Galen turned to him once more. "Safe travels to you, Siri. It is likely just mountain clans. No need to be a hero. Your father only wants to show the people that protection is paramount, and that justice is served."

Sirich nodded. "I shall. Besides, I am stopping by Waterside Landing to get Doc. Certainly he will accompany me to Alarya. It has been too long, and I'm sure he's tired of the sea."

"Good," replied Galen. "Just remember—this is not one of your adventures into the wood to hunt and hawk. Give Amari my regards." Galen followed Sirich to the door. "Sleep well, boy."

"You too, old man." Sirich's voice echoed behind him as he took his leave and walked down the narrow corridor.

Galen blew out the sconce next to his door in the hallway. Maybe this would discourage any more visitors, allowing him to rest. He closed the creaking door and slid the iron lock into place. As he turned to continue his journaling, he thought he heard light footsteps. He paused and listened.

That was fast. Perhaps more weighs on the boy's mind.

The light footfalls stopped. He thought he heard a low growling. The footfalls started once again, but this time they were lighter and seemed to double with light clicking noises. The household guard occasionally walked this hallway, but typically it was one guard in heavy boots and the clang of his scabbard against the stone wall. He opened his door once more only to see the sconces down the hall flickering as if someone had passed. Perhaps it was a guard with one of the hounds.

He thought no more of it until he looked down and saw a small roll of parchment on the floor as if someone had meant to slide it under his door. As he leaned down to pick it up, he glanced once more down the corridor. Only the flames from other sconces crackled in the corridor. He backed into his chambers and locked the door once more.

Galen walked to his desk to study the paper. He lit a candle and unrolled the parchment. It had no wax seal, and it was quite old. He opened it to reveal only rune-like symbols that flowed together, written in some language he could not read but that seemed familiar to him. It looked to be penned in a faded red ink.

"What is this?" he mumbled, studying the symbols. Perhaps this was meant for someone else? Or maybe one of his apprentices had left it, thinking he had retired for the night? He would ask on the morrow. For now, it was time to sleep.

Before he stood, his thoughts jumped back to Sirich and his symptoms. Individually, they were nothing unusual, but it was odd for these afflictions to happen at once. Perhaps Theo, who knew the great library better than anyone, would know of an old tome that may hold answers if this was anything to be concerned with. He could write to him in Ashbourne to get his opinion. While he was at it, he would ask about these strange runes on this old parchment.

He quickly penned a note but took time to carefully copy the symbols from the mystery parchment. He sealed it in the wax with the ancient glyph that was the sigil of his house: a circular line resembling a serpent reaching for its own tail. His ancestors had likely chosen it to represent knowledge and healing. He dropped the letter into the wooden chute beside his desk that would take it to a basket in the room below. There, he and his assistants sorted messages going to and from Wolfpine. He listened for the little bell that rang anytime anything was dropped into the basket. Too many letters had ended up on the floor behind the table and were never sent. He thought it was a good solution.

He heard nothing. *Odd.* "Damnit, do I really..." His voice trailed off. He walked to the door again, mumbling under his breath as he exited into the dark hall and made his way around the corner to the stairs.

"Damn these stairs," he growled. His bed robe dragged along the dusty stone floor. He rounded the corner and bumped into someone. "My apologies." He turned to see only long dark hair vanish down the staircase, the lingering scent of a sweet aroma in the air. "No manners, these children."

The old door creaked as he entered the small room beneath his chambers. He walked over to the corner, the room dimly lit by one sconce. He glanced out of the only window. The city within the outer walls was winding down for the night. Little fires were being lit in the distance as the house guards took to their posts. The basket was in its usual place, the bell as well. He gave it a shake and the chime echoed in the room.

There lay his letter, right under the bell as it should be. He picked it up and checked to be sure. His wax was still warm, but one end of the seal was slightly loose. To be sure, he carefully peeled the seal back so as not to tear the paper. He lit the small tealight under the wax cup and waited for it to melt while rummaging through the various stamps on the table. He found his sigil and once again sealed the letter. This time he blew it dry to be sure. He put his letter back into the basket and turned to leave. He made his way back toward his quarters.

Can anything else keep me from my bed?

He entered his room and locked the door for the last time. He blew out the remaining candles in the chamber and finally settled into the comfort of his featherbed. Although his body ached, he faded into sleep thinking he would dream of being young again.

Chapter Five

Amari

Amari rowed toward the docks after a fortnight at sea. His fishing cog rocked behind him, anchored in the deep waters of Glass Water Bay. A small crew remained to gather the bounty of fish, primarily blue gill and bloodfin, that had wandered into his nets. Sweat glistened on his ebony skin, the breeze refreshing in its coolness. As he approached, a voice cut through the lapping of water and the cries of birds.

"Doc!" yelled the familiar voice. He turned to spot the silhouette of his small keep. To the right, a figure stood on the closest dock. It looked to him a shadowed image—what he imagined a small dragon would have looked like flapping its wings. He continued closer as the voice grew louder through the breeze.

Sirich waved his arms as if he were lost on an isle and

hoping for rescue. Amari reached down, grabbed a rope at his feet, and threw it up to him.

"My prince!" he smiled. "High Lord Sirich Blacksun of Vaegomar in Waterside Landing? Am I in some trouble?" he asked, laughing. He noticed the mounted men behind him on the shore.

"Have you committed a crime, my friend?" Sirich paused. "Oh yes, you called me your prince, which I am not." Amari laughed like he had in the old days. Sirich had teased him since they were just boys running the yards of Wolfpine.

Sirich reached down and took his hand to help him up to the dock. "Going to battle?" Sirich asked. Amari wore a faded black gambeson over a simple white undershirt with grey cotton breeches. "Or is that now standard fisherman's clothing?"

"Helps with the cold wind at sea. I've no plans to go off to war anytime soon," Amari replied as he got his balance and embraced his friend. "What brings you this far south?"

"Oh, just an adventure to Alarya to see what occurred at some village. An adventure I thought might need a proper traveling companion..."

"I am not sure who that could be," Amari replied. "Does it look like I have time for an adventure? Besides, by the look of it you have fifty or so companions." He glanced at the men behind them.

"They are not you, old friend. I have your horse at the ready, and a wagon of provisions for the road. I may have heard there are a few brothels between here and Valton to keep us warm at night."

Amari smiled. "I have no time. I—"

"Nonsense, Doc," Sirich interrupted. "As your former prince, I command you to ride with me." He offered a teasing smile.

"And that, my friend, is the beauty of it," Amari responded. "You haven't been my prince since we were boys. You cannot command me."

"Yes, yes, but I command you all the same. First, however, I want to see your lord father. I have missed Uncle Amaru."

Amari's smile faded. "Father died nine moons ago, Siri. Almost a year gone now. A fever took him."

Sirich's smile faded as he placed his hand on Amari's shoulder. His eyes started to glisten. "I am sorry, Doc. I wish I had known." Sirich looked down. "Father would have certainly come to pay his respects. Amaru was a good man, an uncle to me."

For a moment they stood in silence before Amari cleared his throat. "It is alright. I have come to terms with it. And besides, my work keeps me busy."

Sirich hugged him once more. "I pray the Elder keeps him."

Amari nodded. "It's good to see you, Siri."

The two men turned toward the old stone keep behind them. As they walked, the old wooden dock creaked under their feet. Amari thought back to his days at Wolfpine. His father had fought alongside William in the last rebellion. He had heard all the stories.

"So how is your father?" Amari asked. "I hear William has been quite busy."

"Yes, the council just convened. I do not fully understand his reasoning for all this, but I *am* trying. Can we not just go back to the good old days of hitting each other with sticks, chasing girls, and—"

"When you would have been the next king, you mean? Look, I understand. A boy born in your position, and that was all taken away. I do not fully understand William's decision myself, but my father told me it was a brave thing.

William called on him first to join the council, but he wanted a simpler life. Father just loved the open seas and fishing."

As they made their way toward the small keep, Amari looked up at the old grey stone, thinking back to when he and his father had first come here. It had been a small castle at one time, whoever it had belonged to. The walls still stood, but some sections had crumbled and fallen. Piles of blackened stones lay in place of a wall, as if a large fire had raged. Tall grass and moss had overtaken much of it. His father had a simple wooden gate constructed where the walls were no more. He had focused on the docks by the water, now a proper fishing port. The keep was in better shape, but some areas were still in disrepair. He reminded himself to hire some masons to finish what his father had started. As a child, Amari had never understood why his father had chosen this location. Now he better understood the charm of this old place.

Amari looked back at Sirich. "Sometimes, we do not understand what our fathers are up to. They may have a vision that we do not fully comprehend."

"I know, Doc. I am trying to understand all of this, it just seems so much easier for Aahsgoth to have one ruler and advisors as it has always been. But I know your father would have been a great addition, whatever becomes of it."

They entered the small hall near the kitchen. Amari poured them both a cup of beer and handed one to Sirich. "Let us drink to the good old days in Wolfpine, and to our fathers." They turned up their cups. "Slow down, Siri! We have many moons ahead of us to get drunk. This trip of yours will take time."

"So, you *are* riding with me!"

"Of course. We have a lot to catch up on. Besides, I have

a lifetime of the sea ahead. Not to mention, Abana is a better fisherman than both of us."

"I would not bet against it." Sirich raised his cup. "And where is your sister? I want to see her."

"Right behind you," a voice responded.

Amari smiled, watching Sirich and Abana embrace. Sirich gave her an audible kiss on her forehead. "Beautiful as ever." Sirich walked around her while holding her hand as if to dance. Her loose tunic was bright yellow with blue and red interwoven patterns sewn throughout. She wore traditional matching Ethoryan breeches, wide at the bottom of each leg. She ran her free hand playfully through her curly hair and smiled.

"Thank you, my lord." She returned a kiss to each of his cheeks.

"Easy, sister, that's the prince," Amari said, laughing.

Sirich glanced at him out of the corner of his eye. "And how have you fared down here with this madman?"

"Please, take him away from here—and find him a good woman!"

"I shall, although I can only promise a good woman for a night," Sirich smiled widely. Amari playfully smacked him on his chest.

"Begone, brother," Abana urged. "I may go myself. I need to go visit our family in Ethorya. I can have Adori run the boat."

"Why now? Wait until I return, and I will go with you," Amari said, concerned.

"I wouldn't go alone. I will ride with a few men after sailing east. How long will you be gone?"

Amari looked at Sirich. "How long will this little adventure take us?"

Sirich's lips pursed in thought. "Two moons?" he said, uncertainty in his voice. "We will go to the village, likely to arrest some savage mountain clan, and be on our way."

"There you go," Amari said to Abana. "Stay here, and I will come with you when we return. We'll accompany Siri back to Wolfpine on the way. I would like to see our family as well. We haven't returned since Father died..." Amari's voice trailed off.

Sirich looked down for a moment. "I'm sorry, old friend, this is a bad time. If you need to go to Ethorya, then do what you must."

"No, it is alright," Abana said quickly. "There is no hurry." She turned to Amari. "Go help your friend, and I will wait until you return. Just bring a good woman back with you. You two catch up. I'll leave you be."

Amari motioned for Sirich to sit at the table. He walked over and grabbed the flagon of beer. "So, how are you really doing, Siri? You seem... different." Amari poured both cups to the brim.

"I thought you said to slow down?" Sirich pulled his cup closer.

Amari sat across from him. "Ah, to hell with it. Might as well get started."

"I am doing alright, I think."

"You think?"

"Galen thinks I have some infection."

"Sirich Blacksun going to see a 'ceptor because you have a sniffle?" Amari laughed. "By the thirteen gods, you *must* be dying." He smiled and drank.

"Maybe, but if I do, might as well be with beer in my belly on the open road with good company." Sirich held out his cup. Amari tapped his cup to Sirich's, foam sloshing to the table.

"It is settled then. Before we ride, let us eat," Amari said. "Relax! Have another drink. I will fetch us supper."

Sirich thought of the men outside waiting. "I will, but first let me tell these riders to go ahead. We will catch up to them."

"You two sit," Abana said, walking back into the kitchen. "I will have Steven bring you something. You don't want Amari cooking for you unless you want to stay on a chamber pot all night. Then you will never catch up to your men!" Abana laughed and walked toward the kitchen.

Amari and Sirich looked at each other with a smile. Amari raised his cup. "Just like old times."

Chapter Six

Theodor

Theodor hated training birds. He would rather be reading some history of Aahsgoth or the Eastern Kingdoms, but it did have its perks. The aviary reached for the clouds. It had been built on the northeastern corner of the great library. He could look in all directions, and today, the view ranged far and wide. He paused to let the last of the setting sun warm his face on the ledge. He could look upon the mountains to the west on a clear day, and gaze upon green fields beyond the town as far as he could see. Small plumes of smoke rose from distant farming villages scattered through the landscape.

The letter the magpie carried had been for him. He had delivered many to various members of the order all day, not expecting to receive one himself. He had not heard from his father in many moons and had last seen him the year before,

on his most recent trip from Wolfpine. He hoped one day
to take his place there. He had enjoyed the few times he had
traveled there, and it was cooler in the north regardless of
season. Perhaps he would visit again soon; he was overdue
for his annual trek. Theodor had been in the order for only a
short time relative to his father, but he had risen to apprentice within only four years of becoming an acolyte.

He pulled the small, rolled parchment from the bird's leg
and put her into the designated cage. He tossed in a reward
of rotten fish and gagged as usual, shooing away the flies. He
walked down the winding staircase to the ground level. If it
were not for the windowed door, he would have wound up
in the cellars again, his distracted thoughts on his father.

Could he be ill?

He entered the yard, walking toward the long wooden
barracks that housed him and his colleagues. The library
and its massive white columns rose behind him. White stone
carvings of historical figures wrapped around the top of the
building. They represented the thirteen aspects, the gods and
goddesses of the old religion. Some thought they were just
various kings and queens from the old days that had shaped
the realm in one way or another. He made his way through
the giant shrubs that most visitors found to be a maze. He
knew every turn to take; he had walked it so many times that
he could likely do it blind.

His quarters were small. Just enough room for a straw
bed, a wash basin in the corner, and a privy that opened
directly to the stream running beneath the building. The
stream had been rerouted from the Longneck River so that
no one had to empty chamber pots. They had since aptly
named it "Shit Creek."

Theodor walked over to his small desk, the wooden
surface barely visible under stacks of parchment and piles

of scrolls. A small window behind his desk let him see the sun while doing tedious scribing work, at least. He laid the parchment on his desk and washed his hands in his basin, the smell of fish still clinging to his nostrils. He washed his face and ran his wet hands through his curly black hair. He had let it grow lately, now almost to his shoulders.

Theodor sat and broke the wax seal, taking off the serpent's head of his house's circular glyph. Theodor wrinkled his forehead as he read.

"Interesting. Odd, but interesting," he mumbled.

His father was inquiring if he had seen such symptoms in a man at the same time, although it did not say who they described. The second short paragraph caught his eye, and he quickly forgot the first. The strange writing of glyphs or runes his father had found seemed to jump off the page at him, but he did not recognize it.

"What ancient language could this be?" he read his father's question aloud.

Not all men and women could read and write, but those that could used the common tongue. He had copied many old books and scrolls in his time here, so he knew there were well over forty languages spoken in Aahsgoth alone, and likely hundreds of dialects between them. This was different, however. The style of the symbols reminded him of the sigils of the noble houses, but they seemed to flow together. They did not seem to resemble anything found in older written languages.

"Ian!" he shouted. He usually heard him through the wall, Ian's quarters being next to his. "Ian, come here!"

Perhaps he is on duty in the library... but usually not this late. He stood. As he was about to walk toward the door, it squeaked open slowly.

"What do you want, Theo?" the boy said, yawning. He rubbed his eyes and wiped the drool from his chin.

"Asleep at your desk again?" Theodor asked, rolling his eyes.

Ian smiled and stretched. "No. I never made it to my desk today."

"You never do. They are going to kick you out of the order."

"So you've told me. What is it?"

Theodor shook his head. "Come and see. Do you recognize this script?"

Ian rolled his eyes. "Always the sleuth," he said slowly, walking around to have a look. He rubbed his eyes once more and studied the parchment. "It looks familiar, but I certainly can't read it, if that is what you are asking."

"I thought so too," Theodor sighed. "I'll check the library tomorrow."

Ian walked back toward the door. "What is that, anyway, and why does it matter?"

"A letter from my father. I do not know—maybe it does not matter. I am sure the king asked him to ask me."

"We have no king, remember? It's been over a decade."

"Right." Theodor paused. "King, overlord... What's the difference? I'm sure the council asked him to ask me."

"At least you get letters from your father."

Theodor looked up. "Thanks anyway, my friend. Go back to scribing, just don't scribe so loudly. These walls are thin, you know."

Ian walked out but reappeared for a moment in the doorway, half-leaning into the room. "Check with Edwyn. He's the language expert. Maybe that's where I have seen it, when I first came here. I started as his steward. He has three times as much shit piled on his desk."

"I'll check with him on the morrow. Someone around here knows, I'm sure." Theodor rolled up the note and stood.

"They might, but remember… if our history is accurate, the plight wiped out more than we can ever remember." Ian disappeared out of sight.

Theodor sat on the edge of his bed. Ian was right—so much had been lost that even the elders did not know what they did not know. *Perhaps I should go see Master Edwyn this evening.* He had never thought the Master Preceptor liked him very much. He was a quiet man and short with his answers, but Theo wanted to help his father no matter how trivial.

"Oh, well. It's not quite dusk yet. Might as well go see him," he muttered. He stood and yelled once more, "Ian, going to see Edwyn and then to the kitchens, would you like—"

"No! I plan to stay here and scribe loudly."

Theodor rolled his eyes. "Fine!" He headed back out to the yards. He made his way through the maze of shrubs and walked the wide stairs to the front of the building. He had walked up these stairs a thousand times, but each time butterflies filled his stomach. The history of this place was tangible.

The first floor was mostly corridors of offices, and if he remembered correctly, Master Edwyn's study was on the west side, near the lesser hall.

"Theo!" a voice echoed behind him. His friend Sam approached. "Where are you going? Come on, let's go eat supper."

"I will, Sam, but I need to speak to Master Edwyn first." He started to walk but stopped again. "You can come with me. Or I'll join you after?"

"I haven't seen him lately. I'm sure his nose is buried in a book. Or he is writing his next one."

"Alright. I will see you in the dining hall."

Sam slapped his shoulder and kept going. "See you then."

He turned back down the hall. *Ah yes, I remember now.* He eyed the two guards beside the double doors to Edwyn's study. He recognized the tall guard, but as usual, he could not remember his name.

He approached to knock, but the tall guard interrupted him. "Apologies, Theo, but Edwyn isn't here."

"Where is he, then? Is this not his study?" Theodor turned to look down the hall again. "Did I not remember correctly?"

"It was." The tall guard looked down.

"Was?"

"He died."

Theodor took a step back, speechless, his eyes wide. He had not known Edwyn well, but his friends had. And although he had a reputation for being stern at times, he was liked by most.

The guards looked at each other, then at Theodor.

The tall one leaned down. "They said he died in his sleep, but Tre here found him face down in a book, two days ago," the guard almost whispered. "Besides, he doesn't sleep in this office." He looked back up at the other guard. "A *bloody* book at that."

Theodor's stomach sank. He did not know what to think, what to make of it. He looked around; not many people were still here at this late hour. "Are you saying someone killed him?"

"No. I'm saying he died in this room, his face down in a bloody book." The guard stood and resumed his position. Theodor would have to tell his friends.

Or should I?

"Thank you, sir," he said finally, still not remembering his name. He turned with his head down. He decided to go meet Sam as he had promised, but what appetite he'd had was now gone.

Chapter Seven

Neph

The night had almost come. Neph wiped his forehead and watched the sun as it started to sink below the horizon, the fading light dancing through the trees in the distance. It had seemed like an eternity since Neph had been promised the gift. Once the moons rose, the god-king Lucian would emerge to sit on his throne and judge those he deemed worthy after years of service.

I shall finally be free, Neph thought as he walked through the small market in the center of Longleaf. He took in the sights of his small village one last time—the sun-faded tents, the laughter of children, the chickens scurrying out of his way. The smells of various stews and spices hung in the air as he made his way down the narrow dirt road leading home.

He was not eager to get back to his cottage even after a

long day in the fields. Although today he had not worked as hard as usual, knowing it was almost time. He could leave this place forever. This was the last time he would go without a bath for days, smelling of grain and soaking his blistered hands from hours spent in the scorching sun. He would no longer have to work his strip and manage the others. He would no longer have to worry about having enough coin to feed his family or pay his taxes.

He was a candlemaker by trade, but Lucian had requested for him to serve as field reeve. He managed the fertile lands outside the walls of Bloodstone, making sure the other peasants kept at work and did not steal. He would typically pour candles at night, after long days in the unforgiving sun. His only son, Seth, helped him now that he was older, learning the methods of wax and wicks. It was hard living here, and he would get what was promised to him.

As Neph entered his cottage off the main road, the door creaking behind him, Aza greeted him with a kiss on the cheek. Little Neph lay fast asleep on his bedding in the corner, sweat glistening on his forehead from being near the small firepit. The hint of a smile came to his face as he paused to look at his son. His lips tightened.

He will be fine.

Neph had taught him well, and he would be a grown man soon. Neph smelled the fresh rabbit stew, steam pouring out the edge of the large black kettle hanging over the fire.

"What's wrong, my love?" Aza seemed to sense his thoughts were elsewhere as she added more carrots and onions.

He sat to remove his sandals. "It's nothing... just that the king is holding court. I must eat and go. It's almost dusk," he said with a slight sigh.

"The king is back?"

"Yes."

"Where does he go for such long periods and what does he want with candlemakers and farmers anyway? At night, no less."

"I am not just some farmer. I..." Neph paused, his face flushing. He was twenty-nine years old but aged by the sun, his shoulder-length dark hair getting lighter and thinner every year, his black-stubbled face skinny and already showing signs of age. Aza turned and must have seen angry eyes staring back at her.

"I know you see to his fields, but why does a king bother to call smallfolk to his court?" she pressed. "You already bring light to his temple and food to his table. Surely his lords and advisors can serve his pleasures."

Neph sighed more heavily this time. "He is no regular king."

"He is no god, Neph. He is a sorcerer, nothing more!"

"Keep your voice down," he whispered, wanting to scream. "He is..." Neph interrupted his growing anger. "He has but only a few guards and fewer advisors. Maybe two thousand men in his garrison, yet with war all around us, no one dares try to take this land. How do you think he keeps his crown?"

She took a moment, rolling her eyes. "I just told you—sorcery. This land is cursed. All the while, he carves out his own kingdom, and men build temples in his honor. What would he have you do this time, anyway?"

Neph hesitated. "He has called us to judge men charged of theft and rape, and a woman of heresy. Like you, here and now, speaking against him..." His voice trailed off as if someone were listening.

Aza did not respond. She adjusted her faded bodice

and walked to the basin. Her white cotton dress swept the dirt floor behind her. Neph watched her for a moment. She pulled her long brown hair over one shoulder and blew the remaining stray hairs out of her eye. She splashed water on her face, but it did not seem to satisfy her. The heat could be oppressive here. Some days during summer, he would help her by fetching water from the river. On those days, the pail of water was warm by the time he made it home.

She dabbed her face with a cloth. "Do what you must. He will do nothing for you as long as you keep doing things for him. I do not know what he promises."

If only you knew.

"We should leave this place," Aza continued. "We should go north to the new fishing village... Water's Edge, I think they call it. My sister lives there, last I heard. It would be better for our son. Besides, they need candlelight as much as any place. Work for your family again, not this so-called king."

Neph sat in silence, turning his eyes from her, looking down at his bowl of stew.

I will leave this place.

Chapter Eight

Ashaya

*H*e should have been home by now.

Merek had not returned, and Sirich had not seemed like himself as of late. Perhaps he had caught the pox or another affliction from some whore in the brothels he frequented. Galen had given him some herbs for the journey south to Valton and had even suggested bloodletting the morning he left. Her goodbye to Sirich had been short, but her father would not have approved of her leaving, so she had snuck out after dusk and sworn the stableboy to secrecy.

Her father would not notice, not with the council assembled in Wolfpine. They would argue for days to come, but mostly they would drink and tell old stories of battles past. Her father could only keep the lords on topic for so long before the wine overflowed. Sirich had not wanted her to come either, but he knew he fought a losing battle. Both were headstrong, but he did demand Mitch come along. If she had gone to her father and he thought that Merek was in some danger, he would have sent an army.

Mitch rode beside her. He had been quiet since they had left two days ago. He moped like a stray dog, barely keeping up along the trail. She had wanted to come alone, but Sirich was right. Mitch had just come from the south and knew the route they had taken. She knew the quickest way was to hire a boat from one of the many fishing villages and go straight to a nearby village or the isle itself—but they may miss him if he came back the way he had gone originally.

"Do you think he'll come back this way?" she asked, trying to break the silence.

"I'm not sure, my lady."

My lady?

"He did mention coming home by sea, as I did." Mitch did not look over at her. She glanced toward the trail ahead and noticed her hair again blowing in her face. She had heeded Sirich's advice and had Clara dye her hair. She did not wear anything with a sigil either, so as not to draw unwanted attention.

Ashaya wore a simple black leather tunic over a white undershirt, with matching riding trousers, her hair now almost as dark as her clothing. She had Acorn fitted with a black saddle. Mitch wore plain brown clothing and no armor, but they did have their swords, and her bow in its usual place over her shoulder with a quiver full of fresh-fletched arrows. Her bow was the only companion she needed, and likely more talkative than Mitch right now.

"The inn is near," Mitch reminded her, in a mumble. "Left at the next crossroads and down to the main road."

She looked up, the sun sparkling through the canopy of

trees above. The path was wide enough here for a wagon, but most of this trail they had ridden single file. Ashaya enjoyed hearing the birds chirping all around them and seeing squirrels dart from tree to tree. The strong scent of purple lilac reached for them through the trees from either side of the path. She brought Acorn to a stop and leaned over to pick a bundle, bringing them to her nose. The aroma was sweet but strong. "Mitch, remind me to take some to Wolfpine on the way back. Clara would love this as a perfume. It smells magickal."

Mitch had stopped ahead of her. "Yes, my lady."

"What is your problem, Mitchel? Enough with the formality and the wounded dog act!" She stared in anger and waited.

Mitch looked down at his horse. "I just—"

"You just what? All day you have acted like a cock, that is what. You have been short with me, and quiet, and certainly not like you're interested in finding my brother. A brother whom *you* serve, may I remind you. I mean, can you at least—"

"I love you!" Mitch interrupted loudly. His face grew as red as the bark of a northern cedar tree. "I've tried to tell you so many times, Ash. We have spent a few nights together, and it seems I'm just a plaything to you, like an old doll you throw out once it is no longer interesting."

Ash sat silent, looking around as if people were listening from behind the trees.

"I'm sorry, Ash. I just… love you," he repeated. "I serve your brother to become a warrior like he is, I do. But I petitioned your father for the role so that I could stay in Wolfpine to be closer to you." For a moment all was quiet; only Acorn's snort broke the spell. "Those nights with you were like the heavens from the songs." Ashaya looked down at the flowers she had crushed in her hand, petals tumbling to the ground below. For a time, only the chirps of birds filled the air.

"I am sorry, Mitch, I..." Ash paused, trying to think of the words. "I thought as much, but to hear it?" Her voice softened. "I like you; I do. But I am expected to... Well, I really do not know what is expected of me anymore. I don't know what to say."

Mitch turned his horse around to approach her. "Say you love me. Or, at the least, if there is something at all in your heart, why not explore it?" He looked into her eyes hopefully.

Ash looked down once more, a tear running down her cheek and falling to her saddle horn. "I cannot, Mitch. At least, not right now." She slowly looked up at him. She saw the heartbreak in his eyes. Mitch turned around once more and rode slowly down the trail. She watched him vanish around a bend in the path.

Only leaves danced in his wake.

Ash trotted out of the woods and came to the crossroads. She looked left down the main road and spied smoke rising above the trees in the distance. She vaguely remembered this place. The main road was wide and muddy, and the wood here was sparse, giving way to smaller shrubs and sand. The smell of saltwater rode the breeze. She had not been here in many years.

"Come on, boy." She turned Acorn left with the reins. She passed a farmer with a wagon full of burlap sacks—likely grain—pulled by two mules. The old man stared at her and

nodded as he passed. She had not even gotten out of Vaegomar but already felt out of place.

Perhaps I should have worn a dress.

She approached the Dusty Rudder, the old inn at the edge
of the Middle Sea and near the border of Vaegomar. She had
stopped here with her father once. Mitch's horse was tied
out front; he was likely already inside with a drink in hand.
She tied Acorn to the hitching post.

The inn did not look too busy—only a few horses waited
for their riders, their heads down as they ate from a trough.
Three hounds lay in front of the barn beside the main building, all panting, watching her but otherwise uninterested.
One man lay against the grey, wooden building, snoring
loudly. The faded sign hanging above the door was an old
boat rudder, suspended from crossed oars that squeaked in
the wind as they moved.

A feather bed would be nice tonight.

This would be the last time for a while she could bathe
and sleep under a proper roof. At the edge of Vaegomar lay
the Expanse, as most called it. The long natural land bridge
ran for hundreds of yards above the Rocky Straight.

The inn's tavern was quiet. Only a few men sat alone with
their cups, and two others shared a table, whispering among
themselves. A bard sat with his bowl of stew, his lute forgotten on the table beside him. His hand was wrapped around
the spoon, and he did not bother to look up. The sun shone
through the windows, dust twirling in the defined rays. The
clanking of pots and pans filtered in from the kitchen behind
the bar.

Mitch sat at a table by a window, a cup to his lips, drinking deep with his head thrown back. He put down his cup,
looked up at Ash, then looked down, wiping away the foam
mustache with his sleeve.

"The ale's good then?" she said, approaching the table. She hoped they could get past the conversation back on the trail, at least for now.

"There she is!" a voice called from the back. The lady dropped her towel on the bar and untied her apron. She pulled her black curly hair behind her neck and walked toward Ashaya. "Oh my, how you've grown!" the woman said, hugging her.

Ash embraced her, took a step back, and then remembered. "Carolyn?"

"Yes, my lady. A little older, and a lot wiser. So, what brings you to my inn, princess? Your husband told me you were coming in."

Husband?

"Please, we don't want any unnecessary attention," Ash whispered as she looked around. "This is your place?"

"It is now. Bought it from Old Man Griffin before he died. That was about four years ago. Always wanted a place of my own since I left Ethorya. He took me in, and I helped him run this place for fifteen years. But enough about me! Look at you, the little princess all grown. Your hair is darker! Come sit. Your husband is drinking without you."

Ash tightened her lips as Carolyn led her to the table where Mitch sat. "Oh, he's just a friend. My brother's apprentice," she tried to clarify quickly, before reaching the table.

They both sat. Ash still felt awkward thinking of what Mitch had said.

"So, you're just passing through? Are you hungry?" Carolyn asked, holding Ash's hands across the table.

"Yes, madam. We've had a long ride," Mitch chimed in. Carolyn stood and motioned to a kitchen wench, all while keeping a smile on her face.

"Thank you, Carolyn. We will stay a night, but we're here about my brother, Merek."

Carolyn sat back down. "Oh, Merek, such a fine man-nered young man. And handsome!"

Mitch rolled his eyes.

The girl brought Ash a cup of beer, foam lapping over the sides. "Have you seen him of late? He never came back to Wolfpine after a ranging down south."

"I can't say that I have, not since these two came through here." She thrust a finger at Mitch. "How did this one return without him?"

Mitch started to speak, but Ash beat him to it. "Mer-ek sent Mitch back, but he was supposed to be a few days behind."

Carolyn stood again and yelled to the girl. "Bring some bread, stew, and the whole damn flagon."

"Thank you. We will need..." Ash paused. "Two rooms, if you have them, just for the night."

"We do. Not busy at all right now. It should pick up as autumn approaches. So, where are you two headed?"

Mitch cleared his throat. "The Crescent Isle, my lady."

Carolyn sat back. "Oh, the haunted isle, or so they say. The sailors that dock out back do not go near. Strange tales of that place, but you know how stories go." Ashaya noticed the singer, the man's head now laying on the table, as the serving girl came. She set down two bowls of stew, steam still rising from them, and a half-loaf of bread. Ashaya had smelled the onion before she walked into the inn.

Mitch was already blowing on his first spoonful. "Smells good."

"Duck broth, with carrots, celery, onion, and a touch of lemon," Carolyn said proudly.

"Duck?" Mitch asked, surprised.

"Yes, why do you think you don't see them out back to-day?" she said, laughing.

Ashaya suddenly sighed deep and closed her eyes. As if she were dreaming, she found herself standing in a beautiful forest with light green willow trees, their branches reaching for the ground, sunlight cascading down through the taller trees and casting shadows on the lush moss-covered ground of the forest. She heard trickling water and turned to see a winding brook with crystal-clear water running over smooth stones. A sweetness filled the air. She heard several voices, whispers she could not make out.

"Ash? Ashaya!" Mitch almost yelled. Ashaya opened her eyes to see Mitch and Carolyn back in the tavern. She was now standing. Carolyn pulled at her hands.

"Sit down! Are you alright, Ash?" Carolyn asked in a whisper. Ash looked around to see a few of the men staring at her.

She turned back to them. "Yes. Yes, I am fine. I was just... daydreaming." She took a long drink of ale from her cup.

"I'll get that room ready. You need some rest." Carolyn stood. "I hope you find your brother. How are Siri and your lord father?"

Ash took another drink and leaned back in her chair. "They are well, I suppose. Doing what they do... and who they want." Carolyn smiled. They sat silent for a moment as Carolyn went to prepare their rooms. Ash wanted to say something to Mitch, but she could not find the words. He had laid his heart out, and she thought she must talk about it tomorrow on the long road ahead.

I owe him that at least.

Ash gazed out of the window. Dusk had settled in. The sky glowed a dark orange behind the trees where the sun had left its mark. Dogs barked outside, likely the hunting hounds in the barn around the back. They kept on for a few minutes, loudly growling, and at least one began howling as well.

The front door of the inn creaked open. A man walked in and slowly closed the door behind him, keeping his eyes down. Ashaya noticed that everyone in the tavern watched him enter. He was rather tall and lean, and he wore some type of black drawstring doublet with no undershirt, with tattoos on both arms that Ash couldn't make out from across the room. He wore a long, dark cloak and pulled down the hood to reveal ragged black hair and an untrimmed beard. The man stood for only a moment before taking a seat at the front corner table. He looked up, his deep blue eyes meeting Ashaya's for a moment. She quickly turned her head back to Mitch.

"Alright, your rooms are ready," Carolyn said, walking toward the table.

"Who's the stranger?" Ash whispered to Carolyn.

She looked over at the man. "Oh, he's been in here several times recently. Doesn't say much, just has a drink and then heads out. Leaves a small gold coin every time."

"A gold piece for a *beer*?"

"Sure does." She leaned down and whispered, "Never seen a coin like it, but gold is gold. He seems harmless enough. Smells like a wet dog, though," she said, smiling.

Ash finished her bread and beer while Mitch ate from his bowl of stew. Ash reached for her sack of coins.

Carolyn waved her off. "Oh, come now, tonight is on the house. Besides, someone is paying more than enough for his beer." Carolyn smiled and nodded at the stranger.

Ashaya returned the smile and stood. "Mitch, I'll see you at daybreak?"

"Yes, my lady," Mitch responded in a low tone and went

right back to his cup. Ash paused, not sure what else to say, then turned and headed toward the stairs across the room.

"Last two rooms on the right," Carolyn said. "Take your pick. Should be fresh water in the basin. The privy is out back. Let me know if you need anything. Get some rest." Carolyn walked back down the stairs, leaving her alone in the small hallway.

The room was compact but would do for the night. A small straw bed, a fireplace, and a table with a basin. A stack of firewood lay on the floor. Carolyn had seen to it that someone had a fire going already, as well as a burning lantern on the bedside table. The window overlooked the barn. Ash stood and studied it for a moment. All she could see below was the glow of a torch as someone walked toward the barn. The moons were bright tonight, and only a few stars were visible as they twinkled through the darkness. Ash thought of the place in her daydream, a beautiful place it seemed, although it scared her the more she thought of it. She had never had such a dream while awake. Perhaps she was overly tired. It had been a while since she had ridden for so long, and the day had been warm.

The room was cool, so she added a couple of logs to the fire. She had not brought any extra clothes, and certainly not her sleeping gown. She removed her boots and climbed into her bed fully clothed, pulling the linen blanket over her but not before blowing out the lantern. The straw mattress was firm but softer than the ground had been last night. She reached to adjust her pillow, realizing she did not have one.

This is not Wolfpine, but I'd better enjoy the comfort tonight. She leaned down and grabbed her spare breeches to roll them into a makeshift pillow. *This will have to do.*

Ash closed her eyes and thought of Mitch. She did not want him to be angry with her, but she could not return his love—at least, not now. Maybe she had been unfair to him those few nights together.

Was he still downstairs? Would he drink his sorrows away?

The fire popped and crackled. She opened her eyes to shadows dancing on the ceiling before shutting them one last time. As she grew warm, her thoughts drifted back to the forest she had seen, the stranger downstairs, Carolyn, Sirich, her father, and finally Merek. She would find him if it were the last thing…

Chapter Nine

Sirich

"Did William ever tell you how he met my father?" Amari looked over at Sirich, chewing on a piece of straw.

Sirich had enjoyed catching up on the long road south. "He told me more than once, actually. He tends to forget what stories he has already told me when he's drunk." Sirich smiled. "But one thing he has never told me is why your family left Ethorya in the first place."

"Politics," Amari answered quickly. "Ethorya is a beautiful place, and Father loved his people, but they are resistant to change and overly dogmatic when it comes to gods. The elders tend to look down upon those who do not follow the old ways. Ultimately, he just wanted to see Aahsgoth and get back to the sea. When your grandfather stood with Ethorya against the Eastern Invasion, he knew he would have an opportunity. William was just a young lad, the crown prince. He didn't have to fight but he stood on the field along with everyone else." Amari paused. "Father felt like he owed him after your grandfather died."

Sirich listened in silence, thinking back to the old chair and his father. He felt lightheaded, and his gut hurt again, although not as much as his thighs. The road had been long today as they came into the foothills of the Highlands. "What I would give to see him that young, in his prime," Sirich finally responded.

"Do you know the history of Ethorya, Siri?" Amari asked, looking over at him.

"I know what Galen taught me. And I have firsthand knowledge of the brothels," Sirich laughed.

Amari shook his head. "Of course you do, old friend. Aahsgoth has many gods and goddesses. Many faiths, from the Thirteen to the Elder. But there is only one goddess in Ethorya. All the oral traditions of the Gazi tell the same tale." Amari paused as if he were deep in thought.

"Go on, brother. I do enjoy a good story."

"It is said that the goddess of the earth, Gaziael herself, saved our people from the slavers Old Afarya in the east who landed on the shores. The singers and storytellers say one woman drove an army back into the sea and left it red with blood, giving the Godswar Sea its name. Then she established her kingdom here in the new world."

Sirich turned to him. "The same goddess of earth who is one of the thirteen aspects?"

"That's the one," Amari replied.

"No offense, brother, but one woman—or one man, for that matter—couldn't defeat an army. Then again, a goddess with magick... perhaps." They both looked ahead for a moment.

"Do you smell that?" Sirich abruptly asked.

Amari sniffed the air. "I smell nothing but horse shit. What is it?"

"Smoke." Sirich sniffed again. "And onions." Sirich shook his head. "Gods, goddesses... I start to lose track after a while. I've yet to hear from one, never mind *see* one." Sirich pulled an apple from his saddlebag and took a bite. Hearing the crunch, Amari looked over. Sirich took another and tossed it to him.

Amari caught the apple and raised it as if toasting with a fine wine. "To the gods and goddesses, wherever they may be."

Sirich held his apple up, half-eaten already. They both took a bite.

"Dusk is upon us. Let us find a place to make camp for the night." Sirich looked behind them. "Philip, ride ahead and find some level ground."

"Yes, my lord." The rider took the lead and disappeared down the road ahead. Philip knew this land, being of House Bore, whose ancestral seat of Castle Stoneshield sat to the west on the Crystal River.

Sirich finished the apple and threw the core to the trees. His stomach continued to ache; insatiable hunger had overtaken him.

"You alright, Siri?" Amari had noticed Sirich holding his gut and wincing.

"Yes, brother, I will live." The pain was not enough to distract from the beauty of Borwyn, one of the smaller kingdoms that stretched from Starfall Bay to the peaks of the Highland Mountains. The road was ancient and wide and had been carved into the side of the rockface for many leagues. Large stones protruded from the hills on the right. A slight dropoff and a thick pine forest flanked their left. The trees stood straight and tall, like an army in waiting. Sirich enjoyed the view for a moment. Their horses' hooves clopped on the rocky road and the men quietly chatted behind them. The farther they rode, the more the army of pines gave way to a mixture of flora. Sirich, in particular, noticed the large oak trees towering above them with ancient arms reaching for the light. The sky's deep blue had started to fade. The deeper into the wood they rode, the song of leafhoppers filled the air, almost drowning out the fifty or so horses behind them.

Philip returned ahead of them, nodding. "My lord, up ahead the wood grows sparse. Plenty of room for camp."

"Good. Bring the wagons up and let us pull off the road so I can get off this damn horse. The dead can wait a bit longer." Philip nodded and rode behind them.

"I smell it now," Amari chimed in.

"Smell what?"

"Smoke. You said you smelled smoke."

"Yes, I did, didn't I? And onions. That was a league ago." Sirich looked ahead of them in the distance and saw it. Smoke rose from above the tree line. "Over there." Sirich nodded toward the trees.

"I don't see anything. Over where?"

"Are you blind?" Sirich jested. "Have the years taken your sight?" He watched Amari squint, still trying to see something. "Let's have a look. Perhaps it is an old inn or tavern," Sirich said hopefully.

"Or a witch that wants us in her cauldron. A jinn, perhaps," Amari replied quickly.

Sirich turned to the men that followed. "Go ahead and make camp. We will catch up." He turned back to Amari. "Come, brother, let's go. Perhaps a warm meal awaits." Sirich rode ahead.

"Or we become the warm meal…" Amari shook his head and followed.

Philip had been correct; the woods were sparse here. A small path from the main road was evident but overgrown.

"Looks to be just a small house," Amari said.

Sirich could see the trees move past the cabin as he rode. "Ah, maybe a warm bed in there… with a warm woman to go with it!"

"Or a crone to steal your soul and drink your blood," Amari responded with a stern face.

"You're right, Doc." Sirich stopped his horse as the cabin came into clear view. "Let's not walk the horses up, otherwise we might frighten someone into planting an arrow in our chests."

The trail opened to a clearing. The cabin looked old and unkempt. Amari dismounted and tied his horse's reins to a tree right at the edge. "Wait, Siri."

Sirich stopped and looked back. "Hurry up, then. The light is fading."

Amari took his sword from his saddle and strapped it to his waist, catching up to Siri as they both removed their riding gloves. Smoke poured from a small chimney, rising to meet the darkening sky. Shadows crawled slowly across the yard as the moonlight reappeared from behind passing clouds. They approached slowly.

"What do you want?" a voice called to them. An old woman stood near a wood pile at the side of the cabin. She wore a tattered grey dress, and her silver hair ran over her shoulders, almost to the ground.

"We are sorry, my lady, we mean no harm," Amari called out.

Sirich added, "We are riding south, my lady. We saw the smoke from the pass."

She did not respond.

"My friend speaks true. We mean no harm. We just thought we may find a roof for the night."

The old lady picked up four or five logs as if she were ignoring them. Amari and Sirich looked at one another.

"Do you need help with that? It looks quite heavy," Sirich offered.

"Well, you're here. Might as well put yourself to good use. Gonna be cold tonight, I can feel it in my bones."

Both walked toward the old woman. Her long silver hair covered her face as she leaned down to grab more wood. "All of your men won't fit in here. You gonna leave them to the ground?"

"How do you know we ride with more men?" Amari asked.

"I could hear your horses on the road. You're traveling with a small army, it seems. There a war somewhere?"

"No, we are riding to Valton, in Alarya. I am Sirich of Wolfpine, and this is my companion, Amari of Waterside Landing. We travel from Vaegomar. What is your name, my lady?"

The woman slung logs into his chest as if they were feather pillows. "Knew a woman from Vaegomar once. Haven't been there since I was just a girl. Used to sell at the markets with my father. A lifetime ago." She kept adding wood to their arms. "I'm Althea. Call me Aly. Everyone else does. Or used to, anyway." She piled the last log into Amari's arms and walked toward the cabin.

"Nice to make your acquaintance, Aly. Do you have a surname? And where is your husband?" Sirich asked. Amari looked at him, his eyes encouraging him to shut up.

"My surname? I don't have a surname. Those are for you

high lords. People didn't always have them, you know. I'm just Aly." Aly's expression never changed.

The woman walked faster than both of them, despite carrying her wood. Once she reached the cabin, she added her load to the neat pile of logs at the front door. "My husband is in the back," she finally said.

Sirich and Amari added to the pile of wood. "Great. We shall go to introduce ourselves."

"No need; the dead don't speak. He's been back there for fifteen years now."

Sirich looked at Amari and stopped himself from chuckling out loud. Amari continued, "I'm sorry to hear that. We'll be on our way. We didn't mean to trouble you."

"No need. Come on in. Might as well eat while you're here. Don't get visitors that often. Been years, really."

The little cabin was in some disrepair. *A homely little place*, Sirich thought. The old lady added two logs to the small hearth. A straw bed lay in one corner of the room, a small kitchen table in the other. A few chairs were scattered around the fire. He and Amari looked around at the books stacked everywhere. The cabin smelled of onion, but Sirich could also smell the hint of a musty odor. The woman walked around, lighting various candles from the one she carried.

"Have a seat. I'll add some potatoes to the pot, and more onion. Already had supper going, anyway." Sirich smiled at Amari and rubbed his belly. It still hurt, but maybe this would appease his hunger for once.

"You are too kind, my lady," Amari responded.

"Aly, I said. And I'm no lady."

Sirich raised his eyebrows. "So, you can read, then?" he asked, looking around at all the dusty books. "You seem to have a small library here." The woman kept chopping potatoes and bringing a handful at a time to the pot hanging over the fire.

"It's all I've done since my husband died. A young woman taught me. So many things I didn't know, or even care that I didn't know, for that matter." She kept on cutting, moving on to more onions. Her knife thumped the table with each slice.

"What young woman?" Sirich asked, examining a pile of books.

"The one that healed me. Tall woman with dark hair. I don't remember much. Don't even think I knew her name, but I won't forget her blue eyes." The old woman brought more to the pot, this time carrots. The fire hissed occasionally as the water boiled over, leaping into the flames. "I was lying there dying from some pox. Horrible fever and sore all over. My husband rode to White Oak with all the coins we had, to look for a healer. Didn't think I would be breathing by the time he returned. The woman got here first, beat my husband on foot it seems. Said she could help me, but it would come at a price."

Sirich looked up from the dusty pages. "A price?"

The woman cut more carrots but did not answer. After the next round of carrots, she finally responded, "Said I may live longer than I wanted."

Sirich and Amari looked at one another. Amari shrugged his shoulders without saying a word. "Why wouldn't you want to live longer?" Sirich asked.

"Gets lonely. And tiring," she replied quickly, as if she'd been waiting for him to ask.

"What did she give you?" Amari asked.

"Called it dragon's blood. Asked for a bowl, walked outside, and came back in with a few drops. Said it had to cool."

"Dragon's blood?" Sirich repeated.

"She was right. After a short spell of cold sweats, my gut

hurting and ears ringing, I pulled through. Husband died a year later."

"I am sorry for your loss," Amari said.

"Was she some witch?" Sirich added quickly.

"What I thought, too, but she came by for two fortnights. She brought a few books and taught me to read. Been collecting books ever since. Nothing better to do." Sirich stood and walked to another stack of books and picked one up.

"Siri!" Amari chided in an urgent whisper. The woman never turned around, still chopping more carrots. Sirich did not look up.

"Dragons. You have a lot of books about dragons, Aly." Sirich flipped through a few pages, replaced it, and chose another book, looking through each for only a few moments.

"Turns out she gave me exactly what she said it was. I thought it was some potion with an exotic name. Blood of the dragon is known to heal. Probably why they were hunted down, made into monsters. Worth more than gold in that age."

The old lady walked over and stirred the pot with a long wooden spoon. Her dark woolen dress dragged on the floor, tattered and torn. She scooped two bowls of stew and handed the first to Amari.

"Here, young man."

Sirich put the book down he had started reading. "Thank you, Aly." Sirich stood and took the bowl, sitting back down. The steam cleared out his nose. Amari and Siri both blew on their spoons before taking a bite. The woman pulled up another chair and sat it by the fire. "So, what do you know of dragons then, Aly? I have read of them myself recently."

"Know everything about them, at least what has been written."

Sirich put another book on his leg and alternated between flipping through pages and taking bites of stew.

Amari looked up from his bowl. "Pardon my friend, my lady, for making himself at home. But I must say it is unusual to find a small library in the middle of the woods."

Sirich looked up. "Yes, how does one go about acquiring so many books?" He went back to flipping pages.

"The woman and her friend brought the first of them."

Sirich looked up. "Her friend?"

"Another woman, red-headed, showed up with her once. Said they were the only ones like them. I collected some other books from markets, villages. Used to trade carrots for them if I came across one. One man knew where to get them somewhere in the south. The Greenlands, I think. He would bring them to me every trip he made. Most can't read. I was lucky to meet the dark-haired woman. Like I said, nothing better to do." She leaned back in her chair again.

Sirich drank the last of his bowl, looking down at the open book and wiping his chin. "What a wonderful sight it must have been to see one of those creatures fly by. Wings blocking out the sun," he said, imagining.

"Horse shit," the woman said calmly. Sirich and Amari exchanged surprised looks as Aly went on. "They were creatures of the night. They never saw the sun, although they carried its fire in their throats. Men eventually figured that out on the rare occasion that they crossed paths. They learned their weakness eventually, sun and silver, driving them from their lairs. One old story from a long dead 'ceptor wrote that there were once two suns, like how there are two moons. The first dragons ate one, and the sun god cursed them to never see the sunlight again."

"And you believe that? Likely some bard's tale," Sirich replied.

The woman stood. "Maybe. But either way, their blood does what it does. I'm proof." She collected their empty bowls. "You can sleep on the floor, or there's a small shed out back." She walked to the kitchen. Sirich and Amari stood and followed.

"Thank you, my lady, but we need to get back to our men," Amari said. He looked at Sirich with a pointed stare.

"Yes, we should," Sirich added. "But thank you for your hospitality."

The woman walked over and added more logs to the fire. "Have it your way. Getting cold out."

Amari waved his arm to get Sirich's attention. Amari nodded toward the woman. "Ah, yes. Here, Aly. For your troubles." Sirich dug into his tunic and pulled a sack of coins out. He took a silver piece but dropped it on the floor. Amari reached down and picked it up.

"No need," the woman said. Amari insisted and laid it on the chair.

They walked to the door, and Sirich turned to thank her once again. The woman stared at him as if she were peering into his soul. A slight shiver ran down his spine. He nodded and turned to follow Amari.

"Watch out for dragons," she said as they disappeared into the wood.

Chapter Ten

Theodor

"Did you speak with Master Edwyn yet? About your letter?" Ian asked as they walked past the library.

Theodor looked up and noticed the figures on top of the building. "He's gone." Theodor looked down.

"What do you mean, gone?"

"I went to his study yesterday. The tall guard—"

"Nigel? The tall man from Cherok with the bald head?"

"Yes. He said Master Edwyn…" Theodor looked around and lowered his voice. "He said he died."

"Died? *Really*? Are you shitting me?"

"Lower your voice!" Theodor hissed. "Yes, he's dead. And something wasn't right about it."

"What do you mean? He was old, I suppose."

"No, the guard—"

"Nigel."

"Yes. Nigel said that they found Master Edwyn in his study, his face in a book. A *bloody* book. But the word put out was that he died in his sleep." They started walking again. "Sam said he hadn't seen him in a few days, but I thought perhaps he just took leave."

"Maybe he did. Nigel could have been pulling your leg," Ian suggested. "Perhaps he traveled home to see his family?"

"He has no family, at least none that he cares for. That is why he came to Ashbourne in the first place. Well, according to Sam, anyway. This is all just odd. I do not want to talk about it." Theodor motioned toward the hall. "Come, let us eat."

"No, I'm going to meet Remy," Ian almost whispered.

Theodor smiled for the first time since he had heard the news of the master's death. "Where?"

"In the gardens. I have to go, she is probably waiting." Ian turned and jogged away.

"He will never last here," Theodor mumbled with a smile. His stomach growled, reminding him to continue toward the hall.

Theodor sat at the short table with some of his friends. He ate with one hand and picked at the peeling wood with the other.

"Did you hear?"

Theodor glanced up under his lashes as Sam approached the table with his tray. "Yes, Sam. Keep quiet. We can talk later."

"Just go straight to Old Man Aethon. Certainly, the over-lord would know if anyone would," Sam reminded Theo.

They ate their supper in the dining hall on the west side of the library. "Overlord Aethon wouldn't likely take a meeting with me," Theodor responded with a sigh.

"Ask Ridley. She can set up a meeting. He is her grand-father."

"Maybe, but he *is* a bastard," Theodor added. Theodor looked at Sam, who gave a pointed look at Herman. "I'm sorry, Hermy. I didn't mean it that way."

"It's fine, Theo. Not the worst thing I've heard. And I *am* a bastard." The boys all looked at one another, their lips tight. Sam was the first to laugh, and the rest followed.

Theo took a drink from his pewter cup and laid down the parchment on the table, going back to his venison pie. *I wonder if Remy actually met Ian in the gardens?* he thought with a grin. The food distracted him; he could taste the mulled wine the meat had been marinated in.

"What's that?" Ridley's raspy voice stood out among the sea of noise around him. Butterflies fluttered in Theodor's stomach. He was sure his face was already red.

"Some note Theo got from his father in Wolfpine," Sam replied through a mouthful of food.

Theodor turned to see Ridley carrying her tray, catching her light green eyes. She walked with a confidence about her. "Move over, fat boy," she said as she forced her way between Theo and Sam. The boys moved aside and made room.

Sam dropped his spoon. "Dammit, Ridley, there are plenty of tables over there."

"And there are plenty of pies for all of us, so slow down." The other boys chuckled but no one looked at Sam. Theodor glanced at Ridley. He noticed the way she flicked her curly black hair over one shoulder. He caught himself staring and looked back down at his bowl.

Ridley looked down at the parchment. "I've seen this," Ridley said before blowing her fork and taking a bite.

Theodor looked up again. "Where? Can you read it?"

She took a sip from her cup. "No, just saying I've seen it. Looks familiar."

"Well?" Theodor waited.

She dug into her pie. "Well, what?"

"You said you have seen it, but you didn't say where."

"Grandfather's quarters, on his desk. Remember, I get to dust and sweep and empty his chamber pot when I'm not in the gardens," she said as if it were some honor.

"Does his shit stink?" Sam asked. Ridley rolled her eyes. "Your grandfather, we were just talking about him and—"

Theodor interrupted. "We were just discussing if he would take a meeting with me. What do you—"

"Ask him yourself," she said, looking back at Sam. "And yes, but not as bad as you do right now, fat boy."

Laughter erupted again. Theodor looked back down at his plate. "Fine. I'll ask him, but no thanks to you, Ridley."

She wiped her mouth with her sleeve. "Why does it matter so much?"

"Because my father asked. He is a master of the order and sent this to me." He paused. "I... I want to make him proud." Ridley and the others looked at him. Heat crept into his face; he knew it must be turning blood red. Herman started giggling. The others followed.

"I want to make him proud," Sam mocked him, in some vague rendition of his voice. Theodor could not help the slight smile, but he tried to hold it back. He took the last bite of his crust and rubbed his plate, trying to soak up the last of the juice and crumbs before tossing it into his mouth. He stood.

Herman looked up at him. "Where are you going? You could wait on us."

"I'm going to ask the overlord myself."

The great library was impressive every time he saw it. Theodor walked toward the main entrance, the imposing statues above him looking down over the yard. The hair stood on the back of his neck as if they were watching him with their stone eyes, a little darker now with the setting sun. He walked towards the overlord's quarters and hoped he would find him there. Preceptors of all disciplines went to and fro, most finishing up their duties for the day. Gardeners, linguists, scholars, and artisans all walked the great halls, their footsteps and conversations echoing off the marble floors.

Theodor approached the great wooden doors of the overlord's chamber. He paused and took a deep breath, looking upon the huge, wooden double doors. The bird-like winged glyph, the sigil of House Aethon, adorned the center of both doors. As he raised his hand to knock, one of the doors slowly creaked open.

"My lord!" Theodor said, startled. The overlord was a short man, but he carried a presence about him. Theodor always thought he looked old and wise, like some wizard from some far-off land. He walked with a cane and a limp, his white beard hanging to his belly.

"What is it, young man?" he asked with a wheeze.

"My lord, if you have a moment, I have something I

would like to show you." He pulled the parchment from his inside pocket.

"What is it, Theodor? I'm short on time." Theo looked up, his eyes wide, surprised the overlord even knew his name.

"It is this note from my father in Wolfpine, my lord. He wanted to know what this language was, and I have never seen it before. So far, I can't find anything in the library."

Lord Aethon took the note from him, his eyes dropping to the words between his long fingers. He looked over his nose as he examined it. "I do not recognize it, but there are many old languages. What would Galen need of this?"

Theodor hesitated for a moment. "I do not know, but I thought that—"

"It is nothing. There's no need to bother with some extinct language. It may have been one dialect from a single village, thousands of years ago. Perhaps from the east. Or even a child's scribbling. Leave it be."

Theodor's heart sank. "But, overlord, if he sent this, I'm sure it is in the service of the king."

"We have no king, boy."

Theodor took a step back. "Yes, my lord, you are probably right. I'm sorry to have bothered you." Theo slightly bowed. The overlord walked past him.

"My lord?" The old man stopped and turned. "May I have the note back? I will inform my father."

The old man held his hand out toward Theo. "Give Galen my regards."

"I will. And I am sorry to hear of Master Edwyn."

The overlord sighed, glancing down at the note once more before returning it to Theo and continuing on his way.

Theodor stood there for a moment. *Maybe it is nothing.* He turned for his quarters, his shoulders slumping. He wanted to come through for his father, no matter how small the request. "He *is* a bastard," Theo mumbled, walking with his head down.

Two hands grabbed his shoulders and stopped him. "Shit, you scared me!"

Ridley laughed; he was sure it was because of the look on his face.

"So, what did grandfather say?" she asked. "I just passed him."

They continued toward the main hall.

"He says it's nothing and not to worry about it. I guess you saw something else. He's never seen this language."

"Bullshit. I know what I saw." Ridley stopped. "Come on." She took his hand.

Theo looked down and blushed again. "Where are we going?"

She pulled harder on his hand. "To his chamber."

He pointed with his thumb over his shoulder. "We just left his chamber."

"Come on, Theo! I know another way."

Chapter Eleven

Ashaya

L eaves crackled underfoot as Ashaya made her way into the forest from the sea behind her. A smile stretched across her face as the sunlight sparkled through the canopy above. Each tree she passed, she ran her hand across the white bark, a texture of thick parchment both rough and smooth simultaneously. Each tree was unique, with weeping branches reaching for the ground, their roots twisting around each other, racing for the earth. Leaves had started to fall, but most trees were still full and colorful. It was warm here, and a hint of sweetness rode the cool breeze.

She walked deeper into the forest along a red stone path. The stone looked to be wet, and the short walls on either side melted together as one. The deeper into the wood she went, the bigger the boulders became. At first one would lay here and there, then more complex formations, as if giants had played a game of knucklebones with pebbles.

She stopped to look back at where she had been. It had seemed gradual, but she realized the change had been abrupt. She made her way on the winding path around the boulders, each step becoming more difficult. The hiss of the sea behind her was now almost inaudible. *What is this place?* Ashaya stopped once more to get her bearings. She looked around, the wind whispering to her—or perhaps it was just the air wheezing through the stones and caves that surrounded her.

"Ah... Shay... Ah." She heard the whisper more clearly this time.

Her eyes widened and she gasped. "Who's there?" Goose pimples rose on the back of her neck, and the hair on her arms stood.

"Ah... Shay... Ah." The whispers continued from every direction.

"Hello?" she shouted. "Show yourself!" She reached for her bow, but it was not there. Her sword was gone too.

"Wel... come," the breathy voice said this time, among other whispers she could not make out.

She ran in the direction she faced, jumping over stones and dodging tree limbs, not looking back. She came to a large clearing, stopping to catch her breath. She put her hands on her knees, gasping for air, her bare feet bleeding.

"Where are my boots? My clothes?" she said aloud.

She stood in the center of a massive circle of stones, covering herself. The blood from her feet ran into the markings in the stone that she stood on. She backed up, covering her chest with one hand and reaching behind her with the other.

"Ah... Shay... Ah," she heard again. She looked down. The sun glyph of House Blacksun was carved into the center stone where she had been standing, the deep lines now filled with her blood. "Ah... Shay... Ah."

"Where am I?" she screamed.

"Ah... Shay... Ah."

"Stop!" A breath was hard to come by; tears leapt from her face to the stones below.

"Ah... Shay... Ah," the whispers called again.

"Please! Stop it!"

"Ah... Shay... Ah... Ashaya! Ash! Wake up!"

Mitch shook her shoulders. She sat up and scooted backwards away from him, pressing into the leaves behind her bedroll. Sweat beads on her forehead ran down the contours of her cheeks. She looked around the campsite, the fire still burning.

"Ash, are you alright?"

"What, where..." she tried to ask.

"You were dreaming. You were talking in your sleep and swinging your arms as if you were in a fight." Mitch tried to calm her. "Look at me." He gently grabbed her shoulders. "It's all right, it was just a dream." Ashaya looked into his grey eyes, still breathing heavily.

The fire was dim now, but the moons and stars were bright tonight. Their horses stood where they had tied them while making camp. Mitch handed her his water pouch. "Here, just breathe."

She took a deep breath and drank. "I'm sorry, it was—"

"No need to apologize, it was just a dream. A bad one, apparently."

Ashaya was glad he was here with her. She took another drink. "It was so beautiful and then... Well, it wasn't."

He added more logs to the fire from the pile. "Only a few hours until sunrise. Are you hungry?"

They packed up the horses after breaking their fast. It was bread and jerky again, along with a few blueberries from her pack. They had passed the last tower a few days prior, leaving Vaegomar for the first time, and Ashaya had been uneasy ever since. The Expanse had been easy riding, but long and hot. The land bridge was high over the sea, which crashed against the sharp boulders waiting below. They stayed on the inner coast all the way through Ethorya and into Thurel, hoping to see Merek heading home.

"Mitch?" she said, after a long silence while she found the words.

"Ash?"

"Thank you."

He looked over to her. "For what?"

"For coming with me." Mitch half-smiled, adding a nod. Ashaya took a deep breath before going on. "And thank you for telling me how you feel. I suspected as much, but it does mean a lot that you said the words. I just need time to think, but my concern right now is my brother. I hope you understand."

"I do. And I agree. Merek is my mentor, and I never should have left him. I am sure he is fine."

The trail here was wide open, with sparse trees to their left and the sea to the right. "How far to the next town?" Ashaya asked.

"Not far now. Another hour or two."

She looked forward to a hot meal and a bed and perhaps a bath. She even missed her room in Wolfpine, and she could imagine her father cursing after finding out she had left. "I wonder what Father will do. Do you think he's behind us somewhere, looking for me?"

"William? He may send an army after you," Mitch said, smiling. She returned the smile and patted Acorn, bringing him into a canter.

"There," Mitch said, pointing ahead. "I see smoke and seagulls swarming. Water's Edge awaits."

As they got closer, she thought back to her strange dream. *Hopefully, I can sleep well tonight.* The town was as Mitch had described it. A quaint little fishing village—mostly wooden buildings, small boats tied to docks, an inn, and likely a brothel. They followed the main road through the settlement; only a few people wandered the streets, going about their lives. Some carried fishing poles, some buckets or tools. The clank of a blacksmith hammering on his anvil rang out in rhythm.

They approached the inn and dismounted from their horses. As Ash tied Acorn to the post, she looked up and noticed the building across the road. A dark black horse stood out front. "Wait," she said to Mitch as she removed her gloves. "I know that horse. Is that—"

"Shadow?" Mitch finished her sentence. The horse was tied outside what looked to be a brothel, a wench loitering out front, her bosom almost escaping her corset. The town was mostly quiet, the woman desperate to lure in the next man or woman to walk by.

"Did Merek frequent brothels? Siri, no doubt, but Merek seems to be much more of a... romantic."

"Not to my knowledge. At least, not when I was with him."

"Come, Mitch. Maybe we will catch him with a lady of the night."

He stood still. "Why would—"

"Come *on*, Mitchel."

The stone foundation of the building did not seem to match the shoddy construction of the wooden walls of the building. A young boy sat on the edge of the foundation, chewing on something. He looked up as she approached the horse.

"Shadow?" she asked, as if the horse might answer. The horse grunted and raised his head, whimpering. "It *is* you." She patted his neck. "Excuse me, young man. Have you seen a tall man with silver hair? This is his horse."

The boy looked at her, then looked around. "That's my uncle's horse, my lady."

Ash stared at the boy. "Really? With a mark of the saddler in Wolfpine of Vaegomar? So, I will ask again, have you seen the man I described?" The boy ran inside, the door squeaking as it closed behind him. Ashaya looked at Mitch, her lips tightening. "Merek could have been robbed, or worse."

As she approached the door, two men walked out. Ashaya noticed the boy looking outside from one of the windows. "Can I help you?" the bearded man asked.

"Yes, perhaps you can. I am looking for someone. I seem to have found his horse. Is he inside? Tall? Silver hair?"

The men exchanged glances, but neither answered. The bearded man walked toward her, and the other—clean-shaven and bald—walked toward Mitch, who was out in the road. "Young lady, this is my brother's horse. You must be mistaken."

Ashaya slowly moved her hand to the hilt of her dagger. She glanced back at Mitch, who had started to speak. "This horse belongs to my master. We came through here a while back. We don't want any trouble. We're just trying to find him."

The man laughed. "Your master? You some kinda servant, boy?" Mitch did not respond. The bald man smiled, showing his green teeth.

"Enough!" Ashaya cried. "This is my brother's horse. I would know. He was supposed to be mine."

The man ran his hand through his beard as he inched closer. "Your brother?" The man thought for a moment. "The dragonborn?" He looked over to the bald one. "A moon or so ago."

"Where is he?" Ashaya's face flushed in anger. She stumbled backwards into the road toward Mitch as the bald man approached from the other side. In an instant, Ashaya had pulled her bow from her shoulder and nocked an arrow, aiming at the bearded man.

"I'm going to ask one last time, where is my brother?" Mitch grabbed the hilt of his sword and partially drew it. The bald man quickly moved behind Mitch and put a blade to his throat.

"Not so fast, lad."

Ash turned the arrow toward the bald man's head. "Let him go!"

"Your friend here will die if you kill me." He pressed the dagger against Mitch's skin, and blood started to ooze from the edge of the blade.

The bearded man rushed Ashaya, leaving no time for her to aim the arrow back at him. He tackled her to the ground, and after a short struggle, he lay on top of her and reached for the dagger in his belt.

The man leaned in close to her face. "First, Imma kill you, bitch, then gonna fuck your corpse. Or would you like it the other way around?"

Ashaya smashed her forehead into the man's nose, blood gushing from both nostrils and onto her face. Even in this moment, she noticed the warmth, could taste it as it dribbled into her mouth.

The man forced her wrists together and held them on the ground. As she continued to struggle, a strange feeling came over her. The whispers she had heard in her dreams echoed in her head. She saw quick flashes, almost like short visions. A candle flickered, a naked woman rubbed her face, a plate of food at a table waited as if she sat in front of it, a horse beneath her trotted over red sands.

"Neph, go get your father, boy!" the bearded man yelled. Ashaya opened her eyes, still struggling as the man reached for his dagger. His blood continued dripping onto her face. He raised the dagger above his head. A coldness came over her and time seemed to slow. The dagger approached her face but as if it were moving in slow motion. The sounds around her seemed to muffle and lengthen. She could hear the man's heartbeat. The vein in his neck pulsated with each thump. Anger covered the man's face, along with blood from his broken nose. She freed her arms with ease and reached toward the blade. She easily caught his wrist as it slowly approached. She pulled the silver dagger from his hand and drove it into his throat, then she shoved her hand straight up into his chest, sending him backwards. His eyes widened as he slowly moved away from her.

She got to one knee and had time to think it was strange that he was still in the air as if he were floating. She looked over at Mitch. The bald man still held the blade to his throat, slowly turning his head to watch the bearded man go by him. Ash picked up the bow that had been under her back, pulled another arrow from the quiver, nocked it, and aimed at the bald man's head once again.

She stood as he turned back to her with his mouth open. She loosed the arrow. It moved almost as slowly as everything and everyone else. She ran toward Mitch, passing the arrow in flight. His eyes were now closing to a squint. She grabbed the man's hand and pulled the dagger away from his throat. Ashaya had time to notice his filthy fingernails. She turned to see the arrow pass close by her face and bury itself in the man's eye.

As quickly as this had all started, everything sped up to move normally again. The man dropped behind Mitch. The bearded man hit the ground with a thud about ten paces from where they lay. Mitch dropped to his knees. Ashaya was breathing heavily and knelt beside Mitch as he grabbed his neck. For a moment, she heard a racing heartbeat again and noticed the blood on Mitch's neck. He wiped it away and looked at his hand. For a moment, neither spoke.

"How did you... I mean..."

Ashaya looked around to get her bearings. The bearded man lay on his back, the dagger in his throat. Blood pooled beneath his head. The bald man lay in a heap, her arrow buried in his eye.

"What just happened?" she asked after catching her breath. Mitch stood and reached out to help her up.

"You moved so fast," he said, shaking his head. "Like the wind. You got to both of them before I could even..."

Ashaya took his hand and stood. "I do not know. I just..." She thought for a moment. "They moved so slowly."

"No," Mitch snapped. "You moved that fast." Ashaya looked around. A few people had come out from the other buildings.

"Come on. Merek may be inside." Ashaya walked over to the bearded man, now lifeless, and took the dagger from his neck. She noticed the small marking on his wrist. She knelt and looked more closely.

"What is it?" Mitch asked.

"A small tattoo of a burning candle," she replied as she stood. Mitch followed her to the door.

The boy was gone from the window. They walked in and the woman who had been outside approached her. "Hello there! Looks like you could use a break." She looked over at Mitch, "Would you both like to... dance?" The woman reached for Ashaya's face. She smacked the woman's hand away and noticed her own, bloody and shaking.

"Have you seen a tall man with silver hair?"

The woman pulled her hand back and ran upstairs. "Been no one here that had silver hair, but lots of tall men. You kill them? Heard the screams," the woman said, nodding toward the door.

"It was us or them." Ashaya was struggling to process what had happened. She had trained and fought for years with her brothers and the warriors at Wolfpine, but she had never killed anyone.

Mitch stepped forward. "Who were they?"

The woman went back to wiping glasses. "Oh, they come in from time to time, don't know their names. They ride with a bigger group. Locals call them *dragon slayers.*"

Ashaya looked up at the woman then over to Mitch. "Dragon slayers?"

The woman rolled her eyes. "Men and their little groups. Guess they gotta feel important."

Ash turned back to the door but stopped herself. "What did they want with my brother? Why do they have his horse?"

The woman wiped her hands. "He heard them talking. Some kind of religious zealots, I suppose. Call themselves the Nepharium."

Chapter Twelve

William

The council meeting had been in progress for nearly a fortnight. Lord Mehla Nahmen had come days late from Nahmana. Once a kingdom of its own, the large tropical island was home to many exotic species, and he had walked into yesterday's session with a monkey on his shoulder. William was sure he had been late on purpose, as he seemed to crave the attention. His wife, Salah, had apparently brought two tiger cubs when they docked in Clearwater Bay.

Most of these fools do not take this seriously, William thought.

"Will?" came a voice, alongside two knocks before the door cracked open. Galen peeked into the room.

"Yes, I'm coming." William sat at his desk, his hands under his chin, supporting his head.

"Would you like me to postpone the meeting until to-morrow, my lord?" Galen stepped in the door and closed it behind him.

"Maybe," William said with a sigh. "No—we should finish today. But I do not know how much more I can take. Is all of this worth it, Galen? Perhaps Sirich is right. It's much easier to be king and just make all the damn rules."

Galen sat and William could almost see him thinking before he spoke. "Only the histories will know. It is easy for people to just accept a ruler and do as they are told. The concept of self-rule is foreign to most, but you are saving people from a future tyrant."

William nodded but did not respond. He stood and put on his overcoat. "I wish Amaru were here. I could use his council right now."

"Should I send for him? Perhaps he would change his mind."

William grabbed the small, rolled-up note from his desk and handed it to Galen. He noticed Galen's unsteady hands. Galen read it and looked up. "I'm sorry, Will. I know he was a dear friend."

William walked over and looked out of the window. "I can't blame him one bit. He left all this and took to the sea for a simple life. Gods, I miss him. I should've been there."

Galen walked over to William. The old man's hand landed on his shoulder. "You cannot blame yourself. It's what he wanted: a simple life with his family. You couldn't have known."

William took a moment, his eyes glistening in the sun and his heart heavy. He had read Sirich's note at least twenty times. He had been so focused on building this council that he had not taken the time to at least go and see his old friend.

He wiped his eyes and cleared his nose. "All right, let's get this over with. What's the agenda for tonight?"

Galen glanced at his notes. "Roads and armies, it seems. And that small matter of filling the remaining seats."

William led as Galen followed him from the room. "I've been at this for almost a decade, and what do we have? Nine? They all want to remain lords, but most do not want to bother beyond their own borders and their own taxes. If the histories say there were twelve original clans, we need twelve to answer the call." Galen bumped into William's shoulder as he stopped walking. "I know what would get their attention."

"My lord?"

"We could hold a vote to remove someone."

"That might be a bit extreme, Will. You may be asking for war. Besides, you can't legislate away a man's blood."

William paused. "You're right. Surely it would not pass a vote, but they may take it seriously enough, knowing a few votes could be changed the next time." William continued walking.

"I suppose it could at least make a point," Galen finally responded. "Even just raising the motion."

"Exactly."

Galen trailed behind him. "Do you mean to do it today, Will?"

"Maybe, but who would I raise the motion against? Which one of the bastards cares the least?"

They were now in the inner courtyard, walking toward the main hall. William stopped again. He saw Heath Promen talking to his daughter Elya quietly by a tanning rack. Various pelts rocked in the breeze. She whispered something with a look of concern. "Him?" William asked.

"Lord Promen?" Galen almost whispered. "Do you think he deserves a motion to be brought against him?"

William scratched his chin. "I don't know. I just don't trust him."

"That is the point of a council, my lord," Galen was quick to respond. "No one has absolute power, and him no more than the rest."

"I'll think on it." William once again turned toward the hall, almost tripping over a rogue chicken beneath his feet. "Not a word, old man, not a word." Galen smiled and continued to follow.

Promen must have caught them in the corner of his eye as they passed, for he turned and nodded.

"Did he hear me?" William murmured.

"I don't think so, Will. I barely did."

Seeing Elya made William think of Merek. He had spoken of her before he left. He wanted to marry her. William knew what a man of his age was going through. Love and duty all came at once.

"Is Merek not back yet?" William asked.

"Not to my knowledge," said Galen. "Perhaps it's time to go find him?"

Marcus III of House Lucian was starting to take back control of the Bloody Sands from his small fortress on the sea, Castle Lachlan. It stood northeast of Bloodstone, but the waste was still a lawless and dangerous land. Merek had wanted this ranging, and he was a grown man now. William had not been able to say no. He felt pride in his children, and he was especially pleased that Sirich had volunteered to ride south. He would set an example for the other lords of the council.

"Galen, go fetch Ashaya. I want her to attend today. If we are to discuss a unified army, we must speak of training bowmen. She could easily fill that role, if interested."

Galen looked over and smiled. "Yes, my lord." Galen turned back toward the outer yards.

"She is likely on one of the ranges or in the stables with one of those boys that follow her around like lost pups."

"Which one?" Galen asked.

"Hell if I know."

William walked in and took his seat. He immediately grabbed the flagon of wine that sat on the table. "My lords!" he said as he raised his cup. A few turned and nodded, but most were not yet in the hall. Lord Daniel Nephane of Sharpstone, down in the southern storm lands, had arrived first and was the only one to come and greet him.

"My lord," Daniel nodded and smiled. "I must say you look spent, William."

"I am beyond spent, my friend." He took another drink. "Half of these so-called lords don't seem to give a damn about what we are doing here." William stopped himself. *Have I said too much?* He had known Daniel for many years. If anyone here could be trusted, it would be him.

"You're doing the right thing, Will. They just want to ensure they remain in power. Once they understand that their last name will not keep them there, that only their service to the people will, they will fall in line."

Daniel patted William on his shoulder, smiled, and walked back to his table. Will felt reassured. "At least someone understands," he muttered under his breath.

A few more councilmen entered the main hall. Elya followed her father. "My lady Elya!" Will raised his voice and motioned to her. Elya noticed and approached. Will walked around the table to greet her.

"Yes, my lord?" she said with a slight curtsey.

"No need for that, my lady. I was wondering if you had seen Ashaya this morning?"

Elya thought for a moment. "Yes, my lord. I believe she left early to go on a hunt for a few days in the wilds."

Ashaya often ventured out with her brothers, but never during council meetings. William thought for a moment.

"Will that be all, my lord?" she asked.

"Yes. Thank you, my lady." The girl bowed slightly and walked away.

Dammit, Ash!

The meeting went on for a few hours. Galen's apprentice scribed in his place. The council had agreed on road improvements and had started discussing council positions of war, the treasury, and what remaining councilmen they needed. William had argued for thirteen members total, representing the original twelve kingdoms and their lands, and a tie-breaking vote as overlord. William had wanted House Eve of Cedar Lake in Aethonya and a representative from the Gazi of Ethorya. William had thought that would be his old friend Amaru, but not anymore. He hoped he would be looking down from the heavens, now with the Elder for all eternity.

Osmond Thorne of Thurel was speaking when William noticed Galen enter at the back of the hall. He scurried toward William. "Forgive me, my lords," he said as he approached.

"What is it, Galen?"

He leaned down to William's ear. "It's Ashaya, my lord. She's left Wolfpine."

"Yes, so I've heard."

"You have?"

"She chose to go hunting at a bad time."

Galen raised his eyebrows. "No, Will. She left many days ago with Merek's apprentice, that boy Mitchel. They went to look for Merek."

I swear by the thirteen... William stood and turned to leave the hall.

"William, where are you going?" asked Heath Promen.

William ignored him. "Galen, find Jordan, and have him gather one hundred men!"

Lord Promen stood and said, more insistently, "William?"

"I'm going to find my daughter."

Chapter Thirteen

Amari

"Siri, wake up."

Amari pushed on his shoulder. The past few days, Sirich had gotten worse. He complained about his gut and occasionally retched from his horse.

Sirich rolled over. "Alright. I'm awake." Sirich was pale and sweat glistened on his skin. He brushed away the wet hair sticking to the side of his face.

"You look like shit! You need to get to a preceptor."

Sirich sat up from his bedroll. "There's a 'ceptor near Valton. Should be, anyway."

Amari shook his head. "There are no preceptors in a small village. Hell, you said everyone was dead." Amari handed him a waterskin.

"No, but Valton stands in the shadow of Black River. There's a small castle there, home of the Blackthorns."

"Fine. So, get up and let us get this done. I told you that old woman was a witch. She put a hex on you, brother." Sirich managed a smile.

The men around them were breaking camp. Campfires hissed and steamed as men doused them with water from the stream. Amari took a moment to admire the beauty of this place. Through the thick canopy above, the sun had finally returned after a few days of rain. Birds whistled, and the smoke in the air took the shape of sunrays that fought their way to reach the earth. Morning dew lay on the large leaves of the ferns and creeper plants that covered the ground. The large boulders shone so brightly as to almost be painted green.

"My lords, we should reach the village by midday," Philip reminded them as he walked toward the horses.

"Thank you," Amari said since Sirich seemed to be ignoring him. Amari shook his head as he watched his friend struggle to stand.

"Eat something." Amari offered him a pan of deer sausage he had cooked from last night's kill.

"I'm all right, Doc. No amount of food seems to satisfy me. Besides, I crave…"

"I have a jar of honey left, if something sweet is what you crave."

Sirich waved it off. "I don't know what it is I crave, but it's not sweet."

It did not take long before everyone had packed up, mounted their horses, and gotten back on the trail. Amari hoped that Philip was right; Sirich was in no condition to be riding for long. Soon the wood thinned out a bit, but the trail was narrow and mud puddles concealed the rest. They rode single file, Amari keeping an eye on Sirich just ahead of him. He had worsened the past few days and had been unusually quiet. Amari feared he had taken some pox.

"Just ahead, the trees thin and the trail is widening," Sirich said from the front, looking up, his hand blocking the sun from his eyes.

They came to a wider road with a better view. The southern edge of the Highland Mountains showed to the west. Amari could see the clearing ahead, and the small village. Two men stood guard at the wooden gate. "My lords," one of the guards proclaimed. Sirich had draped his horse with a caparison to display his sigil. The men behind them displayed a dozen different banners as well. Amari recognized the fire glyph of House Promen that adorned the chest plates of the guards.

"What happened here?" Sirich said, dismounting. Amari and the others followed.

"We don't know. We were sent here to await your arrival. There was no one around when we got here almost a fortnight ago." Sirich looked back at Amari.

"No one?" Amari said.

"Well, a woman and a child are all."

"That *is* someone," Sirich snapped.

"Sirich!" Amari faced him. "They are on our side, brother," he said in a low voice. Sirich looked over Amari's shoulder at the guards and sighed.

"I do apologize for my friend. It's been a long ride." The two men looked at each other, then nodded.

Sirich turned back to them. "Let me speak to her." One of the guards opened the small gate.

"Not what I pictured it to be," Amari mumbled.

Valton was just a tiny village, no more than thirty houses.

Amari covered his nose and mouth; the smell of decay was overwhelming.

A guard noticed him wincing. "You'll get used to it, my lords."

"I hope not," Amari replied.

"We moved the bodies to a grave but haven't buried them. We wanted you to see first." One of the guards led them through the village square, past the framed building left unfinished. Amari's eyes were quickly drawn to the center of the square, where an ominous stone statue towered above them. He had never seen such a statue. Blackened by the sun and broken by time, the figure of a woman with the wings of a bat kneeled. One of the wings and half of her face was missing. The arms reached down and what remained of the hands looked as if they were holding something long gone, the palms facing the sky. Amari noticed the rusty chains hanging from one of the wrists.

"They were everywhere, my lord. The bodies, I mean," the guard said.

Sirich stopped and retched. Amari almost followed but held back, gagging. Sirich wiped his mouth with his sleeve. Death clung in the air.

"This way, my lords."

They followed past the last house and toward an old barn. Amari noticed the dark clouds moving in.

"Every one of them was the same. Their necks looked to be torn open," the guard said. Amari gagged once more as he looked into the pit. Pale, bloated corpses littered the hole. The guard was right: a wound showed in each of their necks.

"Wolves, perhaps?" Sirich turned. "These marks are not from a blade."

The guard shook his head. "Never seen no wolf do this. Especially to this many people. As I said, some were still holding tools or buckets in their hands before we dragged 'em over here."

They all stood silent for a moment until Amari spoke. "So they didn't run?"

"What, Doc?" Sirich turned to him.

"They didn't run, so they never knew what happened. You see wolves attacking your neighbors, most would have made it inside."

Sirich look back at the guard. "Are you the captain of this garrison?"

The man stood taller. "Yes, my lord."

"What about the mountain clans? I hear of them raiding villages down here, stealing food and sometimes women. I have dealt with a few myself up north."

The captain thought for a moment. "Ran into them a few times, but they usually won't venture down this far south into the foothills." Amari turned to see the mountains in the distance, a white fog hanging in the air near the rounded peaks.

"Philip!" Sirich called.

Philip approached from behind. "Yes, my lord."

"You know these mountains. Take twenty men and head up that trail," he said, pointing to an opening in the trees past the flimsy gate. "See if you can find anything, I'll talk to the woman." Philip nodded. "Oh, and Philip..." He leaned close to his ear. "Have *you* seen the mountain clans ever do anything like this?"

"Not like this, my lord, but they don't have good steel either. Their shit weapons could have made those wounds. Savages." Amari noticed Philip moving quicker, barking orders with a hint of excitement in his voice.

"Are they truly? Savages, I mean?" Amari asked bluntly.

Philip turned back to him. "Some of them." He turned to gather his men.

Amari put his hand on Philip's shoulder. "We should try to avoid any needless killing. The mountain clans can't all be—"

"Where is the woman?" Sirich interrupted.

"In her home, my lord. This way." They turned to follow once again. Amari was relieved as the smell was at least tolerable the farther away they were from the pit. He had never seen Sirich in a leadership role. He only had memories of playing in the yards of Wolfpine. *I can see a bit of William in him.* "A bit brassy, maybe, but taking the lead nevertheless," he mumbled under his breath.

They approached a small house, the only one in the village with smoke rising from the small stone chimney.

Sirich rapped on the door. "My lady? May I—"

"Who are you? I've said all I know," a voice came from behind the door.

"The council in Vaegomar sent me to find justice for your village, for the tragedy…"

Amari heard the footsteps as Sirich spoke. The door swung open.

"You're a little late for justice." The woman wiped under her eyes with her finger. "I told you, I've already told these men everything."

Amari let her finish. "My lady, we're here to help. Perhaps we can learn something with new eyes and ears."

The woman stood there for a moment. "Fine, come in. You're likely not to leave until I speak with you, anyway."

Sirich entered and stopped beyond the threshold. "Come, Doc."

Amari had planned to look around but turned and followed. The others waited outside, some going back to their posts.

"What happened here?" Sirich asked bluntly.

"I already told them." Sirich looked frustrated with her already.

Amari spoke calmly. "Please, my lady, you have been through a lot, but perhaps we can help. What is your name?"

The woman sighed. "Bella."

"What did you see here, Bella?" The woman paced in her stained green dress. She swept the knotted brown hair from her face. She sat after checking on her baby, sleeping soundly in a small wooden cradle near the fire.

"I was in here after hangin' some linens to dry. I was feedin' my boy." Amari thought the woman to be about twenty-five years, the baby only a few months old. She wore a ragged grey dress, and a bonnet covered her dark hair.

"So, you heard nothing?" Sirich kneeled in front of her. He was more relaxed now.

Bella thought for a moment. "That's just it, I heard everything stop."

Amari looked at Sirich. "What do you mean?"

"I heard old man Colin beating on his steel, the children playing, the men hammering on the new temple..." She paused. "It all just stopped. All I could hear then was the chickens and that damned ol' rooster."

Amari looked at Sirich and turned back to Bella. "Then what?"

Her eyes teared up. "I put the baby down and walked out." She put her face in her hands. "Everyone was dead, some still twitching. Never heard a scream." She paused and wiped her cheeks. "My husband was helping to build the temple."

Sirich stood and walked to the window. "Was this temple to be a shrine for the Elder?"

"No—a new temple for the dark queen, the one you see right outside that window. Old one burnt down last year."

Sirich turned to her. "The dark queen?"

"She was born here and returns from time to time, at least that's what the priests and priestesses says when they come 'round here." Amari noticed Sirich roll his eyes and turn back to the window. "There were no gods here that day. Only Lucian, the fallen one, forever banished to the underworld."

Amari looked over at his friend; his face still held a stern look. Bella lowered her head again. Amari walked over behind her and put his hand on her shoulder. "I'm sorry for what happened here. What will you do now? You can't stay here alone."

Sirich turned to them. "She can take her son to Wolfpine." Bella looked up and wiped her eyes, swollen and red.

"Do you have any other family?" Amari asked.

"My sister used to live in a town, on the other side of Black River, but I ain't seen her in years. Where is Wolfpine?" Siri looked at Amari. "That a castle?"

"The capital of Aahsgoth," Sirich replied.

"I've never left Alarya."

Amari walked over to Sirich and leaned to his ear. "Remember, most of these people don't know anything beyond their own village."

Sirich turned to her. "After we finish here, you're welcome to come north. We will escort you and your son to Vaegomar."

"Oh, I've heard of that! Where the king lives."

Sirich's jaw tightened. "He's no longer... never mind."

The woman stood and looked at her son, still sleeping. "I guess I don't have a choice. There's nothing here for us now."

Amari and Sirich sat around a large fire with some of the men from Mudstone. Amari had never seen it, but he remembered his lessons back in Wolfpine.

It is peaceful here. If you can forget the smell. The song of leafhoppers and crackles from the many fires filled the air. A few men talked to one another, but most were quiet after burying the bodies. Many could not eat supper. Dusk had come, and Philip had not yet returned. Sirich sat beside him with heavy eyes. He was not sure if it was the ale or his condition.

"It's pretty here, despite the circumstances," Amari said. Sirich nodded in agreement, the fire reflecting in his eyes.

"I have to piss." Sirich stood and stumbled toward the gate behind them. Amari heard it creak open and turned to see his old friend walk out.

"Guess he had to do more than piss," one of the Alaryan men said, chuckling. Amari smiled to acknowledge him. He looked toward the path that rose into the distance behind the fence. He expected to see the torches of Philip and his men at any time, but it could be a day or more. Amari caught himself yawning and realized Sirich had been gone a while. He had to go as well. He grabbed a torch and walked toward the open gate. As he got closer, he heard a voice.

Is he talking to himself again? Perhaps propositioning a tree? A smile came to his face. *Perhaps Philip had returned.* He went toward the voices. "Everything all right, Siri?" He came to the old tree that stood across the road. Sirich stood in front of a man casually sitting, leaning against the base of the ancient oak.

"Siri?" the man said. "Is that what they call the prince of Aahsgoth these days?" The man's white teeth flashed as he smiled.

"Amari, this is…" Sirich paused.

"Call me... Ethan." The man had short dark hair and bright blue eyes, although Amari squinted at the darkness that fell around them. He got closer and held up the torch. The stranger looked to be wearing a dark leather jacket with drawstrings on both the front and the long sleeves. Leather straps crossed his chest and buckled above the pockets.

"This is my friend, Amari," Sirich continued.

"Amari? Of the Gazi clan."

Odd. He had never heard anyone call his birth name a clan, much less a commoner in the south. "Amari Docksider. What is your surname?"

The man looked up. His eyes seemed to glisten in the dying light. "I do not have one. I come from a time when people didn't."

"Do you not mean a *place*, dear brother?" A woman approached.

The man turned to her. "Ah, sister, what are you doing here? You should be... asleep."

The woman stepped into the torchlight from behind the tree. Long, straight red hair laid over one of her shoulders. She wore a similar leather jacket, only lighter. Amari noticed their matching blue eyes. The man turned back toward Sirich and Amari.

"Pardon my sweet sister, she can sometimes sneak up quietly—like a snake in a tree," the man said, smirking.

"What are you two doing in Valton? Perhaps you know what happened here?"

"And how do you know who I am?" Sirich added.

The man stood. Amari was surprised to see how tall he was. Sirich was tall, but he looked up to the stranger. "Your sigil, of course. House Blacksun of Vaegomar. How could I not?" the man asked. "Not everyone down here is uneducated, my lords. I come from a nearby town. We heard the news of this place." The man still wore a grin.

"Our mother used to live here," the woman added.

"Your mother?" Amari asked. "Did she know anyone here? Perhaps we can speak to her?"

The stranger spoke without looking at them. "No, she's sleeping, I am sure. Besides, that was long, long ago." He turned back to his sister. "Perhaps you should go check on our mother. She *is* very old."

"Stay out of trouble, brother." The woman turned and vanished into the night.

"Why are you here again?" Amari asked the tall man.

"Me?" The man kept his smile as he bowed. "I am here to serve the prince of Aahsgoth. How may I assist you, my lord?"

Amari shook his head. *Who is this man?*

Chapter Fourteen

The Beast

Her scent was strong here among the salty air. The princess had come this way. *Close.*

There ahead, the trees were smaller, and the winds were stirring.

The lands here were easier to run compared to the tall lands where the sun fell.

It has been so long.

Not so many stones and sharp edges. But some of the greens here drew blood.

There. Ahead through the pointy greens. The floating trees rested in the water. They gathered in these places. *Stop and look. Quiet.*

There in the clearing. Two of them lay cold. *A meal, perhaps? No, we cannot risk it.*

The black flyers were already taking their share.
It was her; she has tasted it.
Keep going.
It has begun.

Chapter Fifteen

Theodor

"Are you ready?" Ridley asked.

"For what?" Theo replied.

"I told you, I know another way in."

"You want to sneak into the overlord's... into your grandfather's quarters?"

"Well, yes. Don't you want to help your father?"

"I do."

"Then come on." Ridley grabbed his hand. She led him all the way past the library toward the gardens. He had never been down to the water gardens at night. With his hand in hers, he was sure he was blushing.

"Theodor!" she growled, pulling him along. "Are you listening?" The sound of her voice and the bubbling stream nearby snapped him out of his trance. "This way."

Ridley let go of his hand. *Damn.*

The water gardens were beautiful during the day but treacherous at night. Winding pathways, rock gardens, and large boulders were everywhere. Luckily, the moons shone brightly tonight. Theodor looked up for a moment and noticed they were a bit further apart. The small red moon was no longer hiding behind the blue. Theodor ran into the tall grass before the narrow bridge that crossed the creek. The blades came up to his face.

"Shit!" he hissed, yelping. A blade of grass cut his cheek. "I don't understand." Theodor admired the height of the grass still tickling his cheek as he backed up. Ridley stopped and turned to him.

"This is Shit Creek."

"Smells like it."

"It makes the plants down here grow bigger." There was enough moonlight for him to see her roll her eyes.

"Really?" He felt stupid, but this was her area of study. They walked across the bridge to a stone path that went toward the other side of the gardens. Small stones crunched under their feet. He could no longer hear the trickle of Shit Creek, but the rushing water grew closer.

"Right here, I think." She left the path through the bamboo thicket. Ridley seemed to be leading them back toward the cliff where the great library stood above.

"Pfft!" Ridley spat. "Damned spiderwebs!" Theodor stopped behind her, grabbing the trunk of a tree. He smiled as she cleared the web from her face. She tried flinging the webbing from her hands in a dance of sorts.

"So graceful," he said, snickering.

"Shut up!" They walked on, dodging short tree limbs while others grabbed at their clothes. Theodor thought they must have walked at least one hundred yards before coming to a clearing. The waterfall was loud, and its mist encircled them. They were standing on a large wet stone, but there was no river.

"Where does the water go?" he asked, looking up at the falls. It seemed to appear from the rock face above.

"It flows underground."

Theodor had read of underground rivers but had never seen one. The water kept going down into the black hole before them. "Think anyone has fallen down there?"

"Likely. *I* about did, the first time I came back here."

"Where do you think it leads? The underworld? Or maybe just to the sea?"

"Of course it runs to the sea, you idiot." She smacked him lightly on the back of his head. "Alright, over here," she pointed.

"Where?" Theo looked around. There was nowhere to go but back the way they had come. Ridley walked closer to the falls, paused, and leapt into the water.

"Ridley?" Theodor tried to keep his voice down, although it was unlikely anyone could hear them here.

"Come on!" Her hand appeared through the falling water, motioning to him. Theodor walked closer, his hair getting wetter.

"Just jump forward."

Theodor was unsure. *I cannot let her see me afraid.* He took a deep breath and leapt forward. He landed on a flat stone behind the waterfall and almost slipped.

"You see?" She motioned behind them. They were standing in a small cave, almost pitch black except for the moonlight glistening through the water behind them.

"It's not too far." She disappeared in front of him as he tried to follow. They walked slowly, Ridley reaching out in front of her. *She has no fear.* He could barely see her now. Theodor almost bumped into her when she stopped.

"Can you see?" He barely made out her smile. After a few moments, his eyes started to adjust. She was right. A small steel door stood in front of them, seemingly leading through the solid stone wall. He could only just make out a large circle with a strange glyph that resembled a bird in the door's center, stretching to either side. *A bat, perhaps?*

He ran his hands along the cold steel. "How did you find this place?"

"I followed grandfather here a few times."

Theo looked around trying to see anything, but he could find no lock near the steel handle. "How do you open it?"

"Push?" she said, unsure.

Theodor pushed on the door; it did not budge. He rubbed his eyes. "I wish I could see at night."

"Like a cat, you mean?"

"Yes, like a cat," he answered, distracted. The stone here was smooth. Theodor felt no mortar between them. "Wait." His hand came over what seemed to be a loose stone.

"What is it?"

"Just a loose stone, I suppose."

"Are you sure? I have never seen any stonework like this." She moved him out of the way. "Let me try." Ridley felt around the stone. "There!" As she pushed on the stone, leaning into it, they heard a click.

"That's it!" He checked the door. It had opened a few inches. He pushed it open further. "I've never seen anything like this!"

"What's next, a room full of pirate's gold, like the stories?" Ridley said, nudging past him.

"With a talking dragon that guards it, perhaps?" Theodor added.

The room behind the cave smelled of must and smoke. They walked slowly.

"Here." Ridley had bumped into something. Wood screeched across the stone floor like a horn. "A candle!" she said in an excited whisper.

"We need something to light it." Theodor rummaged through his pockets.

"You mean like this flint and steel? You didn't come down here expecting torches to be lit for us, did you?" she snickered. "Here, hold this. And come closer to the door so I can see."

She handed him the candle and used the flint and steel. The sparks reflected in her eyes as she concentrated. Finally, the wick took a flame. The room lit up like the sun had risen. Theodor winced at the brightness. He held the candle out, squinting, trying to see as his eyes adapted.

"There, the stairs." Ridley walked over to a corner where there was a staircase. Theodor followed. They ascended only ten or twelve creaking steps and came to a solid wall.

Ridley slapped the wall. "A stairway to nowhere?"

"Wait." Theodor thought for a moment. "This is under the southwest corner of the library, right?"

"So… it's under grandfather's study." Ridley finished his thought.

"I thought you had been here before?"

"Not in here. I only came to the waterfall. Grandfather was not there, but he was in the main hall soon after."

Theodor pushed on the wooden wall. "It's heavy," he said as it creaked open slowly. His eyes widened. "A door of some kind."

He opened it just enough to slide through. Ridley followed, and they found themselves standing in the overlord's study. He looked back at the bookshelf that they had just opened like a door. Theodor smiled. "My father told me about these passages existing in some castles, but I've never seen one."

"I told you!" Ridley almost clapped but caught herself in time. She smiled and turned, her elbow knocking a book from the shelf. The pages of the heavy book fluttered as it hit the stone floor with a loud thud.

"Damn." They stood in silence for a moment before they heard the voices outside the double doors.

"Come on!" she whispered loudly. "We'll have to look around up here another time." They hurried back behind the bookshelf, and Theodor pulled it closed behind them.

"Wait, the book!" He slid the door back open, picked up the book, and laid it on one of the shelves. Once again, he shut the door behind him. They walked down the stairs to wait and listen. "I don't hear anything, but we can't risk it." Theodor walked toward the sound of the water.

Ridley followed but stopped and grabbed his arm. "We snuck in here. We can't leave without at least looking."

Theodor held the candle out in the darkness. "Maybe we still can." He spied what looked to be old wooden shelves. He walked closer. Rows of shelves were full of books and crumbling scrolls, and stacks lay everywhere on the floor.

These are old.

"Wait here." Ridley took the candle. Theodor stood in the darkness, watching her ghostly silhouette, the candle almost floating toward the door. She leaned it sideways to light another she had found. "Here." She brought the candle back, now holding her own.

Theodor kneeled in front of a stack of books. These were ancient, leather-bound, and covered in dust. He blew the dust from the one on top and opened it. It was sticky with cobwebs. He recognized the Old Tongue. He knew enough from his studies to realize that it was pertaining to the rising and setting of the sun.

"Here!" Ridley whispered excitedly.

Theodor ran over. "That's it!" Theodor's heart raced. "That's the same writing." An old parchment lay in the center of the table, torn and tattered, with the same glyph-like writing as the note his father had sent. The parchment was ragged, the red ink chipped and fading. Some darker red splotches adorned the edges of the paper. "It's so light, I can barely make it out with only a candle," he said.

"Not this one." Ridley had been rummaging through another stack of papers. "It's a copy."

Theodor took it and laid it beside the original. "You're right. It's a copy, and not that old." It looked to be a single paragraph. "How can I possibly translate with no reference or key? If we could find something that said the same thing in the Common Tongue..."

Ridley walked around behind him to the other side of the table, looking through more old piles of parchment. "Like a map?"

"Yes!" She held what looked to be an old map of Aahsgoth, labeled in this strange tongue. "If I can compare this to a current one, I can figure out the structure, the vowels—"

"Yes, I get it," Ridley interrupted. "We have to go." She started blowing out the other candles. She pointed up. "Listen!" They could hear faint footsteps above.

"Let's go. Besides, the sun will rise soon." He took the copy and the map and blew out his candle. They walked back outside to the roaring water, the mist greeting their faces. Theodor pulled the door and heard it latch as they made their way back into the night.

Chapter Sixteen

Neph

The bell tolled from the temple; the time had come.

Neph had just climbed out of the wooden tub and put his best tunic over a light cream undershirt and black breeches, his hair still wet. Seth had awoken and was sitting at the small wooden table, eating what was left of supper. Aza sat with him, giving him a reading lesson.

He did not know many people could read, but her mother had taught her. Aza had told him of the pale woman who had come upon their village in the Greenlands where she had grown up. He had heard the story a hundred times. She would often speak of home and the beauty of the never-ending forests, rolling green fields, blue lakes, and rivers that cut through the landscape.

Although it had no name, her village had been outside the new town of Ashbourne, where a huge stone structure was to be built by some queen. Her family had fled when war engulfed the area. From time to time, she would talk of the strange black-haired woman who seemed to vanish before the fighting began and wondered what had become of her. He listened to his wife tell Seth how she had learned to appreciate the beauty of the written Vedician language, as if the glyphs flowed into one another. Now, this new tongue brought over from the east was predominantly spoken here.

"I must go." Neph walked over and sat beside his son. "Make sure you talk to the beekeeper coming at the morning star. Our wax is running low." Seth nodded.

Aza looked up at him. "Will you not return tonight, so you can talk to him yourself?"

"Yes, but likely late. You two will be fast asleep." Neph sat for a moment longer. He stood and ran his fingers through the boy's hair, then walked around the table and leaned over to kiss his wife on the top of her head.

She pulled back and looked up at him. "Is this goodbye? Kiss me when you return, and more," she said with a slight grin.

Neph returned a glancing smile and pulled his hand slowly from her shoulder. He walked toward the door and looked back at his family as they continued their lesson, the old wooden door screeching behind him as he left.

Neph made his way through the dirt streets toward the red temple on the hill that overlooked the village. It was dark now, and firelight showed in almost every window. Most were in their homes, but a few people still wandered. Stray dogs searched for scraps of supper, and the wolves started their nightly song in the distance.

An orange glow danced in the alley ahead as he approached the few stone buildings there. He heard the ring of iron on steel as he approached the smith's shop.

"Still at it?"

The old man turned with a bitter look and sighed. He picked up his tongs and plunged the sword into his slack tub to quench the blade. The water hissed and steam poured upward around the man. "Have to be. The damn king has me and my boys here all day and night now. Seems he's building an army. Hell is coming, but it pays good." The old man scratched at his long beard and turned back to his work.

Neph climbed the stairs leading to the temple. Torches lined the path and shone on the wall. The red stones looked as if they were bleeding in the flickering light, and he knew where this place had gotten its name. The iron gates were open, with two guards standing on either side. Neph paused, not knowing whether to stop or keep walking. The guards crossed their spears in front of him.

"What is your business?"

Neph cleared his throat. "The king summoned me to—"

The guards brought their spears back into position in order to let him pass.

"Candlemaker, he is expecting you," the guard on the right said, looking straight ahead.

Neph nodded and passed through the gates.

The courtyard was ripe with activity, workers toiling on into the night. The moons were bright tonight. Masons worked by firelight, raising new foundations and adding to the walls. A man climbed down the bell tower on the side of the building. The bell still swung, light gleaming off its smooth surface. Ten men worked some type of treadwheel, holding large stones over fire as if to melt them. The statue of the woman now lay broken and crumbled. Once, it had stood beside the main cobblestone path to the temple entrance, across from the statue of Lucian himself, still as pristine as the day it was erected. It stood tall, a solemn face of bloodstone, the wings of a dragon adorned on his back. Neph felt uneasy as he passed under the statue and walked toward the massive columns that lined the entrance.

He walked up a staircase as wide as the temple itself and stopped, leaning on a column to catch his breath and gather his thoughts. Sweat beaded on his forehead, his stomach alive with butterflies. He gathered himself and walked to the entrance, a wall just inside the threshold. He stopped to look at the massive glyph in the center. Neph held his own wrist. Lucian had taken this as his personal sigil—two markings starting at thin points at the top curling outward, getting thicker until they came together at the base, resembling a droplet of some type. *Water, wine, perhaps blood?* The flower-like glyph beside it had been mostly chiseled away. Only sharp points remained untouched around the outside.

Neph could have gone either way, but he turned to the right and walked around the large wall, entering the main hall. Massive columns reached for the ceiling. Large, incomplete paintings had been started above him, perhaps commissioned by the high priest or Lucian himself. The scaffolding stood empty. He stopped for a moment to look up, but he could not make out anything other than random patches of color and various figures that seemed to dance in the torchlight. He had been here many moons ago, but he had never noticed that there were no windows here. If not for the massive wall sconces that lined both sides of the hall and the various candles scattered about, no light would see this place.

Neph walked toward the front, where circular stone stairs led up to the bloodstone chair sitting in wait for its master. Only eight guards stood in the hall, four on each side, spears pointed to the heavens. They wore black, boiled leather and polished steel half-helms. Their eyes did not move from beyond the nose guard that continued down from the point of the helm. Only the crackle of the flames and the echo of his footsteps stirred in the chamber. Two others waited at the base of the stairs. They looked to be commoners as well, the old man wearing a dirty brown jerkin, torn breeches, and worn sandals. The other, a clean-shaven younger man, looked around nervously. He turned and spotted Neph as he approached, then he looked down at the floor. "You here for the trials?" Neph asked quietly.

"Trials? Is what you call them?" the old man replied.

"What do you mean?"

"He already knows their fate."

How would he...

The younger man paced, wiping his face with the sleeve of his white cotton shirt, still silent.

Chapter Seventeen

Ashaya

"We need to rest," Mitch reminded her again. "I don't think anyone followed us."

They had been riding hard since they left the village. Mitch led Shadow behind his horse like a pack mule.

"We need to find Merek. If he went to the Crescent Isle, then we—"

"Ash, I'm sure he's well…" His voice trailed off.

"There is no other reason that these people, whoever they are, would have his horse." Ashaya stopped Acorn and looked over at Mitch. Sweat carved lines on his dusty face. She could still smell the blood on her clothes. "I have to know, Mitch!" She dismounted and sat in a clearing beside the old king's road.

Mitch climbed down and sat beside her. "I know you do, and I'm with you all the way, but we cannot run the horses to death."

He put a hand on her shoulder. Ashaya looked him in the eyes for a fleeting moment, then put her head between her knees and closed her eyes. The faces of the two men still haunted her.

"Who were they? The woman said they called themselves dragon slayers. What does that mean?"

Mitch shook his head. "I don't know. Likely some religious fanatics. But what would they want with Merek?" Mitch looked at her more closely. "Your eyes."

"What is it?"

"They look... lighter than usual."

"Lighter?"

"Bluer, maybe." Mitch paused. "And what *was* that back there? How did you—"

"I do not know, Mitch. It was like... everything moved so slowly around me." More tears caressed her cheeks. "I killed two men, Mitch! I have never killed anyone. I do not know what is happening. Where my brother is and..." She put her head down again. They sat in silence for a moment.

The aroma of pine here was strong, just like back home. Dusk had already fallen, the moons shining on the sparse wood. In the clearing where they sat, bats dived for pinflies. They had plenty to eat; they'd buzzed around Ash and Mitch all day. The old road here was in shambles, cobblestones lying everywhere but where they were supposed to.

Ash finally spoke. "Where are we, anyway?"

"Not far now. Once we pass through the waste and get back into the wood, the isle should be close." Mitch walked to his horse and pulled an old map from his saddlebag. "We follow the road until it ends, and then we turn west into the

Whispering Wood. We should water the horses and get some rest. It'll only be a few hours' ride, and we do not know what to expect or how long we'll be there."

Ashaya nodded and stood. "Fine. Let us get off the road, just in case dead men speak and send their companions after us."

They led the horses well off the road and found a small clearing of tall grass beside a stream. Mitch tied the horses near the water while Ashaya took their bedrolls to lay out beside the large oak at the edge of the clearing. She sat down and leaned against the trunk.

"I'm cold and hungry," Ashaya mumbled. Mitch had started to gather kindling, kneeling to light a small fire in a pit he had scraped with his boot. Ashaya watched. He tossed her a pouch of venison jerky and nuts. "That wasn't an order to warm and feed me, Mitch. But thank you."

"Anything for the princess," Mitch smiled. "Besides, you saved our hides back there." Ashaya looked down, and Mitch frowned. "What is it, Ash?"

"It's just that... I can still see his face," she said, almost whispering.

"You killed two, remember?" Mitch japed. "I'm sorry Ash, I didn't mean to..."

Ashaya managed the hint of a smile. "It's fine, I just don't know how I am supposed to feel about it." She thought for a moment. "You ever kill anyone?"

"No. Maybe. I tried once. The time I went with your brothers to run off the Mudfoot Clan that came up north into Vaegomar, causing trouble. They were raiding villages. It was a small skirmish, and this man charged at me with an axe. I shat myself, but I was able to dodge and cut him," Mitch said in a shaky voice. "He ran off with the rest, bleeding." He sat on his bedroll and snapped off a piece of jerky, staring into the flames. "I'm sorry I couldn't help back there. I felt paralyzed. And once you moved the way you did, I froze more. How did you move like that?"

"We have gone over this," Ashaya sighed. "I do not know. I barely remember what happened. I just… reacted." She took a drink from her waterskin. "Lately, I hear things. And see things. I don't know what's happening to me."

"I don't understand. Do you see things in your dreams? What kinds of things?"

"Not only in my dreams." She hesitated. "I cannot explain it. I do not understand myself."

Ashaya threw her empty pouch beside her, still hungry. She lay back, looking up at the stars through the old oak. Mitch walked back to camp, retying his breeches, and lay down beside her, his hands under his head.

"Is there anything I can do to help? What do you see and hear?"

"I do not know, Mitch. Let's just find Merek tomorrow." Ashaya closed her eyes.

It seemed like only a few minutes had passed when she opened them again. She lifted her head. The fire was not much more than embers, and the woods around them were alive with leafhoppers. She looked over at Mitch. He had not moved, and she could hear his heavy breath. She rolled to her side, facing him. The little bit of firelight that remained contoured his face. His jawline, his stubbled chin, his messy dark hair. She had never really looked at him before, but now she studied him while he slept.

An urge came to her. A hunger. She slid over and laid next to him. She smelled him and listened to the rhythm of his heart. A grin came to her face. She knew she should not continue, but something drove her. It was if she were not in control, although she did not fight it either.

She put her hand on his chest and slowly slid it under his shirt. Chills ran up her arm at the touch of his warm skin. Mitch cleared his throat and inhaled, still deeply asleep. Ashaya carefully removed her trousers, leaving them wrapped around one leg. She slid her other leg over and straddled him. She leaned down and gently kissed his neck, making her way up to his lips. Mitch awoke.

"Ash, what—"

She covered his mouth with her hand. The other reached down and untied his breeches. "Shhh..."

His eyes widened, but he did not say another word. Mitch struggled to take off his undershirt. She leaned down and kissed him deeply, both breathing heavily now. She reached between her legs and took his manhood. They both gasped as she guided him into her. She slowly rode him, looking into his eyes. His hands gripped her hips, his head leaning back. She closed her eyes, her hands on his chest. She moaned as she rode him faster and faster. Mitch grunted, his grip tightening around her waist.

He grunted louder. "Ash." She kept going, but he spoke again. "Easy." She moaned in rhythm with her hips.

"Ash!" Mitchel grabbed her wrists. She opened her eyes and stopped. She looked down to see him bleeding where her hands had been. She brought her hands up in front of her face. Her nails were long, and blood stained the tips of her fingers.

"I'm sorry. Mitch, I—" She rolled off him and back to her bedroll, desperately trying to cover herself.

"I do not know what came over me. I didn't mean to hurt you." Tears streamed down her cheeks as she struggled to pull her trousers back on and lower her shirt.

"It's alright, I just..." Mitch said, unsure. "You didn't have to stop. I mean, you know, just..."

Ashaya looked at his chest. "Please forgive me. I just felt...
I don't know."

Mitch sat up. "I'm fine, just scratches." He reached for
his water. "I just thought... We talked, and you were unsure.
About us, I mean."

Ash wiped her face. "I am. I think. I don't know." She
stood and walked to the small stream to rinse her hands. She
got a small cloth from her saddlebag and wet it in the stream
and wiped Mitch's scratches. She did not look him in the
eyes, but she could feel his gaze. She handed him the cloth
and went back to her bedroll.

She lay down without saying anything. She turned away
from him, not fully knowing what had just happened. She
heard him sigh as he settled again. A wolf howled in the distance as she stared off into the darkness.

Chapter Eighteen

Theodor

Ridley sat on the edge of the desk, her eyes fixed on the map. Ian picked up the parchment with the strange markings for what seemed like the thousandth time, leaning back and sighing. They had returned to the secret room again the previous night, but they did not enter. Theodor had an odd feeling, like they were being watched.

"If we assume the names on a modern map were translated to the Common Tongue, then we can match the symbols to their meanings… but there is no way to know phonetics," Ian said.

Ridley rolled her eyes. "No shit. You've said that at least a hundred times."

Ian looked at her. "What are you doing here, anyway? Don't you have trees to plant, or—"

"Enough, Ian," Theodor cut him off. "She's the reason we have what we have."

"Well, then. Theo's standing up for his love."

"Shut up, Ian," Theodor snapped.

"Stop, both of you. Let's take a break. Get some air." Ridley dropped the map and walked out.

"She's right. Come on."

The three of them walked into the small courtyard. Dusk had settled in. The moons shone full tonight, bright enough for Theodor to notice their shadows. The chirps of leafhoppers had almost overtaken the trickle of Shit Creek behind them.

"How hard can this be?" Theodor pondered.

"Hard enough for someone to have spent almost thirty years studying languages and hold his own office in Ashbourne."

Ian raised his voice. "Yeah, Ridley, and who has now mysteriously *died*."

"Quiet!" Theodor stopped. "We have to be careful. We don't know who can hear us."

"Hear what?" a voice rang out behind them.

"Shit," Theodor muttered under his breath. They all stopped and slowly turned back.

"Sam, you bastard!" Ridley smacked him in the arm.

Sam took a step back. "What did I do?"

"Quit sneaking up on people like that, idiot."

"I'm sorry! I called your names three times. It's like you were all in a daze. What are you doing out here after dark? Want to play some knucklebones?"

Ian spoke first. "We are trying—"

"Nothing, Sam," Theodor interrupted. "Ridley here was just explaining how the creek feeds the plants in the gardens.

Did you know that shit makes them grow bigger?" Theodor glanced at Ridley, unsure.

"Boring. I will find Hermy, then. He'll play, unlike you bookworms." Sam turned back toward the library. "Oh, and Ian—don't forget the scribing on animal husbandry from the Old Tongue is due tomorrow!" Sam yelled without looking back.

"Yeah, got it."

They all stood silent for a moment, watching Sam walk into the shrub maze.

Ian turned to Theo. "Why didn't you want Sam to know?"

"I don't know, but something isn't right here. A secret doorway to a basement, secret languages, and Edwyn dead?" Theodor took a deep breath. "I think the overlord is up to something. No offense, Ridley, but the passage leads from his chambers to the basement."

"None taken. He's never really acknowledged me, anyway."

"So, what now?" Ian said as they started to walk back.

Ridley took the lead. "What do you think? We go back and try again."

"Wait! That's it!" Theodor cried.

"What's what?" Ian asked, confused.

"Yeah, what?" Ridley added, her eyebrows raised.

"Sam said it—the Old Tongue. That is the key. If this language is older than the Old Tongue, it was likely translated to that first." Theodor took a breath. "Or the Old Tongue itself originated from this one!"

Theodor started moving faster toward his quarters. He looked back to see Ian and Ridley exchanging a wary glance. "Come on!"

Theodor sat down at his desk, rummaging through stacks of paper.

"What are you looking for?" Ridley asked.

"A map marked in the Old Tongue."

"I have one." Ian hurried next door to his room.

Ridley's face lit up. "So… if we compare the map we found with Ian's, and the names of places were the same during that time, we can use the phonetics to see if the markings on that note makes any sense by translating twice."

Theodor slapped his desk. "Exactly."

"Here." Ian walked in and handed him a map, then slid a stack of papers over and sat on the front of the desk. Ridley leaned down closer to Theodor. The floral scent of her hair caught his attention.

Ian snapped his fingers. "Let's go, Theo!"

"Yes, sorry." He met Ridley's eyes and quickly looked down.

Theodor placed the maps side by side. "Alright, let's use the Lightfall Sea as a test."

Theodor read slowly, trying to remember. He mumbled a bit in the Old Tongue.

"Close enough," Ridley said with a slight smile.

Theodor's face warmed from her gaze. "If we now try and apply the phonetics of the Old Tongue to these symbols, perhaps…"

Theodor grabbed a quill and inkwell. Ridley slid him a piece of clean parchment. He copied the symbols from the old map and wrote what he had read in the Old Tongue beneath them.

He sat back. All three stared at the paper, Ian cocking his head sideways.

"Wait!" Ridley pointed to the writing. "Start with the word *the*. It's an article that defines a noun. If you can isolate it, the structure will match if it does indeed say 'The Lightfall Sea.'"

Theodor counted the symbols and started writing again, this time separating them. They sat and watched him for what seemed like an eternity. Theodor felt the sweat beading on his forehead. Ridley replaced a few candles that had burned down. Ian stood, yawned, stretched his arms, and eventually flopped down on the bed.

Theodor's eyelids grew heavy. He ignored Ian's snoring and noticed Ridley still beside him, trying to keep her eyes open. Her hands held up her head.

"That's it!"

Ridley jumped, and Ian sat up. "It was definitely the origin of the Old Tongue. You were right. *Gisg na graf* would translate to *the*. The rest match up, like the Old Tongue was more or less a substitution system. So *Urgon gedna gis gorun ur* is Lightfall, and so on. So, if I apply this to the letter we found…"

Theo grabbed another clean sheet and applied what he had learned. Ridley brought him a cup of water.

"Where's mine?" Ian held his hand out.

"Get it yourself." Ridley snapped, continuing to watch Theodor.

"That's it! It works. The note is not just a bunch of gibberish!" Theo stood. "We did it!" He hugged Ridley without thinking, quickly pulling back. "I'm sorry, Ridley, I was just…"

"It's alright, Theo," she grinned. "So, what does it say?"

Chapter Nineteen

Galen

William had stormed off in a fury, leaving the council to their own accord. This was to be the day they finished the session, but there seemed to be no order without William. Galen had scribed most of the day as the lords bickered back and forth. *Most do not understand his vision, even still.* Heath Promen had excused himself earlier, after his daughter had come and whispered in his ear. The others were now arguing over how to keep the peace when there was a land dispute.

"What's to stop a mob from murdering someone if they decide collectively that they want to cut down a tree beside his house for firewood?" Marc Dane stood, waiting for an answer. "After all, it is for the good of the village, right?"

Atohi Cherne stood in response. "Each person in a town

is an individual. A man and his family should own the land around his house, the land he works." He was the most recent lord to join the council, coming from Cherok, an ancient nation to the south. "If we are to make this transition in good faith, we must address each *person* in Aahsgoth, as opposed to each village, town, or high lord's castle. Each citizen of the realm has rights given by the gods. Our job here is not to *give* them rights, as has been done throughout our history, but to protect the ones endowed to them already."

Galen's eyes widened. He felt a strong urge to stand and clap. "My lords, if I may? Lord Cherne's eloquent summary is the essence of William's goal. If the last decade of work on this council could be said in one breath, it couldn't be stated any better." He nodded toward Cherne and took his seat. The lords whispered among themselves.

Nivara approached Galen, carrying a small scroll. She had only been in Wolfpine a short time, another apprentice sent by the order. "My lord." She knelt beside him. "A corvid arrived for you."

"Thank you, my lady."

"From Ashbourne," she added.

Galen stood with her. "From my son?"

"It bears your seal," she said, smiling.

"Thank you, Nivara." She nodded and turned to leave, and Galen cleared his throat. "My lords, perhaps a break is in order." No one responded directly, but most stood and stretched. "An hour or two perhaps?" Galen watched as they started to leave. "I'll take that as a yes."

He turned toward the doors at the back of the main hall.

Galen shut the door behind him and sat behind his desk, trying to catch his breath. He poured himself a cup of water from the wooden flagon. "Those damn stairs. They will be the death of me."

He was anxious to read the letter. He peeled the wax seal from the paper, carefully trying not to tear it. The writing was small and blurry. He looked around the stacks of paper on his desk, searching for his spectacles. "I need a damn pair of spectacles to find my spectacles," he muttered in frustration. He found them in a drawer in his desk and leaned back into the light from the window to read.

Father. I am pleased to tell you that I have found the answers you seek regarding the strange writing you sent. I was able to compare a map I found written in the same symbols with a current one labeled in the Common Tongue. Once I had the structure figured out, the translation was not too difficult. The hard part was finding the language in the first place. You should come as soon as possible. There are bigger implications here that I do not yet understand.

Master Edwyn has died. I dare not say too much now.

The note you sent reads...

A knock sounded at the door. Galen stood and put the note on the shelf among the various bottles and candles. *Can I never have a moment alone?* "Come in," he called. Heath Promen entered and shut the squeaky door behind him, carefully latching it. Galen nodded, surprised. "Ah, come in, my lord. I thought you had left Wolfpine."

"I am about to. There is news from Alarya. I must go."

Galen sat back down. "What can I do for you, Lord Promen? I don't have copies of the meeting notes yet. We have one last session shortly."

The man walked toward his desk. "No need, Master Preceptor. I'm not sure that this plan of William's will ever come to pass other than in name only." He leaned over and put both hands on Galen's desk. "And you seemed in a hurry once the girl came to you in the hall. Anything the council needs to know, Preceptor?"

"My lord?"

"The pretty girl that brought you the note?"

"Oh, my apprentice. Yes, yes. Nothing special, only updates from Ashbourne." Galen paused. "Why do you ask?"

"How is Theodor, anyway?"

Galen's forehead wrinkled. "He's doing well. Why do you ask?"

"I am just curious. I wouldn't want him to get into any trouble in Ashbourne. All those leagues away, you know. Boys will be boys."

Galen stood. "And what is that supposed to mean, my lord? What does my son have to do with anything? That is my business alone, and it has nothing to do with the council."

"Take it easy, old man." Promen stood straight and smiled. "Speaking of the council, I am considering leaving it and declaring Alarya an independent kingdom as it used to be."

Galen took a breath. "My lord, why would you do such a thing? Will, and indeed *all* of us, have worked for this for so long. It is finally starting to come together. Besides, Alarya was never more than a territory, according to the histories."

The lord smiled. "I have been assured by a forefather of mine that it was." He turned toward the door. "Do not fret, I have not decided. Once Will returns, I will send word one way or the other. *If* he returns."

Galen stood, but no words came to him before Promen had left the room and shut the door behind him. Galen had never liked the man or his arrogance. *Why would he break with the council?* This was not a good time, while Will was away in search of his children.

He sighed and sat back down to continue reading. He reached for his spectacles once again, only to realize they were still in his hand. He continued where he had left off.

"The note you sent reads: I'm sorry, my love, it is better for them if I leave this place now. I hope to explain one day."

Galen looked up, remembering that day. *Val.* The look on William's face. Joy, happiness, sadness, anger—all at once. He looked back down at the note.

There is more. The ancient text I found was some type of foretelling. Although I have no clue as to what it means, it reads:

'When the sun goes black,

and the shadows cross,

when the twelve become one,

and emeralds turn to sapphires,

the dragon will return to see the light.'

The translation is surely not perfect, but I am confident that it is fairly accurate. Come to Ashbourne, Father. There is much more to show you that I dare not say here.

Yours, Theo.

Galen lowered his spectacles and leaned back in his chair. He raised his hand to his chin and sat in silence for a few moments. *What could this mean?* he thought. *Val must have written this note before she left, but how would she know such a language? What couldn't Theo speak of? And why in the hell is this bastard coming to me asking of my son?*

"I must get word to Will and go to Ashbourne," he muttered. He had to get back to the main hall to wrap up the council meeting. He took his quill to a fresh piece of paper. "Perhaps a rider could catch up to Will. By now he is likely nearing Ethorya, but they will have to stop with such a big group."

Galen finished his letter, rolled it, and sealed it. William had taken at least one hundred of his best men and most of the horses with him. "Perhaps the new girl is a fast rider," he mumbled as he left to go back to the main hall.

"My lady! Nivara, may I have a word?" he almost shouted across the courtyard, watching her walk toward the inner gate.

"Yes, my lord?" She stopped in front of him and nodded.

Galen was short of breath. "My lady, I would ask a favor of you. Once the meeting is done, I need to leave for Ashbourne immediately. Would you be able to deliver a message for me?"

"Yes, Master Galen. Is everything alright?" she asked, concerned.

"Yes, but I must get a message to William. A corvid will not do. You are studying horsemanship and husbandry, are you not?"

She nodded. "I am."

"I am sorry to ask you to leave the comforts of Wolfpine, but as you know, William is on the open road. Could you—"

"Gladly," she interrupted. "It's no trouble to me. I enjoy

the road. Honestly, I prefer it to scribing meetings. I am no writer," she said, smiling.

Galen returned the smile as relief swept over him. "Thank you, my lady," he said, handing her the tightly rolled note. "Take this to Will, and I will scribe the rest of the meeting. I need to pack supplies and leave at first light."

"I'll leave right away." She nodded and walked past him, putting the note into a pocket. Elya Promen nodded as she walked by, but he only half-smiled as she passed. His thoughts went back to Theodor as he walked toward the doors to the old hall.

What could he have discovered?

Nothing came to mind as Galen entered the hall and closed the door behind him.

Chapter Twenty

William

William wiped his sweaty palms on his trousers. The last time he had ridden from Wolfpine in such haste, he had an army with him, and he was king. Although he knew the men with him were loyal, they technically did not have to be here.

"I wonder what the council thinks of this, Jordan?" William asked the high commander of his garrison.

Jordan looked over at him. "May I speak freely?"

"As always. I am not your father."

"Fuck the council, Will. This is about your children. For this ride, you can be king one last time."

William smiled, reassured. Jordan had come to him at a young age, already a renowned warrior. He had risen to lead a group of mercenaries some called "The Bulls." He had ridden into battle six times before reaching his thirty-fifth year, and he'd won them all. He had trounced many legendary men from the east. Some even said he had beaten a man of magick and the legendary Sir Charles, a warlord from the west. William had offered him a role in his army, and he had been by his side ever since. The last time they rode together like this, they were heading to put an end to the last rebellion.

"Ironic," William said.

"What is?"

The last time we rode toward Old Lucian was to kill a would-be usurper." William paused, looking over at Jordan. "This time, I need help from that man's son."

They had just entered the small port town of Myrtle in the southeast of Vaegomar. They were to take the Middle Sea to Water's Edge and pick up Ashaya's trail from there. He tried to hide his worry, but his face must have shown his concern.

"I'm sure they are fine, Will. Ash and Merek can take care of themselves. Besides, Promen's boy rode with her, did he not?"

"Yes, I suppose you are right." William paused, managing a small smile. "But I think it's the other way around. Maybe it is Mitchel I should be concerned about."

The men were loading the horses onto two of William's galleys. The water was deep, deep enough to dock along the piers. His fleet sat in Capeton, but he kept a few ships here. William worked alongside his men, as he always had.

"Sit before you fall down, old man." Jordan slapped him on the shoulder. "These young lads can handle this. You are just getting in the way."

"I hate to admit it, but I miss this. The open road, the wind in my hair, and the prospect of battle. Like the good ol' days." William sat on a crate, watching the seagulls circling above, scouting for their next meal.

Jordan sat beside him. "Only something's different this time."

"And what might that be?"

"We are old men, and you have no hair."

"Fuck you!" William smiled and nudged his friend while rubbing his own head.

The ships took sail and William stood on the bow, looking out to sea. The sun was high, and the day was clear. He could easily see the Eye of Promethial to the southwest, ever watching. He inhaled the salty air.

I have been holed up in Wolfpine for too long.

The breeze cooled his face, and he did not mind the saltwater spraying him from time to time. "I see why he loved it out here," William mumbled, looking down at the passing swells and thinking of his old friend. Jordan had handed him a small loaf of wheat bread. He had no appetite, so he tore it into pieces, tossing breadcrumbs to the gulls that followed them from the docks.

"Loved what?" Jordan joined him and leaned over the railing.

"Oh, nothing. Just reflecting on an old friend. When this is over, I will go see his children." He paused. "I have been so focused on this damn council. I didn't take the time to—"

"Stop beating yourself up, Will. You are doing the right thing." Jordan grabbed a handful of crumbs from William's hand and joined him in feeding the birds. "So, *The Emerald Princess*? I had forgotten the names of half the fleet."

"Yes, aptly named for Ashaya when she and Merek were born. I had two ships commissioned for them by the best. She had the deepest, emerald-green eyes I had ever seen. I was instantly in love with her." A smile came to his face as he continued to stare out to sea.

Jordan broke the silence. "Who built them?"

"James the shipwright, of Starfall Bay. Sirich was jealous, but I reminded him at the time that he was to be king," William said with a sigh. "Then I took that away, too."

"He seems to understand, Will. If not, he will change. At some point, we all do."

They stood and fed the birds until they ran out of bread. "This voyage won't last long with the wind at our back." William could already see the lands of Thurel; Water's Edge was not far beyond.

The gulls above did not stay long after the crumbs were all eaten. William could see the smoke rising from the small town as they got closer. A few people stood and watched the ships approach. One man pointed. William chuckled. "They probably only see fishing cogs around here, not two warships pulling up to their backdoor."

"My lord, the water is too shallow to dock here," the captain reminded him.

"We'll row." William walked past him.

"See, we *are* too old for this shit," Jordan said with a sigh.

They dropped anchor and took skiffs to the dock. William, Jordan, and ten others were on the first one, rowing toward the shoreline. The other men stayed behind to prepare the skiffs for the horses.

Jordan threw a rope to the dock, stepped up, and wrapped it around a pole. He reached for William to help him up.

"My sword." William pointed. Another man handed him the sword he had laid beside him.

He wore only a red tunic with no armor, his half-cape snapping in the wind as he helped a few others out of the skiff. "Let's go."

Jordan put a hand on his shoulder. "You don't want to wait on the horses?"

William pointed behind them. "We aren't too old to walk to that tavern. If Ashaya came through here, someone in there would know. You know the gossip of a tavern. Besides, we aren't going to kill anyone... hopefully," he said, smiling.

The men followed William through the door, half-hanging from its hinges. Only a few patrons were sitting around drinking. A serving wench sat with one, while the other stopped where she stood. One young man sat at the bar turned to them. His eyes widened. "My king!"

A few of the others then stood, looking at each other. William had not heard someone call him king in quite some time, but he did not mind it so much.

"Have you seen a young woman come through here? Hair like the sun, green eyes?"

No one said anything.

The man at the bar stood. "My king, I—"

"Who are you?" William cut him off.

"No one, my lord. Just a singer. I sang for your birthday feast in Wolfpine last year."

"I see. So, have you seen the girl I described come through this town? My daughter?"

"I'm sorry, I just got here last night, so I—"

A voice rose from behind them. "There was a girl here I haven't seen before, about a fortnight ago. Killed two men outside the brothel." William turned to see a woman standing in the doorway.

"Two men? A brothel?" William looked over at Jordan.

"Not the girl you describe, though," the lady said. "Not quite."

"What do you mean, not quite?" William felt his face flush.

"Girl had dark hair." The woman paused. "She came in after those men attacked her and her friend, asking about her brother."

Jordan looked at him. "Has to be her, Will."

"Show me what happened," William said, walking toward the door to follow her out.

"Right over here." The woman pointed. "Two regulars walked out here after little Neph ran in."

"Who the hell is Neph?"

"Just a boy, the son of the leader of some zealot group out of the Bloody Sands. Anyway, they came out, and next thing I know, they was dead. She came in asking about her brother. They had his horse, I gathered. Blood all over her face, but I don't think it was hers."

"She killed two men?"

"Laid 'em out right here." They stopped in front of the building. "I didn't see how, just a blur through that dirty window. Heard the screams."

William looked at Jordan for a moment. A smile came to Jordan's face. "I told you she could handle herself." He turned to the woman. "And this zealot group, you say... They come in from Old Lucian?"

"Old Lucian?"

"The Bloody Sands," William reminded her.

"Yeah, some temple they always mention."

Jordan stepped toward her. "Where did they go, this girl and her friend?"

"Hell if I know. Took the horse and headed south."

"So, if she found Merek's horse..." William's voice trailed off.

"You and your men want a drink, or maybe..."

"Gods, no." William walked toward the docks. The others followed. "Get every man and horse ready."

Jordan whistled and motioned toward the ships to continue. "So we head south and track her there. Should be easy to pick up her trail."

"No. First, we ride for Bloodstone."

"The ruins of Old Lucian?" Jordan asked.

"My lord?" a voice approached from the dock.

William looked over to see a young woman walking toward them. "Yes, my lady? Nivara, isn't it?"

"Yes, my lord."

"What brings you here? Are you alright?"

"I am, my lord. Galen sent me after you left. I boarded the other ship before it sailed. He had a message for you after hearing from his son in Ashbourne." She pulled a note from inside her riding breeches.

William took the note and broke the seal. He began to read. "He doesn't need my permission to visit home. He knows better than to…"

"William? Is everything alright?" Jordan walked back to him and must have noticed the tears welling in his eyes.

"Will? What does it say? Is Galen alright?"

William did not respond. His heart raced; butterflies tickled his gut. He looked up, wiped his eyes, and took a deep breath.

"Will, what is it?" Jordan faced him with both hands on his shoulders.

"She's alive…"

"Who?"

"Val."

Chapter
Twenty-One

Ashaya

Ashaya walked slowly through the open field. The tall grass tickled her palms. The sun above warmed her skin. She stopped when she spotted someone at the edge of the tree line. The figure with dark hair and blue eyes turned, disappearing into the forest.

Ashaya started to run, but she was barely moving. Her hands burned. She raised them to see her palms bleeding. The blades of grass might as well have been a thousand swords, all reaching for her and biting into her naked body as she passed. Thunder cracked and clouds rolled in, blacking out the sun.

She glanced down; ankle deep mud held her in place. A man lay in front of her. Dying fish flopped around him, gasping for air. Blood pooled in the mud below his neck. She reached for him but kept sinking lower. Tears ran down her cheeks, and blood from the corners of her lips. She tried to scream, but nothing escaped her throat. She reached for the man once more, but it was too late. She was sinking faster and faster until her head went under. Only her arm remained, reaching for the sky.

Ashaya sat up from her bedroll, gasping for air, wiping sweat from her brow. Her undershirt stuck to her body. She took a deep breath.

"It was just a dream," she mumbled, trying to gather her thoughts. Embarrassment still hung over her about last night. She looked at Mitch. He remained asleep, breathing deeply. *What was I thinking?* She could only remember the urge, the hunger. An appetite had taken her that she had not experienced before. And she had hurt him. She shook her head but did not mention it.

The sun sparkled through the trees above and what was left of the last night's fire smoldered. A small plume of smoke rose from the ashes. Ashaya stood and stretched, her stomach reminding her to break her fast.

We have no time. We have to find Merek.

"Mitch, wake up." He stirred but did not open his eyes. "Mitch, get up, we need to go," she said, a bit louder this time.

"I'm awake." Mitch sat up, yawning. Ashaya avoided looking at him.

"Did you eat?" he asked as he stood and went to relieve himself behind a tree.

"No time. We need to find Merek. Let's get to this isle."

He walked over to the horses and grabbed a pouch. "Here is what is left of the jerky," he said, holding the pouch out toward her.

"Go ahead, you eat it. It will only tease me, anyway. I want something more. I'm so thirsty." She drank deeply from her waterskin.

Mitch walked back to pack the bedrolls and spoke as he chewed. "Speaking of teasing, what was that about last night? I thought..."

Ashaya took a deep breath. "I'm sorry, Mitch, I don't know what got into me. I did not mean for that to happen."

She avoided his gaze while she packed. Mitch did not respond. Only the birds of the wood around them spoke for a while.

"Let's go," she said finally.

They continued south on the old road. Some parts were old cobblestone, most of it crumbling. "There." Mitch pointed to the right. There was carved a wide trail, overgrown but visible, heading west. "This is the Whispering Wood, where we rode in."

He led the way. The chirping of birds, the buzzing of insects, and the ripple of water echoed in Ashaya's head all at once. She closed her eyes for a moment and tried to focus. The scent of pine and salt in the air was strong. A wisp of decay rode the breeze with a tinge of sweetness.

"You smell that?"

Mitch looked back at her. "Smell what?"

"I don't know, smells like... rot. Let's keep going. We're close."

Mitch slowed so that she could ride up beside him. "How do you know?"

Ashaya thought for a moment. "I just do." She pointed to the crumbling ruin of what looked to be a stone wall. "Here!"

Mitch stopped his horse. "It's just some old ruins. Why here?"

"I don't know. There is something familiar about this place." Ashaya dismounted Acorn. The horse grunted as Mitch followed her to the stone wall. She knelt and ran her hands over the smooth stone. She heard a muffled scream.

"Did you hear that?" she asked, turning back to Mitch.

"I suppose not… unless you are talking about the birds?"

She stood and kept walking.

They came to a clearing where a small stream trickled, red lotus flowers covering the surface where the water pooled. She knelt, looked into the clear water, and splashed her face. She brushed some of the flowers aside and studied her reflection. Her dark hair rippled. The dye had washed out, but it remained darker than it had been before. Her eyes were lighter now, almost blue, as Mitch had noticed. A short scream escaped her throat and her face morphed into her brother's.

"Ash! What is it?" Mitch ran to her. "What happened?"

She had scooted back from the stream's edge. "I saw, I saw…"

"You saw what?"

"Merek."

"Where?" Mitch stood and looked around.

"No, Mitch. In the water. I saw his face."

Mitch looked into the stream. He ran his hand along the top of the water. "It was just your reflection. You are twins, for the gods' sake." He knelt again and reached for her. "Ash, we need to go home. You need to see Galen. I don't know what the hell is going on, but you are not well!" She just sat there as he crouched down beside her. "I'm sorry, Ash. I do not mean to raise my voice, I just don't know what is going on. I only know you have been acting strange as of late."

"It is alright, Mitch. I wish I had answers," she sighed. "I killed two men. I have trained for it for years, but I still see their faces. I see the shock and pain; I see their blood. I taste it."

Mitch did not respond. She sat beside him a while longer. Only the breeze whispered through the trees.

"Come on. I didn't come this far to just turn around. Let's finish this." Ashaya stood and reached her hand out. Mitch shook his head and took her hand. They both went back to searching the clearing.

"You were right. This was a camp," Mitch said, standing over what had clearly been a stone fire ring. "Do you think Merek stayed here?"

Ashaya continued to scan the area. "Yes," she replied, bending down to look at the dark spot near the fire ring. It had rained here recently; the spot looked to be muddy ash with bits of doe skin scattered in the soil. The hint of something burning filled her nose.

"Why are you sniffing the air like some beast?" Mitch asked with a slight chuckle.

She ignored him and ran her hand along the muddy ash. It was cold and hard, and the ground had cracked as it dried. She heard another scream and saw what looked to be two bare feet on the ground as if she were in a daydream. Ashaya lifted her hand and gasped.

"Ash?"

"Here. He was here." Tears filled her eyes and streamed down her face. She touched the area again and saw a flash of silver, a pool of blood, and embers reaching for the sky.

Mitch put his hand on her shoulder. "What is going on? What is wrong?"

Her tears fell to the ground. She covered her face with both hands, sobbing, coldness creeping into her and numbing her insides. "He died here, Mitch."

Chapter
Twenty-Two

Theodor

Theodor stared at the stacks of paper in front of him.

"Theo, what is going on with you?" Ridley asked.

"He should have been here by now. Father, I mean."

"I'm sure your father is fine," Ridley responded as she sat on the edge of Theodor's desk. She lit the lantern from a small candle. Dusk had come, and the tin roof made the pitter-patter of rain sound heavier than it was.

"Yes, I suppose you are right. It's just that by sea it's only a few days' journey."

"He probably hasn't even left yet. He's a master of the

order, and Wolfpine is likely the toughest assignment one could have. Big place to manage."

"I suppose," Theodor sighed and lay back on his straw bed, cupping his hands behind his head. He glanced over his nose at Ridley, making eye contact for just a moment. He quickly went back to studying the ceiling. His lips tightened to hide his faint smile.

"Hey, so we figured out the old language on paper, but I still want to know what it sounds like. We can't exactly speak it." Ridley walked over and reached for him. "Come on."

"Where are we going?"

"Where do you think?"

"We are going to get caught. We have been back half a dozen times."

"There are too many old books and scrolls in that dungeon. There has to be something in them."

"It's too early, don't you think? The overlord may still be in his chambers."

"Maybe, but it's dark and raining. Most of these old men are likely already in their beds."

"Fine." Theo took her hand and stood. He held on longer than he should have, and she looked back and grinned. She tugged him toward the door before taking her hand back.

They made their way down to the gardens. Ridley had been right—the rain had driven away anyone who may have still been outside. The rain grew heavier, and its song filled the air, covering any noise they made.

By the time they reached the waterfall, they were already soaked. Theodor went through the usual routine and immediately found the stone latch. They entered and lit the candles after Ridley had dried her small silver blade to strike the flint. They stood still for a moment, listening for footsteps above.

Ridley wiped away the curly black hair that stuck to her face. "I think it's clear." She took a candle with her as she started to search a bookshelf.

"What could we possibly find? We've at least glanced at almost every book in this room."

A voice rang out from the dark in the back of the room. "Not *every* book."

Ridley and Theodor turned in unison. A slight scream escaped Ridley's throat.

"Who's there?" Theodor held the candle out in front of him toward the darkness. Blue eyes stared back at him, glistening in the light.

"What are you hoping to find here?" the woman said in a raspy voice.

"Stay back! We don't want any trouble! Come on, Ridley." Theodor reached for her, holding the candle out toward the woman. Ridley hurried toward him, her eyes wide and fixed on the woman. She pointed her small blade in the woman's direction.

She approached slowly and came into the light. "Relax. I will not tell anyone you are here." The woman stopped a few feet away. "But please, put away your silver." Theodor did not realize they had been backing up the entire time until his elbow hit the stone wall near the door.

"Why would I put my dagger away?"

The woman took a deep breath, and before he could blink, Ridley's dagger flew out of her hand, clanking off the wall to the floor. Ridley jumped and covered her mouth.

"Calm down, before your heart beats out of your chest. I mean you no harm. Especially you, Theodor," the woman said.

"How do you know my name? Who are you?"

"Do you work for my grandfather?" Ridley asked, moving closer to Theodor.

The woman smiled and walked over to the desk where they had found the notes and map. She started looking through the various stacks of parchment and scrolls without answering. Theodor and Ridley exchanged a glance and turned back to watch the woman.

Her straight red hair hung over one shoulder. She wore a black leather sleeveless doublet, four straps on the front, the drawstrings loose and revealing. Theodor had never seen such clothing. The matching leather breeches looked foreign, with a flare below the knees and thin laced bracers that ran from her forearms to the backs of her hands.

"Are you from the east?" he said finally, after studying her for a moment. For the first time since he had known her, Ridley seemed quiet and afraid. She held on to Theodor's arm tightly.

"No, Theodor. Aahsgoth is my home. Take a deep breath—that heart is still pounding."

"How do you know?"

"I can hear it." The woman turned to them. "So, I ask again, what are you two doing down here?"

"How did you know we were—"

"We have eyes everywhere," she continued, looking through the papers.

Ridley looked over at Theodor, her eyes asking for forgiveness. "We were studying some ancient language. One that my grandfather seems to be hiding."

"*Una, gonmevon vanun gal graphvehgon undru?*"

"You... You speak it?" Ridley blurted out.

"That is what you took the note for, is it not? You are here to learn of Vedician?"

"Vedician?" Theodor repeated. "How do you know it?"

"Some called it the language of the gods. It is my native tongue."

Theodor stepped forward. "Who *are* you? And how do you know about this place?"

"I helped build it, along with my sister."

Theodor looked back at Ridley, who was already looking at him, her forehead wrinkled. He shook his head. "Where are you from? I do not understand."

"I told you, Theodor. Aahsgoth is my home. I believe what you are asking is, *when* am I from?"

"What does that mean?" Ridley seemed to finally let her guard down.

"Have a seat. I am not here to hurt you."

Ridley sat in the one chair at the old desk. Theodor slowly collected a stool from in front of one of the bookshelves and blew the dust off.

The woman paced the room. "It seems your grandfather, the overlord, is working with my brother. The bastard of our little… family. He must have been told this place was here. I had this room built when my other, much older brother planned to sack Ashbourne. I knew everything would burn, and I was not strong enough to stop him. I had all of this taken underground before he arrived with his army. I got what I could." The woman raised her arms and looked around.

Theodor shook his head again. "Your brothers? I don't understand."

"The plight, you mean?" Ridley chimed in.

"The girl gets it," the woman said, pointing to her.

"But the Plight of Ashbourne was what, 1050 ADD? That was over a thousand years ago, or so the histories say."

"Yes, I suppose it was. After the first century, who keeps track?" the woman smiled.

Theodor studied the woman. She had a presence about

her. Her face was young, but her eyes held wisdom. It reminded him of some of the elders of his order. "Are you some historian? Are you just telling us something that you have read? You cannot have—"

"Are you... religious, boy?"

"Well, not really. House Serwyn prays to the thirteen, but I never really—"

"Ah, yes, my sweet sister's clan." The woman paused and looked back at them. "So, you would know the names Lucian and Promethial, then?"

"Yes," Theodor and Ridley answered in unison.

Theodor continued, "Promethial, the god of fire. Lucian, the god of war, although some call him the god of blood."

Theodor paused and looked at Ridley. Her eyes never left the pale woman, who still paced the room, smiling as she listened, rubbing her fingers over dusty books.

"What about them?" Theodor pressed. "I walk past them every day, the carvings on the top of the library."

"Yes, a nice touch, if I do say so myself." The woman walked back toward them. "They are my brothers, and Promethial is up to something."

Theodor stood and rolled his eyes. "What does that mean? Your brothers are named after old gods?"

The woman reached out and grabbed his arm. He tried to pull away but could not budge. Her hand was an anchor, holding him in place.

"Sit, boy. I'm trying to help you." Theodor looked up at her, chills running down his spine as the blue gleam in her eyes seemed to brighten. "You have no idea. Your history has been all but erased. *Men* made my brothers into gods. And the rest of us, I suppose. I tried to save some of it—in this very room."

Theodor looked to Ridley, her eyes wide again, her hands trembling.

The woman continued, "And now, your grandfather schemes with my brother because he found an old foretelling, a bullshit prophecy written in a strange tongue."

The woman stood and walked back toward the dark side of the room, her hands running through her hair.

"I am sorry, my lady." Theodor stood slowly. "We just don't understand. What you're saying seems like a fairy tale."

"Sometimes, I wish it were."

Ridley took a deep breath and stood. "So... if... if your brothers are who you say they are, then what is your name?"

The woman smiled. "I am Aethial. Where do you think you get *your* surname?"

Chapter Twenty-Three

Sirich

Most of the men lay around asleep by their fires. Others boiled rabbits. A few had taken over the small houses in the village. Some of them had expressed their disappointment in not finding a fight. Philip and his men had not yet returned.

"Where are they?" Sirich paced back and forth in front of the old statue. The many campfires distorted his shadow on the stone woman.

"Perhaps we should go see if they are in trouble?" Amari suggested.

"I'm sure your men are fine. The mountain clans pose no threat to anyone except perhaps an unarmed child," the strange man offered.

The one they called Ethan had been at Sirich's side since he had appeared a few nights ago. At first, he seemed a nuisance, but Sirich had come to enjoy his company. Amari did not seem to like him. The man would leave the village every night before dawn and return by dusk the next. For a commoner, he seemed well educated, well spoken, and witty.

"This man cannot be trusted," Amari mumbled under his breath.

Sirich closed his eyes and covered his ears. The whispered words had sounded like a scream in his head. He turned from Amari when he winced, hiding his pain. He needed to finish this for his father.

"So, what shall we do, brother?" Amari asked. "Ethan here seems to have your best interest at heart, but I have known you for thirteen years. He has known you for, what? Two days at best?" Sirich noticed Amari cutting his eyes to the man, only to see him wearing his usual smile.

"What can we do but wait, Doc?" Sirich replied impatiently. "And what the hell is that supposed to mean?"

"Nothing, Siri. Nothing."

"Once Philip reappears, we will return to Wolfpine and take the girl with us." Sirich pointed to Bella, sitting by a fire, rocking her babe.

"And what if he does not come back? What will we tell your father?" Amari asked, sitting down heavily.

"Perhaps your friend is right," Ethan offered. Sirich could almost feel the man's gaze. "Send more men to make sure. I don't think the attackers are coming back."

"Fine." Sirich walked toward his horse.

"Where are you going?" Amari stood and walked with him. "You are in no condition to go anywhere but to a 'ceptor."

"I need to do this myself. Besides—"

"Your friend of the Gazi is right once again, my prince," Ethan said, nodding. "The foothills are no place for a man in your condition."

Sirich took a deep breath and pointed to one of his men. "You there, take ten men and your horses and go aid Philip, if need be."

"Yes, my lord," the man said, standing.

"Beats sitting here, twiddling our thumbs," another added.

They had watched the men mount their horses and ride toward the mountains before Ethan spoke again. "You should not worry about your father. Why tell him anything?" Sirich turned to see Amari roll his eyes. "This is but a show. There is no justice here. Besides, your sister rides south, looking for your brother. Perhaps she needs—"

Sirich opened his eyes wide and walked quickly toward the man, reaching for the hilt of his sword. "What do you know of my sister? How would you know that?" he demanded.

Amari stood as the remaining men heard the commotion and approached, the sound of steel against scabbards, half-drawn and at the ready.

"Easy, my prince." Ethan paused, a slight grin still on his face. "You seem quick to anger. You told me last night, remember?"

Sirich tried to think. His head was foggy, and he had not eaten. He backed away slowly and released his hilt. He raised his other hand, rubbing his eyes and then running it through his hair. "I'm sorry," he said with a sigh.

The others went back to their fires, and Amari patted him on the back. "I'm sure our new friend can forgive you. You need to rest. Better yet, you need to see a 'ceptor at Black River or Mudstone."

"Perhaps you should go to your sister," Ethan suggested. "On the way, stop at Ashbourne. There is no shortage of healers there, if you think that is what you need."

"And what of this place?" Amari snapped.

"Take the head of any man back to your council. They will be satisfied. Perhaps your friend Philip will bring one back," the man said, almost mockingly.

Sirich sat and took a drink from his waterskin. "Someone bring me wine. This does nothing but tease my thirst," he shouted at the others.

One man must have tossed him a skin, as he turned to see Amari reaching to catch it almost as if he were moving in slow motion. Sirich heard a low whizzing noise, only to turn and see the wineskin moving slowly toward his face. He noticed the flames of the nearest fire steadily dancing, and he reached up to catch the skin before it collided with his head. He turned, and in an instant, everything was normal again.

Amari's eyes were wide. "What in the hell?"

He looked at Ethan, who chuckled. "Nice reflexes. Almost... unnatural."

Sirich felt confused and weak. Amari must have felt the same. "How did you know..." Amari stopped and sat beside him. For a moment he only heard the leafhoppers in the wood around them. "I think we should sleep and get to a 'ceptor at first light. Your condition is only getting worse."

Sirich noticed Ethan grinning as he listened. He knew Amari was right. These strange bouts of nausea, odd hearing, obscured vision, and now a burning in his veins had gotten worse. He did not want Amari to worry any more than he already did. This had gone on far too long. He continued to sit in silence, drinking his wine. "Perhaps Ethan is right. There is nothing else we can do in this place."

"Siri, you can't just leave—"

"I can, Doc. These men are capable of finishing up here once Philip returns. Ethan is right. I need to go to Ashaya. The road is no place for a woman. She might as well be alone with Mitchel at her side."

"You are in no condition to help anyone. You need to see—"

"Didn't you hear the man, Doc? Ashbourne is on the way. We can hire a fishing cog to take us to Ashbourne, get patched up, and then go east." Sirich drank the last of the wine. "You don't have to come, brother. I know you need to get home."

Amari sat up straight and met Sirich's gaze. "I came with you for whatever adventure this would become. I will not leave you like this. Besides, I want to see Ash. It has been too long. Whatever you do, I will be by your side. Someone has to watch out for you." Amari cut his eyes to Ethan, who just watched them. Amari leaned closer and whispered in Sirich's ear, "I don't know who he is or what he wants, but I don't trust him."

Sirich looked over at the strange man. Ethan sat quietly, his mouth closed, but the same grin as always painted his face.

Chapter
Twenty-Four

Neph

They had been waiting quietly for some time.

Certainly, these two weren't promised as well, Neph thought, wiping his palms on his breeches. *An old man with one foot in the grave, and a man still as green as the fields he worked.*

Footsteps sounded behind them, and Neph turned to see a young girl approaching. The girl was maybe twelve or thirteen. She walked slowly and looked around as if she were lost. Her dirty white dress brushed the stone floor behind her. She stopped beside the younger man, and he leaned down and whispered something in her ear. The girl nodded and whispered something in return, but Neph could not make it out. She looked unsure. Neph moved over beside the girl, but as he was about to speak, she turned and sat on the floor behind them.

Then came a sound from the back of the hall. The guards straightened. Two of the king's advisors walked in from a dark hallway located well behind the stone chair. They wore black robes with some type of embroidery, although it was hard to make out. The first, an older man, took his place to the right of the chair. Neph had seen him before; he was sure this was the high priest of the temple. The other, a woman with long brown hair, stood on the other side.

A moment later, the god-king himself emerged from the darkness.

Lucian stood tall as he walked slowly to his throne. The king did not look down at his waiting subjects. His long black ponytail brushed the center of his back. The dark leather lappets at his waist flapped in rhythm with his stride. Neph thought they looked like dark, layered feathers forming a skirt of armor that reached for his knees. His matching black sandals' thick lacing wrapped around his legs like boots. He wore no shirt, and his body looked to be cut from the stone he walked on. A leather spaulder adorned his left shoulder, and a half-cloak covered the lower half of his face, the rest hanging off his left shoulder. Even in the darkness, his eyes seemed to glimmer like blue stars, his pale skin contrasting against the dim hall. The cloak fluttered behind him, blood-red with the black glyph of his sigil contorting the folds of the fabric. He sat slowly and glanced at the waiting peasants.

"The king calls forth the accused," the priest proclaimed through his thin white beard.

The guard nodded and walked into the dark passage from the other side of the hall. After a few moments, he returned with three others, all bound in chains. The iron wrapped around their wrists and ankles, the clanking echoing around the chamber as they stumbled in. There were two men and a woman, all frail, with nothing more than ragged cloth wrapping around their waists and hanging no lower than their knees. Their heads hung low, their hair covering their faces. They had been here for some time.

"This night, you will judge the accused. The lord is fair and will hear their pleas," the robed woman proclaimed. She motioned toward the first man. "You are accused of theft. Step before your god-king and tell your story. Speak freely."

The hunched man stepped before Lucian and started to speak. "Your Grace, I—"

"Kneel before your king, peasant!" the woman admonished him.

"I'm sorry, my lord."

Lucian spoke in a soft but deep and commanding voice. "Continue, my child."

The man stumbled through his story, the fear in his voice permeating the chamber. He admitted to stealing some bread and a broken wheel of cheese, but only to feed his family. He claimed he had suffered a back injury and could no longer work a strip. "I beg your mercy, my lord. I was wrong to take it, but it was for my children," he concluded.

Neph watched as Lucian listened to every word, never taking his eyes off the broken man. After a moment of silence, Lucian motioned to Neph and the others. "What do you make of this man's story?"

Neph lowered his chin, not knowing who should speak first. He was relieved when the old man took a step forward.

"He admits to it. Stealing is stealing." He stepped back into the line they had formed.

"And you?" Lucian nodded to the younger man.

"I believe him to be telling the truth, my lord. He admits to theft, but I would do the same for my daughter if I had no other choice. I don't believe it to be theft in this case."

Neph felt a lump form in his throat as Lucian nodded and turned to him. "And you, candlemaker?"

He stepped forward, walking a pace up the stairs toward the king. "The man deserves no more punishment, my lord. I have a son and understand his plight." Lucian stared at Neph, and he stepped back down with the others, feeling his king's gaze.

Neph's stomach remained in knots as this went on for the next two prisoners, thinking of what he must do. As each was called, they kneeled and told their stories. Neph and the others would then speak on each. The man accused of rape denied it completely. Neph and the others thought him guilty. The woman had denied speaking ill of the king and went so far as to thank him for his blessings. Neph had not been sure, but his wife had done the same many times. The others thought her guilty. Once all three had been called, Lucian motioned for the robed woman.

"*Padonged druge Gisgnagraph Vehvan malfam.*" She left the chamber and quickly returned with a tray containing three goblets. "You have each openly spoken about your matters, and I have taken the counsel of your brethren on each. Now the truth will come to light."

Lucian picked up one of the goblets, pulled down the cloak, and drank. Neph thought nothing odd, until Lucian jerked his head back. His eyes closed, and he tilted his head as if in pain, taking a deep breath. He slowly opened his eyes.

The king gestured to the man accused of stealing. "You are being truthful. You did what had to be done for your children. I will see to it you have work you can perform. I will need many scribes soon. You will learn to read and write in this new tongue. Return to me tomorrow night, and I will see to your injury."

The old man smiled in relief. "Thank you, my king, thank you," he said, elated. He bowed over and over while clutching his back. A guard removed his shackles, and he stumbled down the steps toward the front of the temple, thanking the king once more on his way out.

Lucian did the same for the others. He drank from a different goblet for each. He proclaimed the man guilty, seemingly knowing the details that he had left out of his tale. He even knew the name of the girl he had raped. He knew exactly where: in the back-alley tavern near the stables. The man cried and begged as he was dragged back into the dark hallway to a cell and sentenced to die. Neph wondered how it would be carried out. He had never seen anyone beheaded or hanged in the square.

After Lucian drank from the third goblet and thought for a moment, he stood slowly. Anger overcame his face. Like a flash of lightning, Lucian moved and gripped the remaining woman by the throat. Neph had only seen barely a blur, as if he had vanished and reappeared in front of her. Where she once stood, her feet dangled to the ground. The young girl behind Neph flinched, and the old man gasped loudly.

"You dare doubt me? Blasphemy does not go unpunished!" Lucian spat out.

The woman grabbed at Lucian's arm and tried peeling his fingers back. His hand did not budge. Neph looked down, only hearing the gurgling sounds as she attempted to breathe. Her legs kicked through the air below her in a last attempt to free herself.

"Have you ever known a common sorcerer to command the strength of one hundred men?" Lucian asked with a devilish grin as the woman stopped moving. He leaned in close to her neck as if smelling her perfume, then released her. She fell to the stone floor in a motionless pile. Without being told, two guards came and carried her lifeless body somewhere into the depths of the temple. The priests exchanged a glance with the hint of a smile.

Lucian turned back to his throne, the priests bowing as he went. "You may go, all of you." The old man trembled and left as fast as his legs would carry him.

Neph hesitated. *It must be tonight.*

As he was about to speak, the younger man spoke up. "My king, I would like to make an offering, if it please you."

Lucian turned. "And what would that be?"

"My king, I offer you my firstborn, my daughter." The man motioned toward the girl. "I assure you she is a virgin, and—"

"Enough!" Lucian's face turned crimson in anger. His voice boomed throughout the chamber. "Is this what you take me for? A monster that steals your daughters from their beds? Is this how you speak of me? Is this what you whisper to one another around your fires?"

The man hesitated, unsure. "I'm sorry, my lord. I thought... I... I..." His voice trailed off. Neph kept his head low but turned to see the girl weeping on the floor behind him.

"Take your daughter and go, miller. Go back to your grain before your daughter leaves here alone."

The man was visibly shaking. "Yes, my king." He nodded and turned. He grabbed the girl's hand and hurried toward the exit.

Should I speak? Does he remember his promise?

Lucian walked slowly toward his throne, his back to Neph. "And why are you still here, candlemaker? Would you offer me your daughter as well?"

Neph looked up, his words barely managing to escape his throat. "The... the gift, my lord." The king stopped and turned, looking over his shoulder, his face showing a barely perceivable grin.

"All of you, leave us!" The priests bowed and left as he commanded, the guards following. Only the flickering of the torchlight remained after their footfalls had faded.

When they were alone, Lucian sat. "What do you know of this... gift, candlemaker?"

"My lord, years ago you promised me your knowledge if I served you faithfully. I am the reeve of your fields, the bringer of light to your growing kingdom. I have worked myself nearly to death at your pleasure." Neph paused to take a breath. "I only ask that which was promised."

Lucian sat silent for only a moment. "That was a different time, candlemaker. My queen-mother is no longer my queen. I was her firstborn, and now we are too many. I intend to change that, if they refuse to follow me. We shape this land from the shadows. Aahsgoth, she calls it. I no longer..." Lucian stopped.

Neph took the opportunity. "My lord, a promise is a promise. I—"

"I do not think you understand what you ask, candlemaker. And who are you to ask this of me? Do you consider yourself worthy? Many here work hard. Men break their backs outside these walls as we speak. Why not one of them? Why you?"

Neph did not answer. Lucian leaned forward and stared at him, cocking his head to the side. The god-king's gaze burned through him.

Neph tried to think, tried to speak. "I took your mark, the mark of your clan," Neph blurted, pulling up his sleeve to show the small branding of the king's sigil on his wrist. He had hidden it from Aza for so long.

"So, you bear my mark, like so many others. Did you take

that for a promise? What is your true purpose here? Come before me." Neph ascended the stairs and stood before the god-king. "Would you spill blood for me, candlemaker?"

"Yes, my lord," he answered quickly. Lucian pulled a dagger from the sheath on his belt.

Lucian handed Neph the blade. "Show me."

"My lord, I don't understand."

Lucian smiled. "Spill blood, as I asked. Your own." Neph held the dagger, staring at it. "Spill your own blood, candlemaker." Neph put the dagger's golden handle into his right hand. The steel gleamed in the firelight. Lucian leaned back and watched in silence. Neph placed the razor-sharp edge to his left arm above the mark and hesitated.

"Go on," Lucian said with a smile. Neph looked down, held his breath, and cut deep across his forearm. His scream filled the chamber. Blood filled the wound and quickly flowed down his arm. A river of black streamed from his fingers and dripped off the ends. The dagger struck the floor, the clank of steel on stone echoing around them as he clutched his arm. Lucian leaned down to the pool of blood and ran a finger through it. The king stood as Neph dropped to his knees.

Lucian turned and opened his eyes. "You would leave them, candlemaker? You would leave them behind so that you may go lead a new life? This was to be how you serve me?"

Neph looked up to him. "I just… I thought… I…"

"It's the oldest story in the book, wanting that which you cannot have." Lucian paused. "Tell me, do you know when the last dragon died?"

Neph hesitated. He held his arm tighter. "No, my lord. I don't understand," he mumbled through the pain. "They say a hundred years ago."

"Five centuries ago, the last dragon was slain. But here I

stand, made from the blood of the dragons. Do you think I would bestow something upon you that you have no under-standing of, only for you to take it and run? My queen gave me no choice, but *you* had one. And you chose to abandon those you love to come here, seeking an escape. You are not worthy of the darkness, and your lust blinds you. Besides, you know not what you ask. You came for a blessing, not realizing it is also a curse."

"Please, my lord." Neph felt light-headed, the black pud-dle growing around him.

"You made your choice, candlemaker."

"You promised!" Neph exclaimed, tears slipping down his face.

"Perhaps I did," Lucian responded quickly. "But I will not help you break yours."

Neph looked down as the stone drank his lifeblood. "What now?"

Lucian walked past him and down the stairs toward the front of the temple without turning back.

"You are strong, candlemaker, but not that bright. You could have just pricked a finger." The walls echoed once more. "Now, you die."

Chapter Twenty-Five

Amari

They had left Valton the previous night, after Ethan had shown up at dusk once again. Sirich had left the man they called "Goose" in charge of awaiting Philip's return from the Southern Highlands. The ride had been easy as they approached the coast, but Sirich's condition had worsened, making it a slow trip. Starfall Bay was not far ahead. The salty air made Amari think of home.

I hope Abana is well.

Amari watched Ethan closely. He had been in Sirich's ear since the night Sirich happened upon him leaning against the old tree. Sirich seemed to have taken to him. Sirich had not been doing well, with bouts of dry heaving and continued weakness, among other things. He was sure Sirich was trying to hide the worst of it. His stubbornness matched that of a boulder refusing to budge. His new friend Ethan did not seem to care.

"Where is Doc?" Sirich called, looking back from his horse.

"I am still here."

"So, Amari of the Gazi clan, you say you have a ship here?" Ethan asked, walking beside Sirich's horse. He never seemed to tire.

"No, I said I know a man who does."

"And who may that be?"

"James the shipwright. He works out of Glass Rock Grove, where the Green River meets the bay."

"And how do you know this shipwright?"

"Does it matter?"

"Why so hostile? I am just trying to get to know my traveling companions. I assure you, I'm here to help."

Amari did not respond for a moment. *Perhaps I am being too harsh?* "James is the best shipwright in Aahsgoth. He has built all my cogs."

"How do you know he is here?"

"I don't. But if he is, I know where he will be."

"I hope you are right. For his sake," Ethan said, nodding toward Sirich beside him. He rode slouching in his saddle. He must have been listening after all, for he turned to Amari.

"What is the matter, Amari?" Sirich waited. "*You* look like the sick one."

"I just hope Abana hasn't run off all the help. I bet she left for Ethorya already," Amari confessed.

"She will be fine. She is much more intelligent than you, my friend." Sirich managed a smile.

Amari returned the smile, trying not to reveal his worry. Sirich had become pale, and Amari was afraid he would not make it on horseback.

A few hours had passed, the moons now bright above them. The woods had thinned to only sandy trails and shrubs. They approached the small town. It had grown since the last time Amari had been here. It used to be nothing but a few buildings along the water's edge, and docks behind them. It now had a proper road, inns, and shops. Amari could once again see the Eye of Promethial in the distance out to sea.

Amari rode ahead of them. "I'll go hire us a boat. Wait here."

"I will go with you. Do you have the coin for it?" Ethan replied, walking toward him.

"Stay with him. I told you I would find James. Sirich is in no condition—"

"I insist." Ethan helped Sirich off his horse and led him to a crate beside a wooden shack. "He will be fine."

"Yes, go, I am alright," Sirich said, waving them on. "Find your man, I will be right here."

Amari rolled his eyes and rode ahead. "Fine. This way." Ethan walked beside him. "He should be over here in the Broken Dish."

"The Broken Dish?"

"The tavern he frequents."

"I see. This was a barren beach last time I was here."

"What do you mean? This has been here since I was a boy," Amari asked, looking down at him.

"Yes... perhaps I am thinking of another place." The man kept his smile.

"Here. He's likely inside." Amari dismounted his horse.

Ethan walked ahead. "I will take care of it. Wait here. What does this shipwright friend of yours look like?"

"He's not going to sail somewhere with a stranger who walks up to him. I will go."

"What does he look like?" Ethan repeated.

"Tall man. Thick brown beard with a touch of grey. Usually wears a flat wool sailor's hat and colorful doublets. Always a smile."

"Stay here," Ethan said forcefully. His eyes seemed brighter in the moonlight.

"Fine. It will not be cheap. Do you need—"

"I will take care of it." The music from the lute and the singer grew louder as Ethan opened the door.

What in the hell? Amari mounted his horse and turned to ride back to Sirich. "He can find his way back. Perhaps he will not," he mumbled.

Sirich sat where they had left him, slumping against the wall.

Amari shook his head. "Who is this man that we find ourselves riding with? He's strange and—"

Sirich sighed. "Ethan is just trying to—"

"I told you, Siri, I don't trust him! And every time we have a conversation, the bastard sticks his nose in it. Can you not see that?" Amari paused. "What do you think he wants, anyway?"

"Someone is jealous."

Amari wrinkled his forehead. "Jealous? Please," he smiled. "Of you?"

"He's just a fan of the prince," Sirich forced a smile through his cough.

"You're not a prince, remember?" Amari reminded him.

"Why not, Doc? Because of father's council? Perception is reality. Who do you think still sits as overlord of that council?"

"William, of course. But you already know that."

"Yes, brother, but isn't that just a king by another name? Ethan is right. What did Father expect back there? For the murderers to run from the woods and surrender to us because of our colorful banners? Besides, if I can be prince a little longer, why not?"

Amari shook his head. "What has gotten into you? This illness has gone to your head."

"He should be king someday," Ethan said, standing next to them.

"Damn, you sneaky bastard!" Sirich managed to laugh.

"That was quick. Do you have us a cog, then?" Amari asked harshly.

"As a matter of fact, I do, Amari of the Gazi," Ethan said, smiling. "I found your friend. He accepted immediately upon hearing your name, of course."

"Well, then. Let us get a room, eat supper, and leave at first light." Amari walked past them.

"No, my friend. We leave tonight," Ethan insisted.

Amari's anger swelled. "Tonight? Not even James should navigate these rocky waters in the dark of night. Have you ever sailed through Starfall Bay?"

"Do you want your friend to get to Ashbourne quickly or not? He is not getting any better, is he, Doc?"

"Since when do you call me 'Doc'? Only he calls me that," Amari said, motioning to Sirich. He was sure his face was flushed.

"I cannot win with you, can I? I call you Gazi, you do not like it. I call you by your Aashgothian name, you do not like it."

Amari moved toward him, his chest leading the way. Sirich managed to stand and put his hand on Amari's shoulder.

"Relax, my friend." Sirich's shiny eyes met his. "Ethan's

right. We might as well go. Besides, the sooner we get to Ash-bourne, the sooner we get to Ash."

"Fine. I suppose we have to risk it," Amari sighed. "If any-one knows these waters, James does."

"Come. He said be at the fifth dock within the hour," Ethan said.

Amari walked beside Sirich, following the man to the docks behind the buildings. They ignored the beggars lining the wooden path. Amari knew they were short on time, and the beggars short on wine.

"Amari Docksider!" a soft voice called.

"James!" A grin grew on Amari's face. "It's been too long, old friend."

"Yes, it has." James took a step back. "How's your old man?"

Amari smelled the ale on his breath and looked down. "My father died last year."

"Oh, I didn't know. I'm sorry to hear it." He patted his shoulder. The grey in his beard had spread, covering most of it. He grabbed his forearm in the customary shake, the old man's hands as rough as the wood he worked with. "Come! Your friend here says you need passage to Ashbourne?" They walked up the small ramp leading to the old fishing cog.

"Yes, this is my friend Sirich of Vaegomar. He's not doing well."

"Oh, my lord. I didn't know. I have worked with your father." James removed his hat and attempted a slight bow.

"No, please, there is no need," Sirich nodded. "Good to meet you. Doc speaks highly..." He grabbed his gut and bent over. Amari steadied him to keep him from falling.

"Yes, my lord. Come, come. Let's get underway. We can be in Ashbourne's port within two hours, depending on the winds. Come."

Amari helped Sirich on board. Ethan walked in front of them. He brought them to the stairs that led to the lower deck. The old sailor motioned. "Down there. He can lie down. It's not much, but it's gonna get wet up here."

Ethan went down first. Sirich followed. "Go ahead. I'll help James get underway."

Amari stayed up top on the main deck as Sirich disappeared into the darkness below. "I'm sorry to get you involved in this," Amari said to James.

"It's fine, Doc. Nothing better to do but drink. Besides, your friend pays well."

"What did he pay you, a few silver pieces?"

"Oh, no." The old man reached into the front pocket of his tunic. He pulled out a small gold nugget as well as a golden coin. "A lot more than that." He handed Amari the coin. "Never seen anything like it."

Amari looked closer at the coin. It was thick and round, with a slight bend in it. He held it up to the lantern hanging from the mast of the old vessel. The face of a woman graced one side, the wings of a bat the other.

"Looks to be hand cut. Maybe from the east?" James said.

"Perhaps. It's similar to an old statue I once saw in Valton."

"Doesn't matter. Gold is gold." He took the coin back and started untying from the dock. Amari shook his head and helped with the other ropes. Amari pushed off from the dock, and they were under way.

The old oak cog creaked in the waves. James stood on the rear deck, steering. He had not said much more, but he had promised Amari he'd fished these waters enough to navigate by the stars.

At least the sky is clear.

Sirich had laid down on a pile of rope netting. The lantern swung to and fro with the slight rocking of the boat; the waters in the large bay were smoother than out at sea. They would not have to travel far to reach the port of Ashbourne. Amari sat on a barrel, and Ethan sat near Sirich on a burlap sack of rice that poured from its many holes every time the old cog shifted.

"Damn!" Sirich almost yelled, clutching his stomach.

"Siri, what is it? What could this be?" Amari saw sweat beading on his forehead.

"I do not know, but it's the worst it has been. This hunger is insatiable."

Sirich continued to grunt as Amari knelt by his side. He looked up at Ethan. "Go tell the old man to raise another sail. We don't have much time."

Ethan laughed, his eyes gleaming blue in the lantern light. "I know what he needs, he just has to be willing to accept it. There is not a 'ceptor in Ashbourne who can do anything for him."

"What the hell does that mean?" Amari had had enough. "If you know how to help him, then do so!"

Sirich managed to speak through the pain. "What do you mean? Do you have some medicine, some herb?" He curled into a fetal position.

"I have given you a gift that you would have obtained anyway, only I've sped up the process. Only one thing can cure you, my prince."

"What the fuck are you talking about?" Amari lunged at him but only grabbed the air where the man had been sitting. Ethan was now behind him, and he'd grabbed him by the neck and shoulder. Amari was astonished by his surprising strength; he could not free himself. "What are you doing? Let go of me!"

Ethan lowered Amari to his knees next to Sirich, who still writhed in pain. Sirich saw the struggle and tried to stand. The man held Amari with one hand and pushed Sirich back down with the other.

"Do you remember that night back in Wolfpine, when you woke right before your precious council meeting?"

"What are you talking about? What are you doing?" Sirich managed in a growling voice. Amari looked over at Sirich before his face was pressed against the thick rope netting on the floor, struggling to free himself. He could only grunt, trying to escape.

"I was there that night, and I visited your chamber. Not to hurt you, but to help you. And I did. Now all you have to do is accept it."

"I don't understand!"

"I have given you a gift."

"What gift?"

"The strength of one hundred men, the speed of a falling star. You will live for eternity, if you choose to accept it." The man paused. "Otherwise, you will die, here and now." Sirich rocked in pain but did not respond. Amari could only mumble, his face pressed against the wet rope. "There are a few drawbacks, of course, for most of us. But for you..." The man paused and jerked his head backward, throwing the hair from his face. "You are different. You will still be able to set foot in the sunlight and drink from a silver cup. You can be king of Vaegomar. Or of Aahsgoth itself, like your forefathers. Only you could rule for all time, if you so choose." The man laughed. "Although I must say, like all good things, it gets old after a century or so."

Amari lay helpless, listening to this man. *This is a bad dream. Or one of those scary bedtime stories the wet nurse told me.*

"I do not understand! What have you done to me?"

"I told you, I only sped up the process of what you were always destined to be. I know your mother, my prince. I know *what* you are."

"My mother? What are you..." Amari could only watch Sirich suffer. He tried to speak again, but the man was too strong, as if he had set an anvil on Amari's face. Time seemed to slow, like it had the first time he fell from his horse.

He saw Sirich open his eyes again. "What do you mean, accept it? What do I have to do? Just take the pain away! Ahhh!"

"All you have to do is drink." The man slid Amari's face close to Sirich's. Amari could see Sirich trying to resist. He could not fathom what the man had just said, but he could see his friend considering it, the pain too much for him.

"Now drink, boy... or die!"

Amari managed to mumble now that the ropes had shifted. "Siri, please!"

Sirich leaned over toward him; Ethan still held his face to the floor.

"You must feed, and you will never feel pain again. Drink!"

Sirich leaned in, tears rolling down his cheeks. He grunted in pain. Amari could see his eyes. They were almost glowing, as blue as the sky on a perfect day. He saw his mouth—drooling, with two sharp, white, fang-like teeth now visible below his upper lip.

"Siri, no! Please!"

"I'm sorry, brother! Please, please forgive me!" Sirich bit deep into Amari's neck. Amari's eyes went wide in disbelief. He struggled, but he could not escape Ethan's grip. His neck burned sharply at first, but the longer Sirich drank, the more a cold crept over Amari. He stopped resisting. His field of vision grew darker still, seeing Ethan laugh over him.

The cold consumed him then, and he saw nothing but blackness.

Chapter Twenty-Six

Galen

Galen packed the last of his things into the burlap sack. As always, he carried a small case of various herbs and potions for the trip.

Where are my old boots? he thought, looking around his room.

"I wonder how Siri is faring," he murmured as he sorted the last of his belongings on his bed. *No news is good news, I suppose.*

Galen had hoped Siri would return before he left. But Theodor needed him, and he wanted to get to Ashbourne quickly. He would ride south to Capeton and make the journey across the Middle Sea. In his younger days, he had preferred traveling by land, enjoying the open road. The sea made him queasy. *Ah, yes, let me not forget the ginger extract—a few drops before we leave the bay should do.*

He walked over to his shelves to look for the vial. *Something seems to be missing*, he thought, squinting over his shelves. *Or perhaps I am losing my mind.* As he rummaged through the dusty shelf, he heard a soft knock on his door. He rolled his eyes. "Can I not have some peace?" he mumbled before clearing his throat. "Come! It is open."

Elya Promen poked her head in. "My lord, are you busy?"

"Yes, I am preparing to leave for Ashbourne, my lady. Is there something I can help you with? My apprentices will take over for me while I am away."

"I was wondering when Sirich would return. Have you heard from him?"

"I have not, my lady. I was wondering that myself."

"I brought you some barley water with honey."

"Ah, my favorite. How did you know?" Galen motioned to his desk. She carried over a small tray with a pitcher and two wooden cups.

"Your assistant told me. I see you constantly running here and there, and I thought you could use it."

"Thank you, my lady." He motioned toward the chair in front of his desk. "Please, have a seat."

She poured each of them a cup, added honey to one, and stirred it. She sat it in front of him, light steam rising from the cup.

"No honey for you?"

"I prefer it without, my lord."

"To each his or her own. So, was there something you wanted to talk to me about?" He tried to phrase the question politely. She had never come to him before in her time at Wolfpine. "Oh, yes— Sirich, was it?"

"Yes. It's just that I worry about him. He seems... different, lately."

"Does he? I have not noticed anything. Wait. Are you

two…" The girl tilted her head, her face blushing slightly. "Oh, I see." He took a sip of his drink. "A nice flavor, my lady, and extra sweet."

"Yes, I added some figs," she said, tasting her cup.

"Well, I do not know if William has plans for Sirich or if he will let him make his own. But we were all young once. Things happen… love happens."

"You said you have a son in Ashbourne. Where is his mother?"

"A fever took her when Theo was very young, I'm afraid." Galen paused. "I could not save her…"

"Oh, I'm sorry to hear that. I didn't know. I didn't know you could marry as a preceptor."

"Oh, yes, there are no laws preventing it. That would be a stupid rule, I think." He leaned back, enjoying his water now that it had cooled a bit.

"So, my lord, do you prefer… younger women?" The girl moved her hair to the other shoulder, smiling.

"My lady?" Galen's eyes widened as he watched her fiddle with her bodice.

The girl giggled. "I *was* hoping to marry Sirich, but I just thought that before he returned—"

"And you shall, little one." Heath Promen interrupted before slamming the door behind him.

"Lord Promen, please be careful with the door, before you knock it off its hinges!" Galen sighed and finished his cup.

"Of course, Galen. But you will not be needing it anymore," Heath Promen said, smiling.

"Pardon me?" Galen stood.

"Well done, little one," he said, his hands on the girl's shoulders. She stood and turned to him, rising on her toes to kiss his cheek.

Elya moved behind her father. "It should be anytime now."

"Leaving, are we, Galen? Headed to Ashbourne to see your son?" The lord sat down where his daughter had been.

Galen felt his face warm. "I am. Why is it your concern?"

"My concern is for what you and your son are up to. What did you send him?"

"That is none of your damn concern! Why are you still in Wolfpine, anyway? The council is adjourned. Should you not be headed back to Alarya?"

"Leave Wolfpine? *Now*? Why would I do that? While the cat is away, the mice shall play. Not to mention, the new king of Vaegomar will soon return, to give me what was promised." Promen took a deep breath and leaned forward. "What did you send to your young Theodor? What has he discovered?"

"I do not know what you are talking about. I must go before my ship leaves." Galen stood, and the room seemed to lean. He grabbed his desk to steady himself. The girl smiled, standing behind her father with her hands on his shoulders.

The lord tightened his jaw and leaned back. "You sent a letter to him. Has he answered?"

"No, he has not, if you must know. It was nothing but a matter of an old translation William inquired about. I must go." Galen rubbed his eyes. He now saw two of the man and his daughter. He blinked constantly, his eyes watering. "What have you done?" The room started to spin, and he struggled to take a deep breath.

"Did you enjoy your barley water, Master Preceptor? What was it, dear?" Promen looked over his shoulder at the girl.

"Snakeroot, I believe it's called, Father."

"Yes, indeed. And is there an antidote for that, preceptor?"

Galen turned and tried to focus on the shelves behind his desk. Blood tickled his upper lip.

"There is no need. Tell me what I want to know, and she will give you the antidote."

"Bastard!" Galen managed, searching his desk. He pulled open the top drawer and found the letter Theodor had sent him. "Here is what you are looking for! Now, please..." His stomach tightened into knots and blood dripped from his nose.

"Ah, yes." Promen scanned down the letter. "So, it *is* true... Ethan was right. The prophecy." The man stood. "See, that wasn't so hard, was it, 'ceptor? Come with us."

Galen used his desk and walked toward them. Promen took his arm.

"Come, old man. Elya will give you what was promised."

Galen managed to stumble to the door, his right hand gripping the man, his left raised to wipe his nose. "Hurry," he managed in a breathy voice. If he had the strength, he would hit Promen, but all he could think of was his son in Ashbourne, waiting for him.

"This way, old man." They turned the corner in the hallway and came to the staircase. Galen held his stomach; he was sure he'd retch.

"Here." The man stopped. Galen tried to pull his arm away. The girl grabbed his other.

"What are you doing? We must hurry. I do not have much time."

"I'm afraid you are right. We do not." Promen's voice almost echoed in his ears. They both let go of his arms and took a step back.

Galen turned. "I gave you what you wanted. Please..."

The hallway twisted now. He sank to his knees at the top

of the winding stairwell. He looked up through blurry eyes to see them both wearing sinister grins.

"Fucking traitors, the both of you. You will burn in hell."

"When *he* returns, I will never see whatever *hell* there may be, my lord." The bottom of Promen's boot raced toward Galen's chest.

As he fell, he heard the thuds and cracks of his own body being pummeled by the unforgiving stone, the pain unbearable. He finally came to a stop, bloody and broken.

Theodor.

His eyes opened wide as he tried to catch a breath, the world going dark around him.

Chapter Twenty-Seven

Ashaya

"What do we do?" Mitch paced back and forth. He knelt at the creek and splashed his face with water. "Are you sure? I mean, how do you know?"

"I just know, Mitch. I cannot explain it. Merek was here. He never left." No matter how many times she wiped the tears from her face, there were always more to come. She sniffled and swiped at her nose with her undershirt again.

Mitch cupped his hands on his head, still pacing. "We should go to the isle, just to make sure. I mean, it is just muddy ashes. None of his things are here. Besides, if he never made it, we should go *for* him."

"Why would his horse be back there, Mitch? Who were those men I killed?" She looked down, noticing her hands shaking. "If they killed him here, they may have taken his body. He deserves better than that. He deserves a proper funeral, if—"

"Ash, think about it. He may have come here, headed home, and simply had his horse stolen. He may be at Wolfpine now, sitting in the great hall, asking where you are." Mitch approached her. "Ash, if you think Merek is… Maybe we just need to go home. We need to tell your father either way. He will know what to do."

"Will he? He probably does not even realize Merek's still gone. Or that I am, for the gods' sake. He's so focused on that fucking council of his." She looked out through the trees.

Mitch faced her. "Ash, let's just go—"

"No, Mitch!" She pushed him away. Mitch flew backwards into a tree, colliding with a loud thud. He gasped, trying to find his breath.

"Mitch, I'm sorry! I didn't mean to—"

"Get away from me, you freak!" He crawled to his knees and wiped the blood from his neck, a piece of a small tree limb stuck to his skin.

"Ah… Shay… Ah," the voices came again.

"Mitch, do you hear that?" He did not answer.

"Ah… Shay… Ah." She looked around. The whispers were louder than last time. "Ah… Shay… Ah."

"Stop it!" She covered her ears and closed her eyes. "What is happening to me?" She kept her eyes closed but saw the man again, the one she had seen before in her dreams. This time, he hung in a fishing net, blood running from where his neck and shoulder met, dripping into a red cloud in the sea below.

"Who are you? What do you want from me?" she screamed.

Then she saw him. Sirich stood in a dark room, his eyes

shimmering blue. He held a crown of bone, blood running from the corners of his mouth. She tried to go to him. He smiled and turned away, disappearing into the dark trees.

"Ah... Shay... Ah," the whispers started again.

"What do you want?" she yelled.

"Come to me..." The whispers became softer, like those of a woman.

Then they were gone. She slowly opened her eyes. She took her hands from her ears. The birds were chirping as they had been. Mitch was standing across the clearing now. She was sitting in the center of the camp, her elbows on her knees.

"What happened?" Mitch kept his distance, his hands reached out toward her.

She looked around again and slowly stood. "It's Sirich."

"Sirich? What do you mean?"

"I do not know, but something is wrong."

"What did you see? How do..." Mitch stopped when she began walking toward him. An insatiable urge overcame her.

His eyes opened wide. "Ash, please!"

She walked past him, brushing his shoulder, toward the horses grazing in the small patch of grass in the sun.

She mounted Acorn and turned back to Mitch, still standing frozen.

"I'm sorry I pushed you, Mitch. Let's go."

"Where? I do not understand what in the hell is going on!"

"The brothel wench said the men rode from the Bloody Sands."

"So? What if she's lying?"

"What if she's not?"

"Alright. Did she say where they come from?"

"No, but I think I know. Only one place it can be for

zealots: a temple." Mitch looked to be thinking back to his geography lessons, but Ashaya spoke again before he could recall anything specific. "Come on, Mitch. We ride to the ruins of Bloodstone."

Chapter
Twenty-Eight

Amari

"Amari, wake up," said a muffled voice. He opened his eyes slowly, an old wooden roof above him, a sunbeam shining through the window. He tried to focus his eyes on the figure silhouetted in the light.

"James?"

"Yes. Just take it easy. You must have lost a lot of blood. Here, drink this." James held a wooden cup to his mouth and helped him lift his head.

"I got you patched up. A nasty wound, it was. Lucky it was more on your shoulder than your neck. A few more inches, and we wouldn't be having this conversation. Must have been one hell of a rat. Seen some the size of racoons. They always find their way down below." Amari drank from the cup, almost choking. "Slow down, young man! There is plenty more."

"How long have I been—"

"A little over a day."

Amari slowly sat up. The room came into focus bit by bit. James sat on the edge of the straw bed. Gulls flew outside the window. Amari shivered under the thick wool blanket that covered him. He recognized the stench of rotten fish. "Are they still—"

"Your friends? No, never saw them. Musta left before daybreak. Once we got to port, I went down under. Only you were lying there in the bloody water." He walked over to the small table. "You hungry? I walked up to the tavern. Emma gave me half a pot of bisque soup she was about to throw out. Still good. A bit salty, but good." James walked over to a table where the wooden pot sat, the bottom blackened.

Amari reached up and felt the bandage on his shoulder. He shuddered at the thought of those blue eyes and the look on Sirich's face. Ethan's laughter echoed in his head along with his own screams. "I'm not hungry, James."

"Eat anyway. You need to regain your strength." He handed him a bowl. Amari struggled to turn his legs to sit on the edge of the bed.

"Thank you."

"So where did your friends go? Maybe they'll come back for you."

"I hope not." Amari tried the soup and almost retched.

"Good, ain't it?" James ate from his bowl. Amari drank more water and set the bowl down on the table. He looked out the window and watched the people going about their daily routines. A part of him wanted to see Sirich, but most of him did not.

"James, do you follow any gods?"

"Can't say that I do. When I was a boy, my mother took up with the Elder when holy men came to Longleaf. Well, what was left of it. Used to be a quaint little village. Anyway, never seen any evidence of any gods. They never listened to what I had to say."

Amari nodded but kept his eyes on the docks. "I need to go to the Crescent Isle. Think you can take me there?"

James put down his bowl. "Are you japing? No one approaches that isle. You know that. You're a damned fisherman. Place is haunted." He finished his soup. "I don't have to have religion to know something ain't right about that place."

"So I've heard. I approached it once, but fog covers it. I turned back when I saw all the dead fish floating nearby. And it smelled like death." Amari sat down across from him. "James, I need to get there. I need—"

"Hell no, Doc. You know I'd do almost anything for you, but I ain't getting close to that place. And even if I get close enough, you ain't in any condition to swim the rest."

"I cannot explain, James, but I need to find Sirich's sister before *they* do." Amari put his hand on the man's arm.

"Look, I don't know what kind of trouble you are in, but I'm sorry, I can't."

Amari sat quietly for a moment. He looked back out the window. "Maybe you are right. Maybe I just need to go home." Amari shook his head, a tear escaping down his cheek. He looked down. *What happened to my friend?* James stood and walked out of the quarters.

Amari put his elbows on the table, holding his head in his palms. *What do I do?* His thumb brushed against the bandage again. He raised his head, his eyes shifting up. He slammed his fist on the table.

Yes, she may know what this is.

He walked up top to the deck, squinting in the sun. He grabbed one of the ropes to help him.

"Oh, no—take it easy," James called. "You've been awake for all of a few moments. Sit!"

Amari walked over and sat on a crate. "You are right, James, I don't need to go to the isle, not yet. But I do know where I need to go, and it is close to home. Any port in the northside of Starfall Bay. Can you take me?"

"Sure. I need to get back. Those damn boats won't build themselves. Where are you headed, anyway?"

"To see an old friend."

Chapter
Twenty-Nine

Sirich

"**W**hat have you done to me? Who are you?" Sirich grabbed Ethan's arm, his voice echoing in the small cave.

"I told you, I only sped up the process of what was going to happen anyway. I gave you the darkness."

"The *what?*"

"The gift."

"What the fuck does that mean? I almost killed Amari!"

"Yes, and you should have. That is the old way."

Sirich pushed Ethan in the chest; he flew backwards, hitting the wall of the cave several yards away.

He stood and laughed, dusting himself off. "You see? Your strength is almost upon you."

Sirich raised his hands, studying them. "How?" He looked

up at Ethan across the large cave. In a blink, the man was in his face, nose to nose. Sirich had only heard the whooshing sound, enough wind to move his hair from his face. Ethan's eyes gleamed a bright blue through the dimly lit cave.

"Sit, boy, and I'll give you the answers you seek. But first, you must give me your word that where we go, you will do as I say. I saved your life. I could have let you go to that stupid library and die on someone's table."

"You made me this way!" Sirich slumped down, leaning against the stone, his forearms on his knees.

"There are bigger implications here that you do not yet understand. Only then will you have your kingdom, if that is what you wish." The man turned, looking toward the dim light from the opening. "You are more important than you know."

"Who said I want a kingdom?"

"Do you not?" Ethan snapped. "You were born a prince. Your father took that from you. Were you not to rule after him as the crown prince?"

"Yes, but he abdicated his crown and started the damn council."

"And you agree with it?" Ethan asked, tilting his head, staring intently at Sirich. "You've questioned your father since you were old enough to understand. You try to please him, but you know in your heart what you want, what you've *always* wanted."

"But…" Sirich leaned back, bumping his head. He could only sit there and breathe. "This is all too much. I didn't ask for it…" His voice trailed off as he stared at the ground in front of him.

"But you did, and now you have the power to take what is yours."

"I have to get back to Amari, to see if he's alright."

"There is no going back."

"I can't just leave him for dead on some boat!"

"You can, and you did." Sirich shook his head. Ethan kneeled in front of him. "You will come to understand all of this in time."

"Help me to understand *now*."

Ethan stood and paced the room. "I gave you a choice. She never gave me one."

"Did you crawl through my window while I slept and turn me into a monster?"

"I told you, you were born this way."

"Wait... who's 'she'?"

Ethan stopped and turned to him. "Your mother."

Sirich's jaw dropped. "My... my mother? My mother is dead. I never knew her." He looked down.

"Is that what your father told you?" the man asked. "Of course he did. Your mother was the first, the maker of us all. Perhaps you have heard of her? Valkarial."

Sirich looked up at him. "Nonsense. My mother was Raina of Aethonya. She died giving birth to me."

"Lies."

"Why would Father—"

"To hide the truth of what you are."

Sirich leaned his head back and stared at the ceiling, snickering. "You are telling me my mother is Valkarial, the goddess of creation? She who is one of the thirteen aspects?"

Ethan wore his usual grin. "How do you think she became known as a goddess? Did you not just drink a man's blood? Or push me across this room like one of your sister's dolls? Have your wounds not healed? And you haven't even begun to know your power."

Sirich stared at the wall. "So, what is the price?" he asked in a low voice.

"What did you say?"

"On the boat, you mentioned a price."

Ethan kneeled by him once again. "Ah, yes. You see, that is where you are different. Like dragons of the first age, I can never see the sun again." The man looked up; his voice quavered. "I have not seen a sunrise in... I do not remember." He stood, his blue eyes glistening.

"Dragons?"

"Where we got our gift from. Val was the first. Her mother was given dragon's blood to save her during childbirth. During that time, it was more valuable than gold. It was too late for her mother, but for Val... it changed her."

"What else?"

"I dare not touch anything of silver. If I avoid these things, sunlight and silver and horrendous injury, I will never die. Some consider eternal life a price, as well. It's both a gift and a curse." He stood with his hands clasped behind his back. "Of course, you already know the most important thing. You will carry an insatiable bloodlust for all time." He faced the wall across the cave. "But you... You only reap the rewards, you see. You will see the sun; silver will not harm you. You have our strengths, but none of our weaknesses."

Sirich just sat there, only hearing the echoing thud of Ethan's footsteps. "How do you know all of this? Why me? Why can I do these things, and you cannot?"

"An ancient foretelling. The secret lies within your blood. William is of the original bloodline."

"What does that mean? Why must you speak in riddles?"

"He alone is the last of the bloodline of Valkarial herself. Her clan became the house of Blacksun two millennia ago. Your sigil is hers, although not quite what she intended."

"Are there others? Other monsters?"

"There are. Not all of us remain. There were thirteen at one time. The crimson gods, some called us back then."

"Us? You are one of the thirteen?"

The man tightened his lips, covering the hint of a smile, and inclined his head.

"Ethan is not your name. You lied about that, too?"

"We have to hide who we are, what we are! At least for now." Ethan turned to him. "And that's why you must do as I say."

"Who are you, then?"

"Promethial."

A slight smile came to Sirich's lips. "The god of fire? Am I hiding from the sun in a dark cave with the god of fire?" Once again, Sirich could only snicker, but Ethan did not take his eyes from him.

"You are serious?" Sirich pressed.

Ethan did not answer.

"The lighthouse on the sea, that is named for you?"

"So they say. But it is not quite that simple." The man turned and walked toward the entrance of the cave, careful not to get too close. "Our stories have morphed over time. Humans have a knack for embellishment."

Sirich felt nauseated, his head spinning. *This is all insanity.* He looked back to the man. "You said earlier that you had no choice?"

"Yes. Your mother should have let me die in that fire. But here we are." The man turned to him and exposed the scarring that covered his chest. "This is your god of fire."

Sirich winced and looked away. "What happened?"

"Another time, perhaps."

Sirich shook his head. "Is that why you are doing all of this? To get back at her?"

"No. I want to live as we once did, as Lucian once believed. We have lived in the shadows for far too long. We once ruled our clans openly. There was no war, only order. Our kind was respected, worshipped. Now, we hide. And for what, to satisfy *her*? Her arbitrary rules?"

"So, you want to kill her, the one you say is my... mother."

"No," he replied in a soft voice. The man paced around the stone room, quietly looking down.

"Oh, I see." Sirich stood. "You love her."

The man continued to walk in circles before finally responding. "I did once. After she banished Lucian, I thought..."

Sirich stood, watching him for a moment. For the first time, the man wore no smile. Sirich ran his hands through his hair. "I feel like I am in some fucking nightmare."

"Oh, no, my prince. You're living a dream, and when you learn what you can do, what you can take..."

"Show me."

"I shall, but you just fed for the first time. You are still too weak. Until then, you need to travel with me, but once you are at full strength—"

"Show me," Sirich repeated.

"I will give you a taste once the sun sets. It will not be long. You have experienced some of these things already. Your senses have heightened, so you must learn to focus. Your strength, as you already know, is great, and that will grow. We have dominion over the night, and you... well, *you* shall walk in the day."

Sirich put his hands on his head. "What have I done to Amari?" he said softly.

Promethial rushed Sirich again, grabbing his neck with one hand, his feet dangling above the ground. If he had eaten in the past few days, he would have shat himself. "You survived. You did what had to be done. You let him live to tell others what he saw. Now we must move quickly." He removed his hand from Sirich's throat. "You must come with me to the Crescent Isle."

"I'm going to find my sister, and Merek. I need to get back home."

"I told you—she is there, looking for him. But nothing will ever be the same again. You will watch them grow old and die."

Sirich turned and put his hands against the wall, looking down. The dirt floor soaked up his tears. Nothing was said for a time, only the sounds of the night filtering in from outside the cave entrance.

Sirich rubbed his neck. "What is at the Crescent Isle that is so important?"

"Our future. You will wake Lucian." The man turned to the opening as the shadows crawled up the walls. "Val is too old, too powerful. He is the only one who has a chance at stopping her."

He looked back to Sirich. "It's time."

Chapter
Chapter Thirty

William

Castle Lachlan, built into the rocky cliffs, loomed in the distance, shimmering on the horizon. William looked back over his shoulder and surveyed the caravan of men behind them. He had sent about twenty men south to make sure they found Ashaya.

"Merek?" Jordan must have seen the worry on his face.

William sighed. "The brothel wench's story of Ash having Merek's horse."

"He and Ash are likely looking for us by now."

"I can only hope."

Sweat ran down his face, drying quickly in the salty breeze. The red sands had subsided to firmer ground. Now they went around the occasional shaggy tree, the boulders growing larger the closer they got to the coast.

Jordan caught back up. "What is bothering you, old friend? Other than the obvious."

"Her."

"Val?"

William nodded.

"I see. I have always wondered why she left. Perhaps she didn't like the idea of no longer being queen?"

"Maybe, but I never sensed it. Perhaps I did not really know her. Her true self. How does one leave two newborn children behind?"

"Maybe you will find her, too, at some point, get the answers you seek." Jordan changed the subject. "So, do you think Marcus has anything to do with this?" Jordan handed William the flagon.

"No. He knows that would be a death sentence. He sits in his castle and lets these bastards run this region." William stroked his beard. "If these zealots have a small army, as the wench told us, they likely already have her. If she is captured, the ruins of Bloodstone are where they would take her."

"We will get her back. We can certainly handle a few pagans with daggers."

"We will speak with Marcus anyway. Perhaps he can bargain with them. He knows this region better than anyone. Besides, he ignored all my council requests. I need to ask him in person."

They approached the gates of the grey stone bridge that crossed the sea below. Marcus did not have many men, but he hardly needed any to defend this place. The castle itself sat on a small island of sheer cliffs, the only entrance being the long bridge from the mainland. The wind was strong; the waves crashed on the waiting rocks below. William looked up. The skies had greyed, and the two moons showed in the day. They were farther apart than they had been: the smaller red moon seemed to be leaving the blue moon behind the grey towers in the distance. The gates were open, and only two guards sat there, their spears leaning against the wall.

One guard finally stood and looked at William after noticing the Blacksun sigil on his chest—or perhaps one of the banners the men carried behind him.

"My king," the man said, attempting to bow but nearly falling over.

The other just sat and laughed at the man and took another drink from his flagon.

William looked over at Jordan and rolled his eyes. "I am not your king, but I must speak to Marcus."

"Yes, my lord." The man wobbled to his feet. "Go ahead. We opened the gates for you. He said you would come. He waits for you on the battlements." The man moved to the side.

Some of the men chuckled behind them.

"Could be a trap, Will," Jordan said.

"Marcus does not have the balls. Come on, lads."

Jordan turned to the men. "Half of you stay here. Watch our asses."

Will and the others rode down the stone bridge, only a four-foot wall separating them from the giant arches reaching down to the sea below.

The hooves of the horses could barely be heard over the water smacking below them. The bridge curved down toward the sea, then back up to the castle, steep and smooth.

"We could have lost here if his father had not met us in the open field," William said softly to Jordan.

"He was a fool, too proud to use his own defenses. Of course, this could have been a weakness, as well. We would have laid siege until he came out begging for food," Jordan smiled.

A voice rang out from the battlements above the gates. "If it is not the old hero of the last rebellion, Killiam himself!"

"Marcus," William nodded. The others followed his lead.

"Why shouldn't I rain arrows down upon you where you stand?"

"Go ahead." William sat on his horse, never taking his eyes from the man. "But I think you want my help, as I want yours. Are you not tired of rotting away here while these fanatics rule your lands—and you?"

"Oh, I see... So you are here to save me? Like you saved my father? I was just a boy when you came here and took my family from—"

"Your father was a damned fool!" William cut him off. "You have no idea what he was doing to his people. And to you. And for what, some fairy tale? He claimed to be a descendant of a god, but he only lusted for power, and he killed all his advisors who warned against it." William shook his head, his lips tight. He could see Jordan looking over at him from the corner of his eye. "Most told me to just kill you and end your line. Or at the least take you to Wolfpine as my ward. I left you and the rest of your family intact, here in your home. If you want to begrudge me for stopping a madman, so be it. Send the arrows."

Marcus stood silent, the guards around him waiting for his command. William's heart raced. *What will he do?*

"I've heard the stories, William. Had I not, I would have given the order to kill you before you spoke. After all, you are no longer my king." Marcus ran his hand through his black hair. "So, what do you want of me?"

William exhaled quietly and glanced at Jordan for only a moment. "I need your help, Marcus. You are not your father. I knew that when I left you here as a boy. They have my daughter. I assume she is at the old ruins of Bloodstone, but

I need to know what you know of them and how many men they have."

Marcus paced above them. "The Nepharium, they call themselves. They claim to be dragon slayers. A frightful bunch. But do not let their stupid beliefs and tattered clothes deceive you—they are armored and well trained."

"Trained by who?"

"Me."

"You?"

"Well, indirectly. Some of my men-at-arms joined them over the years. Some men have a natural bloodlust. That thirst cannot be quenched on training dummies in the yard." Marcus turned and put both hands on the battlements. "You see, William, when you so nobly left us here alive, you left a vacuum of sorts. You may have saved some part of Aahsgoth, but you destroyed another. Once only a small group of zealots that merely robbed passersby to survive, they were then able to get a foothold. They recruited and eventually attracted enough lost men to their cause, and now you come to reap what you sow."

"Why didn't you come to me?" William demanded.

Marcus paced again and turned back to him. "I was but a boy!" He took a deep breath. "You didn't leave us with a book on how to rule, did you?"

William looked over at Jordan and lowered his eyes. Only the winds spoke for a time.

"I apologize to you, Marcus. I failed you. But that is why I have spent the last decade trying to make it right. I have sent countless corvids to you, inviting you to Wolfpine. I want you on the council."

Jordan looked over at William. "My lord. Remember Ashaya."

"Your man is correct, Will. We can discuss this later. Your daughter is in danger. They are likely at Bloodstone, but they live in the small village of Longleaf, below the ruins."

"Are you sure?"

"I may have been but a boy then, but I have learned. I keep a few men among them," Marcus said, grinning. William nodded and turned, but Marcus held up a hand. "Wait. You will need more men."

"I have more riding south."

"I have about fifty men. Leave me a few, and take the rest with you."

William turned his horse back around and looked up at him. "That's not necessary, Marcus. We have men."

Marcus motioned for someone. A young girl came to his side, brushing black hair from her eyes. "I have a daughter, too, William. If she were in danger, I would ask the same of you." Marcus looked around at the men on both sides of him. "Besides, I'm sure they itch to fight." The men around him smiled, some nodding their heads as they looked down at William.

"Why are you doing this for me, Marcus?"

"So that you don't fail her."

Chapter Thirty-One

The Beast

He sniffed the air; the others approached.

There.

The stone was cold beneath his feet. He paced in a circle, his strides clicking, growling in anticipation.

Hurry.

Finally, he sat on the center stone, his breathing slowing, but his tongue still hanging low from the long run to meet them.

Speak.

The others walked in the stone circle, both growling, drool dripping to the floor. They smelled him. They gave each other space, then looked at him almost in unison.

Time.

He had done this thousands of times, but each time it

was almost unbearable. He looked down at his hands on the floor in front of him, watching his fingers narrow and extend, the hair falling from his arms, the long nails left behind on the ground. He heard the cracking of his breaking body and felt his every fiber burn. What took only moments stretched like a century. He leaned his head back and put his hands on each side, feeling his ears shorten and round out. His voice returned with a grunt as he tried to keep himself from screaming.

Finally, it was over.

He was able to get to one knee, then stand. Sweat covered his naked body. He opened his eyes to see the discarded fur beneath him, the rotten breeze already sliding tufts of it across the stone. He took a deep breath. The others were still going through it. For the youngest, the change took longer. As the pain subsided, he took several deep breaths, his thoughts returning to him.

"That is always such fun, isn't it?" He managed a slight smile at the others around him. They all stood naked.

"Thade," the woman nodded. "I wouldn't trade it for anything, my lord."

"You chose this life, Amelia," he said, pointing to her then sweeping aside the black hair sticking to his face. "So, tell me, what have you all learned? We are in the middle of strange times, it seems."

"The boy in Ashbourne succeeded, but the 'ceptor was killed," Raziel answered quickly.

"So Promen has discovered his past, as we suspected. Promethial made promises to him, no doubt."

Amelia looked between both of them. "Of course—he turned the boy, after all. But why him? What would he need from him?"

Raziel stepped forward. "What of the girl?"

"It has begun, but she doesn't yet understand. She will need guidance." He put his hand to his chin. "Wait. The foretelling."

"What of it? You do not believe in such nonsense, my lord, do you?" Raziel said quickly.

Thade thought for a moment. "Promethial thinks..."

"Thinks what?" Amelia insisted.

"That he can wake Lucian."

"He's banished for all time. She would never wake him." Raziel sounded sure.

"Promethial may have found another way." Thade paced around the stone circle and leaned against a column. Ivy had crawled to the top, almost covering it.

"I must awaken her."

"Just kill Promethial yourself. He cannot stand against you," Amelia reminded him.

"That is not my decision to make. It is my sister's." He walked back toward them. "Go. Let the others know. I am not sure how this will play out. We need to keep close watch. I will go down and wake her."

"Thade, are you sure?" Raziel asked, concerned.

"Yes. Promethial will come here, and I will let her decide his fate."

Raziel and Amelia looked at each other, then nodded. They turned and disappeared into the night once again. He heard their song in the distance as he found the large stone covering the entrance to her chamber.

Chapter
Thirty-Two

Aza

Aza lay on her straw bed, waiting for Neph to return. She had been reading by the candlelight, her eyes heavy. Seth snored lightly by the fire. A fresh batch of white candles sat in a crate beside his bedding. She had left the lantern burning for her husband's return, but tonight the moons shone bright. That would have likely been enough to guide him home.

The door opened. Startled, she sat up.

"Neph?" Her eyes hazy, she noticed the figure at the door. Blue eyes flashed back at her from the darkness before the figure stepped into the reach of the candlelight.

"He will not be coming home, Aza," a soft voice replied.

"Who are you? How do you know my name? Where is my husband?" The figure walked closer. Seth had awoken and ran to his mother.

She realized who stood in front of her. "My king!" She clambered up hastily, forced Seth behind her, and tried to curtsey, her white gown almost tripping her. "Where is Neph?"

"He betrayed you, he came to me for... knowledge. He planned to never return to you." Lucian noticed the boy behind her. "Don't look so afraid, boy," he said, studying Seth, who peeked out from behind his mother.

Aza looked around. There were no guards. He had come alone. "I don't understand. Neph went to your court to serve you. What did you do to him?"

"Nothing, my child. He did it to himself."

Seth stirred behind her. "Is he... dead?"

"Yes," Lucian cut him off. "He abandoned you for a better life. Now he has it."

The boy ran at him. "What did you do to my father?" he screamed.

"Seth!" Aza tried to grab him. The boy reached Lucian with his fists clenched, swinging wildly. He hit only the air where Lucian had stood. Lucian, now behind him, grabbed the boy's wrist with only two fingers, picked him up, and gently tossed him onto the bed.

Aza went and clutched him close.

"I grow impatient. I simply came to inform you of what has transpired. I wanted to tell you myself. He lied to you, to both of you." He turned toward the door.

She felt her blood begin to boil as she held her son, huddled on the bed.

"Liar!" the boy yelled.

Aza restrained him, tears running down her cheeks. "He would never leave us! What did you do, sorcerer?" Her voice quavered. "You might as well kill me now, or—"

"Or what?" Lucian stopped and turned back to them.

Aza found the strength to continue. "Or I swear, I will find out what you are and kill you. I swear on my husband's life, on my son's life." Aza sank and began sobbing.

The boy held his mother and looked up at the king. "I will avenge my father. I will kill you in his name, no matter how long it takes."

Lucian smiled, looked over his shoulder once again, and continued walking. "In another time, I would kill you both where you stand. But, for now, I look forward to it... candlemaker."

Chapter Thirty-Three

Amari

A mari leaned against a thick pine tree just off the main road, chewing rye bread. He struggled, tearing it with his teeth, but was rewarded with a garlic flavor. The air was cool this morning, smoke from the remains of his fire defining the sunbeams through the surrounding trees.

He thought of riding straight home to his sister, but it would have to wait. James had dropped him off in the small port town of Kingston. Luckily, they had left all three horses on the boat. He was running low on coins, not enough to feed the horses, but he had enough to grab a few provisions.

It shouldn't be far now, he thought, checking the bandage on his neck. He had been lucky that James had been there to help him get back to full strength. Just as he finished his bread, he heard horses approaching from the south. Only a few had passed so far, mostly farmers and their carts. *Sounds like quite a few men.*

He walked toward the sound of the road, moving tree limbs from his path. Once he got to the road, a familiar group rode up to him.

"Philip?" Amari's lip quivered at the sight of someone he knew.

"Amari?" The men behind Philip stopped when he held up his hand. "You look like shit. Where's Sirich? Is he alright?"

Amari moved the braids from his face, his hand stopping on the bandage. "Uh, yes, he's fine. We made it to Ashbourne, and they patched him up. He's likely on a ship home already," he said, shifting his eyes.

"What are you doing here? The others said you went with him."

"I did, I have to get home to my family. I had a friend sailing into Kingston, so I joined him. Anyway, did you find anything in the foothills?"

"We came across one of the mountain clans. Claimed they didn't know anything."

"Did you believe them?"

"I don't trust them, but it doesn't fit. They would have taken everything they could carry from that village. Nothing else we can do. Anyway, is Sirich with that stranger he met?"

Amari cleared his throat. "I suppose. He was still there when I left. I'm sure he will be heading home soon after he finds his sister."

Amari turned. *I need to get going.*

"Ride with us," Philip urged. "No need to travel alone."

"That's alright. I'm not far now, and I actually enjoy the solitude. Give William my best."

"Be careful out here, my lord." Philip nodded and snapped the reins of his horse. Amari waved as the men passed by. He noticed Bella on a horse near the back, carrying her babe. She looked over at Amari, her face mostly expressionless.

"I think you will enjoy Vaegomar. I hope you find peace, Bella."

"Thank you," she said.

Amari watched them disappear behind the bend before turning to break camp.

Amari headed south, remembering the path they had found was past the road that ran beside a rock face. *Perhaps the smell of onions will lead me to her.*

He saw the opening where they had camped. The smaller pines here hid the trail to her cabin. *It has to be close.* He slowed down. *There.* He turned into the wood, angling toward the old cabin.

He tied his horse and looked around the yard. "Hello! Aly?" he said to no avail. He came to the door and lightly rapped on it. "Aly, are you here?" He pressed an ear to the door. He knocked again, this time the door almost knocking the door off its hinges. "Aly!" he nearly shouted, then he looked over his shoulder.

Amari walked away from the door and put his hands on his head, pacing in a circle. "Fuck it." He walked back to the door and pushed. It creaked open. "Aly?"

The room was dark; only the light that made it through the windows showed him any details at all. Pain struck the back of his head.

"Leave me alone!" She swung again, but Amari backed up just in time. The broomstick whizzed through the air where he had stood.

Amari's arm shot out in front of him. "Aly, it is me, Amari. Remember?"

She held the broom in both hands. Her eyes widened. "Oh. Yes, yes. I'm sorry. What are you doing back here?" She lowered the broom and walked past him.

Amari felt the back of his head and checked his hand. "I'm sorry to startle you…"

"Where's your friend?"

"That's why I'm here. Wait. Why did you attack me?"

"I thought you were him."

"Who?"

"The man who came after you left." She walked toward him into the light. "Did this." She tilted her head to the side; bruises covered her neck.

"What did he look like?"

"Tall, black hair. Strange leather clothes… and those eyes."

Amari shook his head. "Ethan," he whispered.

The woman sat down. "I knew you two were trouble, especially your friend."

"How would you—"

"Those eyes were like hers."

"Whose?"

"The tall woman who healed me. He reminded me of her."

Amari turned and kneeled in front of her. "I need to hear what you know of all this."

"Did he do that?" she said, pointing to his neck.

Amari felt the bandage and paused. "Yes. Do you know what the hell is going on?"

"I have an idea." She looked over at the books, still lying where they had been last. "So, what happened to him?"

Amari backed up into the chair. "He became ill. The more days passed, the worse it got. We met this man in the village we were riding to—"

"He bit you, didn't he?" she interrupted calmly.

"How did you know?"

She pointed to the books. "There are tales in some of those. I didn't believe them. But after you came here and I watched your friend, he reminded me of her. I thought back to her and what she did for me. She didn't have some herbal potion at the ready in her saddlebag that just cured me of the pox and kept me feeling young again. Hell, she didn't even *have* a horse. It was blood magic."

Amari leaned back and sighed. "I don't know what the world is coming to. Gods walking around Aahsgoth, blood magic. What can I do for him?"

She did not answer. For a few moments, he just watched her stare at the fire. "They can't be all bad. After all, the woman helped me."

"Where could I find her?"

"I don't know about her, but I did read of someone who may know something."

"Who? Where?"

She walked over and looked through a stack of books. Amari watched her study the books one by one, blowing away the dust on each before discarding it. "Here." She fumbled through the pages. "Some book that tells of a 'ceptor's journey, traveling the continent over two hundred years ago." She flipped back to the cover and started to read. "*Oddities of Aahsgoth: A Chronicle of the Travels of Grandmaster Mercel Serwin*." She flipped through the book and scanned the pages with her finger. "*The woman claimed to once be queen, she* who now sits here in a small cave near the point of the fang." She looked over at Amari.

"How does that help?"

She read some to herself then continued out loud, "*Old tales say that the last queen never aged and ruled for one hundred years. She then vanished. Likely just some singer who favored her spread the tale, as men do not live that long.*" She looked up from her book. "He clearly is talking about one of these... things."

Amari nodded. "Yes, but where could he have been, this preceptor?"

"Hell if I know. I ain't seen much beyond here."

Amari stood suddenly. "Wait! Read the first part again."

The old woman found her place again. "*The woman claimed to once be queen, she who now sits here in a small cave near the point of the fang.*"

"That's it!"

"What's it?"

Amari paced, the floor squeaking beneath him. "I know this story. I heard it as 'The Lady of the Rock.' An old tale of the first queen who went to live in solitude in a cave."

"That is where he wrote this—the Fang. It's a peninsula."

"And where is it?"

"My home: Ethorya."

Chapter Thirty-Four

Sirich

They were almost to Starfall Bay already. Sirich could still not believe all of this insanity, but here they were.

The southern end of the Crescent Isle lay just across the water. They had run the entire way with only a few stops. He could now run like the wind. It seemed as though everything around him, even time itself, could slow at his whim. A slight smile came to his face. This would have been nice as a child back at Wolfpine, running from Ash and Merek or chasing them in games of tag. During those long training sessions with Gavin, he would have to stop and catch his breath after only a few minutes. Now he recovered so quickly.

"We are here. I could smell it a league back." Promethial approached him and put his hand on his shoulder. "How do you feel, brother?"

Sirich knocked his hand away. "Brother? I am not your brother."

"You are now." He walked past Sirich toward the shore; the moonlight glistened off the water. The few remaining trees cast double shadows on the sands, small waves rippled in the distance among other sounds of the night. Sirich stopped and listened.

Promethial turned to him, smiling. "Focus, my prince. It can be overwhelming, I know. You hear the water, wind, wolves in the distance, creatures crawling among the leaves. Focus. In time you will hear what you need to, when you need to."

Sirich heard a faint clicking noise through it all. He turned back to the trees behind them. As clear as day, he saw a spider building a web as if it were just a few yards away, hearing a faint click every time it attached its webbing to another strand. He raised his eyebrows, his head turning, scanning the forest. He saw what looked to be the silhouette of a small deer, partially blocked by a tree. It had an almost red aura around it. He heard its quick heartbeat, the glow slightly pulsing with each beat as it looked in his direction before scampering away.

"You see? Now you have the eyes and ears of the dragon. You see what you need to survive—any warm-blooded creature. *You* are now the apex predator." Promethial grabbed his shoulders and smiled. "Come." Sirich turned, trying to take it all in, trying to understand.

"You are welcome to swim, or you could simply leap to

the other side, but there is a bridge ahead," Promethial said, leading the way.

"How often do I need to—"

"As often as you like. You will know when the hunger comes—and it *will* come."

"But how do you…"

"In the old days, when we had a deal with mortals, they would bring us their guilty… among others. Some offered virgins and other such nonsense." He stopped and turned to Sirich. "But we are not always the monsters some old tales would have you believe. I don't mind the old way, but there are other ways, depending on where you are."

"What other ways?"

"All your questions will be answered in time. For now, we must hurry." He pointed to his left toward the bridge. Devil's root had overtaken the arches and walls, the long vines covered with green hand-like leaves now wrapped around the stone. What parts of the floor that weren't covered in moss shone like a smooth red stone and seemed to be molded together. The short wall had crumbled in places, but the bridge had mostly remained intact. It arched across the water to the island, the dark waters waiting below.

"What is this place?"

"The isle. It's where we… sleep."

"Sleep?"

"Yes. You will want to take a break from eternity every so often." He laughed as they neared the other side.

The place smelled of decay. The blackened trees rotted near the water's edge. The heavy fog stirred deeper on the island. Sirich caught a familiar scent in the air; he stopped and sniffed the breeze.

"Come, my prince," Promethial said, motioning toward a rock formation deeper into the wood. The stones of the path were rippled by the roots of the twisting trees. The boulders became massive, and they were headed uphill now.

"Here." Promethial led him to what looked to be an opening in the rockface.

Sirich rolled his eyes. "Another cave?"

"Not quite."

Over the opening hung was what was left of the skull of a dragon, carved from the stone itself, one fang broken off, the entrance where the mouth would be. They came into a round room that looked to be chiseled from the cave itself. Four columns stood near the center; a few links of rusty steel chains hung from some of them. Other holes dotted the stone, but only stains remained. Promethial stopped and looked down.

"Thade," Promethial said in a low voice.

"What?" Sirich asked. The light breeze stirred small clumps of thick fur, scattering them across the floor.

"Not what. *Who.*"

"Who, then? Who is Thade?"

"Your uncle." He turned to Sirich. "There's no time to explain. Come on."

"Where?" Sirich said as Promethial approached the back wall adorned with a worn carving, several points in its center, too faded to make out.

Promethial stepped forward and stretched his arms out to the side, grabbing the seams of the wall. He pulled, and the stone moved. Sirich took a step back.

"You are free to help. You have the strength, too."

Sirich moved to one side and grabbed the edge he could now see. They both pulled to reveal the opening. The carved boulder had to be two feet thick. A smile crept to Sirich's face as they moved the massive boulder. The darkness behind it emerged.

"You are getting stronger. Now come show your real strength." Promethial pulled a torch that stuck out from the wall inside and smelled it. "This should do."

"How will you light it?"

The man ran his fingernail across the back of the boulder, and sparks leapt from his fingers. Sirich looked at his own hands. He rubbed his thumb along his fingertips, his nails a bit longer now and hard as steel. The fifth time he tried, the torch took a flame. Promethial did not say a word. Sirich followed him in.

They walked down the winding stone stairs. Promethial would stop and light the other torches on the wall. They came to the bottom, a large round chamber. Promethial walked around the room, lighting the remaining torches. As his eyes adjusted, Sirich noticed the large glyphs carved into each section of the wall, each separated by a half-column that looked to melt into the stone. In front of each section, a large ornate steel slab lay on the ground, each with matching glyphs in their center. A few of the slabs were slid to the side, revealing a shallow opening.

"What are these? Tombs?" Sirich asked, kneeling in front of the one closest to him.

Promethial smirked. "Well, I suppose they could be considered as such. But temporary ones. We can die when we want."

Sirich turned in circles, scanning the chamber. "Wait, I know these glyphs." He pointed to the rounded serpent-like glyph. "This is the sigil of House Serwyn." He moved to the next one. "This is the lightning bolt of the Thornes, this the bow of the Danes—"

"And the one in the center?" Promethial interrupted.

Sirich looked to the center of the room, to a glyph he had not even noticed. The steel slab there carried the sigil of his own house. "The sun of Blacksun?" He put both hands on his head. "What is this? What does this all mean?"

"You have it backwards, my prince. These were not originally the sigils of the noble houses. These are the glyphs of the original clans of Aahsgoth." The man returned to the ones he had pointed out in order. "This is the glyph of Serphial, my younger sister." He pointed to the others. "This is the glyph of Thurel, and that one is the glyph of Dyanial." He paused. "You see, once the clans started getting too big, surnames were introduced. They took these as their own, but as time passed, we faded back into the night. Legends were born, history twisted."

"And this one?" Sirich pointed to his own sigil in the center.

"The glyph of Valkarial, the first of us. Born of the dragon. Your mother."

Sirich stood silently in the flickering flames, only drops of water echoing in the chamber.

"This one. This is why we are here." Promethial stood beside the glyph that resembled a droplet of water.

"Lucian." Sirich knew the glyph. "My father wiped them out in the last rebellion."

"Not quite. Here lies their founder. Their father, I suppose. And only you can wake him."

"Why him?"

"He was the first made by Val. Only she is his elder. Lucian is the only one powerful enough to help you get what you want, what you deserve."

Sirich shook his head. "I do not know what I want."

"If you want to go to your sister and claim your crown, this is the only way. Now, come."

Sirich slowly walked toward him. "What do I have to do?"

"Feed him. Here," Promethial said, pointing to the slab.

Sirich ran his hand over the cold steel. He had never seen metal work this detailed. Many images were scattered across the lid, as if they were telling a story. At the end was carved a face with its eyes closed.

"What does all this mean?"

"Stories for another time. Here." He pointed to the mouth.

Sirich looked closer. The mouth was black, an opening behind the sharp steel teeth.

"All you have to do is feed him, and Wolfpine is yours."

Sirich hesitated. "How?"

Promethial pulled a blade from his hip with a smile. "What, were you just going to bite yourself?"

"I suppose not. But what if…"

"You will heal within moments, remember? It doesn't take much."

Sirich took the blade and gripped it over the watching face.

"Shit!" he said as he pulled the knife across his palm. Blood oozed from his hand and dripped to the steel face underneath, running down the crevices that seemed to channel it toward the opening. It ran into the mouth, staining the teeth.

"How long?" Sirich grimaced.

Promethial did not answer, but as he flexed his fingers, he saw his hand was already healing.

"Now what?" Sirich pulled his arm back and ran his hand over where the cut had been, smearing the remaining blood.

"It will take a while. He's been here for quite some time."

The two men stood and walked back to the center of the room. Promethial turned to him. "Thank you, my prince. When he wakes and regains his strength, he will make you a king."

Sirich knelt and looked at the steel lid beneath him. He

ran his hand over the glyph of his house. "So… my ancestors took this sun glyph as their own?"

A voice sounded from the stairs. "It was never meant to be the sun." A tall woman with dark hair walked down toward them, her icy blue eyes never leaving his. Sirich had never seen such strange leather clothing; it even covered her neck. He turned to look at Promethial, backing up.

"My queen." The man knelt.

Sirich looked around, unsure. Promethial was still on one knee, his head down.

"What is it supposed to be, then?" Sirich asked.

"*Un vehdon gontalfam meddru Urmed gisvanfam.*"

"I'm sorry, I do not—"

"The red lotus. My favorite flower as a child."

She walked past Sirich, almost brushing his shoulder. He moved aside just in time. She looked past him seeing the blood on the steel lid. "What have you done, brother? What game are you playing now?"

"I found him, my queen," Promethial said, standing and taking a step back.

"Lucian was banished, never to be woken for all time. Only his elder can wake him, yet here you are."

Sirich had never seen Promethial so quiet, or without his smile. "What has my dear brother told you, Sirich of Vaegomar? What has he promised to you?"

Sirich did not have a chance to speak before Promethial said, "It's him, my queen, of the prophecy."

She slowly turned her head back to Promethial. "We were not to interfere with their affairs any longer. Lucian lies banished behind you for that very reason. That is our covenant!" Her voice boomed then softened again. "And now, so will you."

Promethial moved like the wind, but she moved more

quickly. It was as if she disappeared, leaving only what looked to be shadows in her wake. The torches all snapped sideways toward them. She now stood in front of him, blocking him from the stairs. Sirich stumbled backwards, watching. He tried to speak, but nothing left his throat.

"Please, my queen. He is your son."

Sirich wanted to speak but faltered.

Promethial continued, "You left him behind at Wolfpine. I'm only trying to—" Her hand appeared around his neck. Sirich hadn't even seen it move. His feet dangled above the floor. She squeezed. Promethial tried to struggle. He grabbed at her wrist and hit her arms.

This man who just moved a boulder might as well be trying to pull the moons apart.

"And what do you know of prophecy?" she asked. "The same prophecy led those fanatics at Bloodstone to obsess over words. Why? So that they could kill my son? So that they can kill all of us?" She took a deep breath. "I did fail you, Promethial, all those centuries ago. But you have played your games for the last time."

"*Mals-ur-graphun,*" he gurgled. "Please..."

She looked over her shoulder at Sirich. Her eyes were like blue fire, and tears glistened on her cheeks. "He is the son of William, but when I left Wolfpine two decades ago, I left behind twins."

Sirich watched the man's eyes widen. They turned red as blood streamed from the corners; it dripped from his ears and nose. She turned back and bit deep into his neck, then snapped her head back with a gasp. Blood ran from her chin to the floor. Promethial fell into a heap on the cold stone.

Sirich fell to his knees, dizzy. The room started spinning, and everything went black.

Chapter Thirty-Five

Ashaya

Ashaya looked into the stream and splashed water on her face. They had ridden for almost a day and had finally crossed the red sands. Finding a small patch of wood and shade again had been some relief. They had almost no rations left, and what little Ashaya *had* eaten did nothing to satisfy her hunger. She rinsed out her hair, and the rest of the dye dripped and clouded the water. As it cleared and the ripples smoothed, eyes as blue as sapphires stared back at her. Her hair remained dark, now only a few streaks of blonde left behind. She turned her head and ran her hands through her hair.

"I told you," Mitch said, stretching beside her. "I don't know what is happening, but it looks good on you."

She stared at the reflection, running her fingers over her lips. She looked closer at the reflection, baring her teeth. The two beside her front teeth were different. *A bit longer, maybe*. She brought her hand to her mouth and ran her finger over them. "Damn!" She jerked her hand away, a small drop of blood welling on the tip of her finger.

"What is it?"

"Nothing." She sucked the blood from her finger and stood. "Let's go."

They mounted their horses and continued toward the small village on the horizon. The landscape here was a vast change from the red sands. Open plains and the occasional small tree lay in front of them. Patches of grass struggled to grow here and there, but otherwise the land was barren, brown earth.

"Looks like these were farmlands at one time." Mitch must have noticed her looking around as they approached. "What village is this?"

"Longleaf."

"How do you know, Ash?"

"The old temple hill above it. The ruins of Bloodstone."

"Are you sure about this?"

"You don't have to come, Mitch. I will find my brother one way or another."

Mitch did not reply.

They approached the old settlement. As they passed through the main road, the women and children watched them. They rode through what looked to have been a gate at one time, the poles tilted in the ground. This place was in disrepair. The old wooden houses were rotting. In some places, woven blankets covered holes in the walls.

"Hello there." Ashaya nodded to the women who watched them pass. Some of them went back to their chores, some sat and sewed, while others stirred pots. A few chickens scrambled out of their way as they headed toward the stone buildings upon the hill. They got off their horses at the small alley. Ashaya looked around and noticed an old smith's shop. Half of a rusted anvil sat on the stone, the rest just a stain around it. A stray dog wandered close, and she knelt to pet it. It approached but stopped short, baring its teeth and growling. She reached for it, but before she could say anything, it yelped and ran out of sight.

They walked up the red stone stairs to a rusted iron gate. Only one door remained hanging by a hinge. Ashaya rubbed her hand on the stone wall inside the courtyard. The stone looked wet in the sunlight, as if it were bleeding.

The courtyard itself was empty, and dry grasses protruded from the cobblestone path leading to the entrance. She looked ahead at the giant stone legs standing on the left of the path. The rest of the statue lay in piles, half-buried. She could only make out the wing of a bat that stuck out above the grass. Part of a solemn face lay broken beside it, half-hidden by time. Beside the building, a large bell lay cracked beneath what remained of the old tower that held it.

"What was this place?" Mitch stopped and kneeled.

"I don't remember much, just the little that Galen taught me during his lessons." She continued toward the entrance. "The people here worshipped the god-king Lucian, or so say the tales."

"I suppose that makes sense. This region was known—"

"I know what it was called, Mitch," she interrupted, looking ahead at the massive staircase—as wide as the temple itself.

Mitch stopped behind her. "Enough!" She turned to him, surprised. "Why do you treat me this way? Am I nothing but a stray dog to you?" He walked past her up the stairs, shaking his head. "I'm only here to help."

Ashaya watched him ascend the stairs, but she did not

speak. She followed him, stopping at one of the large columns. She ran her hand along the stone. "This place seems familiar to me."

"You've never been this far south."

"But still, it's like I remember..." She shook her head.

She caught up to Mitch at the entrance, a massive wall with two glyphs, one barely visible. The other, she could make out, although the chiseled edges were rounded and shallow.

"House Lucian. But what was the other?" Mitch asked.

"Blacksun." The only things that remained were sharp points; the center stones had fallen out or been removed.

"Blacksun? Your sigil?"

"Yes."

"How?"

"I do not know."

Ashaya entered to the right side of the wall. On the other side was the main chamber. There were no windows, but large columns reached for what remained of the figures painted on the ceiling, cracked and chipped away. A beam of light shot through the woman in the center, a large hole letting the sun in. The floor leading up to the rounded staircase was littered with firepits and makeshift bedding. Smoke still rose from some, the wood black and smoldering. They stood still, only hearing the dripping of water echoing from the darkness. They both traversed the scattered beds and piles of stone, approaching the stairs. At the top sat a single stone chair, one of its arms missing.

Mitch stood beside her. "Is this where those men live?"

"Looks like it."

"Wait... when we rode in, did you see a single man?"

Ashaya thought back. "No, only women and children."

"So where are the men?"

"Likely out robbing and reaving." She turned toward the entrance. "Well, let's go ask, shall we?"

They walked out into the yard. "Wait!" She put her hand on his chest. "Do you hear that?"

Mitch tilted his head and looked up. "I hear nothing. What am I listening for?"

"Steel." She stood for a moment. The clank of steel on steel and the occasional scream echoed in the distance. "Let's go!"

"Where?"

"You were right—the men are in battle close by."

Chapter Thirty-Six

Theodor

Theodor and Ridley watched from behind the bookshelf, both of them balancing on the top stair and trying to peek through to the overlord's chambers from where they had snuck in the first night. Theodor stood, leaning to the crack, while Ridley crouched below him. Aethial sat on the edge of the overlord's desk, his eyes indifferent while she spoke.

"What did he promise you? Power? Women? A kingdom?"

"I do not know what you are speaking of. I work for no one."

"Lies," she said calmly. "You found one of the cellars under the waterfall." She looked over toward them. Both jerked their heads back from their spying.

"Did she see us?" Ridley asked.

"I don't know. Did she say one of the cellars? There are more?" Theodor leaned forward to look again.

"Please, my lady, I must ask you to leave. The hour is late."

"Yes, it is. The sun will be up in a few hours, which is why... wait." The woman stood. "Did he offer... *it?*"

Lord Aethon's face grew stern as he stood. "I must go. I do not know you or this brother of yours."

"So, he did. He revealed himself." Aethial pointed to his chair. "Sit!"

"Excuse me." Lord Aethon walked around his desk toward the double doors.

"We aren't quite done." Aethial grabbed the back of his neck by his tunic and dragged him to his chair. The man struggled but could not free himself. She slung him into the heavy oak chair. It was massive, with a tall, ornately carved back and steel to bind the oak together. It looked more like a throne in some massive castle than an ordinary chair. He hit with a thud, his cane flying into the wall behind them.

"Grandfather!" Ridley whispered loudly. "She's going to hurt him!"

Theodor grabbed her arm. "Wait." They kept watching through the crack.

The man now looked concerned.

The woman stood in front of him. "My brother came to you. Why?"

He sat for a moment, not speaking. He stood as quickly as he could and limped toward the door. In a blur, she moved in front of him, blocking the door. She pointed over his shoulder. "*Fam gongis.*"

Theodor looked down as Ridley stared up at him. "Did you see that?"

"Did *you?*"

"How did she..."

"He's an asshole, but I don't want her to hurt him."

"I know, Ridley, but he may know something about my father."

She reluctantly returned to watching.

He backed up slowly, almost stumbling over his chair. His hand out in front of him, he managed to sit again." Alright. Alright, please."

Theodor had never seen Overlord Aethon look afraid, but now fear shrouded his face.

The overlord took a deep breath. "He came to me before I was selected as overlord. He promised that I would be selected. He said he would show me lost knowledge of Aahsgoth."

"And?" The woman paced around the desk.

"He claimed that if I served him well, he would grant me a gift. That things were going to change soon, and that I could live in the new world or die with the old. I am old and already dying. What would you have done?"

Aethial sat. "Go on."

"Frankly, I did not believe him or know what he spoke of until I went behind the waterfall. Everything he said was true."

"Almost everything he says is a lie!"

"When the boy showed up asking about Vedician, I knew something was afoot. He said I had to keep it a secret."

"Did he tell you what that gift entails? What it costs?"

The overlord thought for a moment. "I was prepared to make that sacrifice."

"Are you?" Aethial walked over and grabbed the arm of the chair he sat in, dragging it to the window with him in it. She slammed the chair so hard that the legs went through the wooden floor.

"Guards!" the man yelled.

Theodor looked over at the double doors to his chamber.

No guards came. She sat him and the chair in front of the large window. "Look at it!"

"Look at what?"

"The night. The darkness." She pointed through the window. "It would be all you ever see again. You could never again have the sun warm your face, never see the morning dew glistening in the fields, never see the sparkle of snow-capped mountains, never see the beauty of Aahsgoth." She took a deep breath. "Unless you choose a horrible death. To die like my sister, Serphial. Promethial talked her into his schemes, then killed her when she disobeyed. Do you think that would be worth it to you?" Aethial's nose almost touched his cheek. "Do you think he would let you live after giving you such a thing?"

Theodor and Ridley looked at each other but said nothing. Theo looked back and thought he could see tears running down the woman's face.

"This window faces east. You want the gift? I'll give you what you want." She stomped to the corner of his chambers and looked under the scaffolding, rummaging through the piles of wood and tools.

"What is she doing?" Ridley looked up. "Is she going to hurt him?"

Theodor could not stop watching. "I don't know."

Aethial returned carrying thick rope. In a blur, she had bound the overlord to the heavy oak chair. His arms, torso and legs were almost completely covered.

"Please, I beg you!" The man broke down, attempting to free himself. He tried to wriggle, but the ropes were too tight, the chair too heavy.

She walked over and grabbed the pewter goblet from his desk. "You want the gift? Then you shall have it." She pulled a dagger and sliced her wrist, letting her blood fill the goblet.

Steam rose from the cup. She smiled, looking into the man's eyes as he watched her blood pour from her arm. Within seconds, the bleeding slowed, and the wound was healing. She sat the goblet on the seal of the window.

Ridley gasped. "We've got to help him."

Theodor pushed open the bookshelf. "Stop!"

Aethial did not react, as if she knew they were spying the entire time.

"Wait, please!" Ridley pushed past him into the room.

"Overlord, where is my father?" Theodor asked the man.

"I do not know anything of your father."

"Bullshit! You had Master Edwyn killed, and my father has not yet arrived."

"I swear, boy, I know nothing of Galen."

The woman walked to Aethon and held his head back. She flicked her finger along his neck, and a small red line appeared. She leaned down and touched her tongue to his neck. She jerked her head back and gasped. For a moment, no one said a word as she stood with her eyes closed.

"He does not know. He has only spoken to my brother, but he has not returned here in some time."

Ridley dropped to her knees. "Don't hurt my grandfather! Please, lady!"

Aethial looked back to the bound man before picking the goblet up. No more steam rose from it as she swirled it around.

"Now, drink." She put the goblet to his lips. He tried to resist, but he was forced to swallow or choke. "Take your gift." She pulled the cup away and threw it across the room. "It is done. Enjoy your newfound gift for the time you have. The sun will rise through that window within the hour." The darkness outside the window had already lightened to a dark purple.

Theodor felt only the wind on his face. He turned; the bookshelf creaked on its hinges. Aethial was gone.

Overlord Aethon leaned his head back, breathing deeply. Sweat beaded on his bald head, his beard stained red.

Theodor stared at him. "What just happened?"

The overlord spoke in a near whisper. "Help me, Ridley." The man looked over to her, then up at Theodor. "I will become like her. But once the sun rises…"

Ridley stood and ran to him. "Come on, Theo, we have to untie him. We don't have much time."

Theodor just stood, frozen, staring.

"Theo!" Ridley screamed. Tears ran down her face.

"Right, I'm sorry, I…" Theodor quickly went over to help.

They both worked to free the man. "You have your knife," Theodor reminded Ridley. She reached for it on her hip, but the sheath was empty. "Go find it!"

"There's no time."

The ropes were so tight that they could not get their fingers under them. Ridley worked on untying Aethon's legs, while Theodor walked behind the chair looking for a knot to loosen.

"Hurry!" the man said, breathing heavily and wheezing. Theodor looked up. The window was lighter. He went back to work. He tried to loosen the knot he found, but the rope was too tight. Sweat poured down his forehead.

"Almost!" Ridley said. She had the rope loose around one of his legs. Birds now chirped in the tree right outside the window, and Theo could see the silhouette of the other buildings. He walked over to the window and looked out. Outlines of clouds had started to show, yellow leaking over the horizon.

"Cover the window!" Ridley shouted.

"With what?" They both looked around.

"We can burn the ropes!" Theodor ran over to the desk and came back with a candle, blocking the flame with his other hand. Ridley had one leg free.

"Hurry!" The man jerked in the chair. Theodor held the candle under the knot. The rope was damp, but some of the fibers only smoked. He was getting nowhere.

"Grandfather, do you have a blade?"

"Perhaps in my desk? Hurry!"

Ridley rummaged through drawers, throwing things on the floor. Theodor got through one knot. "This is taking too long!" He looked over at her as she intently looked for a blade. "Ridley, we have to try to push the chair."

They moved to one side and pushed. The heavy oak didn't budge, the legs of the chair driven through the floor like nails. They both grunted as they pushed, and the old man tried to rock.

"It's too late!" the man said, exhausted. Theodor leaned into the chair, looking out the window. The sun peeked over the long stables. The sky turned from a dark purple to bright blue as sun rays shot upward. Light scattered through the trees. Theodor grabbed Ridley and pulled her away. She resisted, still reaching for the ropes.

"Go, child!" The man closed his eyes and turned his head. The sun covered his face.

Theodor held on to Ridley, unable to do anything but watch.

Nothing.

The overlord slowly opened his eyes. He turned his head, looking at the sunrise. A tear ran down his wrinkled cheek. After a few moments, a slight smile grew on his face. He watched the sunrise as though he had never seen one. His smile grew into a tearful laugh.

Ridley ran back to the desk and looked through another

drawer while Theodor watched the overlord. He could almost see his father and how he had acted when Theodor had told him he was accepted to the order. He could only smile.

"Got one." Ridley found a blade and started to cut through the rope. After a few minutes, Aethon was free. The overlord rubbed his wrists, never taking his eyes from the window. He slowly stood.

Ridley brought his cane. "Grandfather, are you alright?" She held the walking stick out to him, but he did not take it.

"Yes, my dear, I think I am." He took a few steps. He stood tall and ran his hand through his white beard. He continued to walk, clutching his lower back. He no longer hobbled with a limp. He walked around the room, smiling and stretching his arms, before turning back toward the window.

"What is it, grandfather?" Ridley still held out the cane.

He put his hand on the glass and took a deep, clear breath. "I do not think I will be needing that for some time."

Chapter Thirty-Seven

Sirich

Sirich saw a dark-haired woman kneeling next to a man, her shadow painted over him, blocking his face. Blood pooled in the mud below him. Muffled clanks of steel surrounded them. The smell of death permeated the air. Sirich ignored the sharp pain in his knee and the taste of iron on his tongue. The woman held something that gleamed in the sunlight. He saw clouds reflecting in sapphire blue eyes, tears leaving trails on her dusty face. The image started to go black in his mind.

"Welcome back," a distorted voice said.

Sirich opened his eyes, the room blurry for a moment as he quickly adjusted to the darkness. His wits came to him, and he sat up quickly.

"What did you see? You spoke in your sleep." Promethial sat against the wall, his neck stained red.

"I thought you were dead."

"Not yet. She just wanted to taste my memories."

"I dreamt of her. I saw her beside a dying man. I couldn't see him well, but it reminded me of—"

"She did marry him, I told you."

"You lied to me. You told me she was my mother. She said she left..." Sirich stood quickly. "Ash. I need to get to Ash."

Promethial pointed to the steel lid that Sirich had bled into. It had been slid to the side. He looked down at his hand; the wound was gone. Only a slight itch remained.

"It worked?" Sirich walked to the empty tomb.

"I told you, only an elder can wake another. Lucian has only one elder, as he was the first made, but your blood woke him. This proves what I said—the foretelling was about you."

Sirich paced the room. A few torches had burned out, the rest held only small blue flames. "She said they killed her son. Was she talking about..."

"Yes. I am sorry about your brother; I did not know. All the more reason for Lucian to return. He will take care of the zealots."

Sirich's face grew hot. He could kill the man with his bare hands, but he only felt numb. His head spun. He leaned over and retched, trying to catch his breath. Merek's face haunted his mind. Memories of them running in the yards of Wolfpine flooded his head.

Sirich slid down the stone wall, tears welling in his eyes along with the anger in his heart. "Who are they? Where are they? I will kill them myself."

"They have been around for almost two millennia. They are the descendants of Lucian's clan."

"Why would they kill my brother? What does he have to do with any of this?"

"They know of the prophecy. They likely thought... You

should go to Wolfpine and take your crown. Your sister will be fine, I am sure."

"She could be in danger."

"If what Val said is true, she will come to you. Go home."

"How do you know all of this? What do you have against your... queen?" Sirich studied Promethial, his downcast eyes and unusually quiet demeanor. "You still love her."

Promethial leaned his head back, looking up. "I loved her once. She made Lucian so she wouldn't have to walk alone." He looked down and shook his head. "It should have been me. When Lucian did not see things her way, I was there for her, but—"

"Enough of your whining. You have lost nothing. You have done all of this for revenge on a woman who would not love you back?"

"You have no idea what I have lost, boy!" Promethial snapped back. He paused and took a deep breath. "It's much more than that! We used to rule, we used to show ourselves. She caged us, made us keep to the shadows. Lucian eventually came to think as I did. He built his clan from his temple, raised an army, and almost destroyed your civilization. Only a falling star did most of the work for him. Not long after, he sacked Ashbourne, and it fell into the sea. What you now call Starfall Bay."

Sirich paced. "I thought that was just a myth."

"No. It blacked out the sun for almost two moons. Oddly enough, we could come out during those hours without burning. Ironically, we could only see a light spot behind the darkened skies. There is no escaping the darkness..."

"So why was Lucian here?"

"After his conquest, he killed his general that he had earlier turned. The rest of his dark army fell. Val banished him here—for all time."

Sirich shook his head and walked up the stairs toward the light. The stone had not been moved back into place.

"We have to wait. The sun has not yet—"

"No, *you* have to wait, remember?"

Sirich walked into the circular room above. Boulders and thick trees blocked most of the direct sunlight, but a few sunbeams reached the floor. *I should have been there with him.* Merek's face remained in his mind. Echoes of his voice stirred. *Big brother, is this correct?* Young Merek would always ask when learning the sword, spear, or bow. He had craved Sirich's blessings and respect.

Sirich shook his head, standing next to a sunbeam. He had to squint, even looking at it askance. His eyes burned as if he had not slept in days. Promethial stood behind him, frozen in the opening of the passage. Sirich looked back at him from the corners of his eyes, his lips tightening. He slowly stuck his hand toward the light, spreading his fingers. He felt the warmth of the sun for the first time in a fortnight.

"Shit!" He jerked his arm back, holding his forearm with his other hand. His fingers had almost charred to the bone. His flesh turned to ash, floating from his hand in the breeze. Blood ran from his hand but turned to smoke, never hitting the stone below. The smell of burning flesh filled his nose. "You lied!"

Promethial turned his head. "It doesn't matter. You are her descendant, one way or the other. Your blood woke Lucian, remember?" He pointed behind them without looking.

"You said I would have all of this, that I could walk in the sun! You bastard!" Sirich dropped to his knees. He watched his hand. It was already healing, new skin growing to replace the old that had been destroyed before his eyes.

"Do you not call that power? What does this change?

You can still have what you want. This is just a minor…
inconvenience."

"*Minor?* Fuck you!" Tears welled in Sirich's eyes. He
stood and grabbed the man by the collar, lifting his feet from
the floor and ramming his head against the stones above the
opening. The stones exploded and crumbled to the floor.
"You used me!" Sirich dropped him and backed away.

Promethial smiled and brushed the powdered stone
from his shoulders. "I freed you. Now get over it, you spoiled
shit. The sun is already setting. Let us go take your castle."

Once the sun dropped behind the horizon, they walked. Neither said a word. Sirich flexed his hand where the sun had
burned the flesh away. It was whole again, only a slight tin-
gling remaining. He did manage a slight grin.

The wood around them had come alive with the chirping
of leafhoppers, the howls of wolves, the rushing of water in
the distance. He could see everything that crawled and slithered around them. The fireflies reminded him of Ashaya.
When she was young, she would run around the northside
of Wolfpine, catching them. Ashaya would bring him a bas-
ketful, trying to impress him. Even if he were bothered by
her attention, he would always thank her with a kiss on the
forehead. Once she went to bed, he would set them free to be
captured again the next night.

Promethial broke the silence. "I am sorry about your
brother. I didn't know."

"I should have been there with him," Sirich whispered.

"You need to stop focusing on what you do not have, and
instead focus on what you do have—and what you can take."

"So, she said she left twins at Wolfpine. Which means—"

"They thought that your brother was you." Promethial said, finishing his sentence.

Sirich's face flushed with anger. "This is all my father's fault. He loved this demon instead of *my* mother."

"It seems you were second rate to your father. It does not matter now. Val could be lying. Only her bloodline could wake Lucian, and you did. To be fair, I do not believe your father—"

"No! Why would she lie? My father discarded my mother like old bath water. Then he discarded me once he had his two prized children with her." Promethial walked beside him and put his hand on his shoulder. Sirich raised his arm, knocking it away.

Promethial stopped. "Go, then. I will see you in Wolfpine."

"Where are you headed?"

"I must go to him, find out the meaning of this. He will know where to go from here."

"Who?"

"Lucian."

"Fine. Just leave me be. I don't need your help."

"You will, and you likely need to feed. You must anticipate your hunger, or you will lash out at them."

"At whom?"

"Mortals. You must start thinking about what you *are*, not what you *were*. On the way home, stop by any old village off the beaten path. Any in the deep wood, far away from the coast. Go to the tavern and ask for a drink."

"What, just ask for some ale or some mead?"

Promethial smiled. "Ask for Vedician Red. We still have these arrangements in some places. Otherwise, you can do it the old way."

"So you just, what? Ambush some innocent man along the road?"

"No one is innocent, and you can do what you wish."

"Why is that?"

"Like it or not, Sirich, you are now a god. A crimson god."

Chapter Thirty-Eight

Ashaya

The figures in the distance looked to be dancing. The old ruins at Bloodstone grew smaller behind them. Men were scattered everywhere in the skirmish. Some in mismatched armor rode against the others with lance, spear, and sword. She saw banners on the backs of the others. Some men rode horses, others ran, others still twitched on the ground. Light blinked in her eyes as the sun gleamed off the various blades spread around the field. She tried to focus, spying familiar sigils. Finally, she spotted her own.

"Hurry, Mitch, it's father!" She kicked Acorn harder. "Faster!"

As they got closer, Ashaya pulled her bow from her shoulder and nocked an arrow. She aimed at the closest man on horseback, her arrow whizzing through the air and into the man's neck. He flew from his horse, rolling into a pile, writhing on the ground, blood escaping between his fingers. She nocked another arrow and struck a man in the back. He tumbled from his horse as Mitch passed him, drawing his sword.

Mitch cut a man down from his horse in front of her. Acorn stopped suddenly, and she was thrown forward into the chaos. Ashaya landed with a thud and rolled to a stop, clutching for her knee. Her breeches had been torn, the gash in her knee deep. She leaned her head back and hissed for a moment, closing her eyes. She stumbled, trying to pull her sword, but the scabbard was bent slightly, and it was jammed. A man rushed toward her in a pointed half-helm, his sword swinging toward her face. She dropped to the ground just in time, the sword swooshing through the air where she had stood. She turned to see him get lost in the battle.

"Ash!" Mitch jumped from his horse and ran toward her.

Steel clashed all around her, dust filling the air along with the screams. The ground shook as horses passed, throwing dirt in every direction. The air smelled of shit and blood. She looked the other way and saw him. Her father, his sword in hand, was standing off against two men. One held a spear, the other a sword. Her father fought for his breath. He held his sword with two hands, pointing it at one of the men as they advanced from either side.

"Father!"

Mitch grabbed her waist and pulled her to her feet. "Come on!"

"Mitch, watch out!" A man approached from behind. She pulled Mitch toward her as the man swung, and he landed on top of her. Ashaya finally got her sword free, scurrying out from under him as he rolled over. She stood to face the man.

He swung widely, bloodlust in his eyes. She sidestepped him and buried her blade in his chest.

She turned back to Mitch. "Are you hurt?"

"No," he said uncertainly. She followed his eyes down to his waist. His dusty tunic turned wet and black under his hand, a large gash above his waist seeping blood through his fingers. He looked up at her in disbelief.

She looked over; her father was still surrounded. She looked back at Mitch. "I'm sorry!" she said as she stood and ran toward her father.

"Father!" she screamed. His eyes shifted toward her. A slight grin came to his face. He turned to the man beside him with the sword as she screamed, running at the spearman. The spear came toward her face, and she dropped and slid on her knees, plunging her sword into his groin. The man's knee grazed her mouth. He fell toward her as she rolled out of the way. She turned to her father as he parried a blow and cut the bearded man's throat.

She ran to him.

"Ashaya? What are you—"

She was too late.

An arrow punched through his chest from behind. William dropped to his knees, his sword tumbling to the ground, his other hand reaching out to her. The screams and clatters around grew muffled, replaced by a ringing in her ears. Her field of vision grew dark. She ignored the taste of iron in her mouth. Her mind was chaos; she could not think. She could not move. She could only stare at her father. *This isn't real.* Ashaya went numb as she sank to her knees.

Reality rushed back to her as she fell to her hands and retched. Ashaya did not realize she had been screaming this whole time. Her throat was dry and scratchy. "No!"

She crawled to her father, but she could barely see through the tears. She dropped to her knees beside him as he lay on his back in the dirt.

"Get up! Please!" she managed, sobbing and looking down at the arrow protruding from his chest. Blood dripped from the shiny tip. "Get up, Father, you will be alright…"

"No, not this time."

The world closed in around them, the sounds of chaos faded. He raised his hand and gently touched her cheek. "I like what you have done with your hair. So beautiful. You have her eyes." He smiled through the tears carving lines down his dusty cheeks.

She managed a smile, tears dripping from her cheeks. "Father." She leaned down to him, her hands on either side of his face. She touched her forehead to his.

"It's alright, my daughter. You and your brothers will finish what I have started."

She laid her head on his chest, sobbing. She did not have the heart to tell him of Merek.

"Ashaya, get up, you must," he whispered.

She lifted her head and held his hand.

"Now, go," he forced through a cough. Blood ran from the corners of his mouth. "Go find her."

"Who?"

"Your mother. She lives." His hand went limp, his cold and open eyes never leaving hers. His last breath wheezed from his chest. She closed her eyes.

Is this real?

Ashaya looked to the sky. Through the muffled sounds surrounding her, she heard a whisper. "Ashaya, you know what you must do." The voice was as clear as if the woman were sitting in front of her. "Go," the whisper said.

A burning anger ignited within her.

The sounds of war slowly returned. She laid her father's head back and stood. She turned toward Mitch, her rage growing. She ran to him and leaned down. His grey eyes never left hers, his now-thin beard covered in blood or mud or both.

"Ash? Am I—"

"No, you will not die today." She put one hand over his wound. Her other hand guided his and placed it over his wound as well. "Keep pressure here and stay still." She stared at the palm of her bloody hand. She tilted her head sideways, and the whisper echoed in her head.

She licked the blood from her hand. All of it.

Ashaya's head jerked backward. The world slowed down around her. She saw flashes of herself on horseback. A quick glimpse of herself through Mitch's eyes during a night together in Wolfpine, sleeping comfortably beside him. A thousand images flashed before her, the last one of her holding a bloody wound and looking up at herself, blood covering her lips and chin.

Fire coursed through her veins. Bloodlust. The battlefield and everyone moved slowly again, like the two men in the fishing village. She reached for her sword; she had left it in the man's groin.

Ashaya raised her hands and looked at them. Her fingernails protruded like claws, thick and black. She surveyed the battlefield around her and moved from man to man. They would never see her coming. This time she noticed a dark, fog-like mist emanating from her when she moved. It hung in the air like wispy clouds when she stopped but dissipated quickly when she moved again, leaving purple shadows in her wake. Her hands were like daggers, swiftly cutting through every man she came to with that mismatched armor. It was no different than a hot knife through butter, and just as innocent. Time was almost frozen as men fell behind her; she would be at the next man before the last one's blood touched the ground.

Slow, deep screams of death filled the air.

She came upon one of the remaining men holding two daggers. He faced her father's garrison commander. Jordan swung his sword straight down at the man, but he dodged and pushed his dagger toward Jordan's neck. Ashaya caught the man's wrist as the dagger scratched Jordan's skin. She held his wrist for a time, watching the man's face contort and his eyes slowly shift to her. With a sharp twist, she heard the bones in his wrist crunch, the dagger almost floating toward the ground. She caught it and buried it in the man's throat, the dagger protruding through the back of his neck. He never had time to scream.

Jordan slowly reached for his neck, and time seemed to move again. She looked behind her as the breeze blew her hair. The low grunts of the injured were all that remained as she surveyed the field. She watched the men who had been in her path fall one after the other.

"Ash?" Jordan said, checking his hand for blood after rubbing his neck.

She spared him only a single glance before running to where her father's body lay. The remaining men looked at each other without speaking, unsure, swords still in hand. Some dropped where they stood, searching for breath.

Ashaya kneeled beside her father. Jordan walked toward her slowly. "Ash, I—"

"Do not!" She stared down at his lifeless body; her father's eyes were still open.

Jordan kneeled behind her and put his hand on her shoulder. "I'm sorry, Ash. He came for you. Are you alright?"

Ashaya gave in and embraced him, burying her face in his neck.

When she opened her eyes, Mitch limped as he approached, holding his side. "I'm so sorry, Ash. William was…"

"This is all my fault," she said, her voice cracking.

"No," Jordan was quick to answer. "You will not place blame at your own feet."

Jordan motioned to the others. "The sun is setting. We need to treat the wounded and make camp. This is no place for that."

"The ruins are close." Mitch pointed in the direction they had ridden from.

"We can't just leave him here."

"We will take him home and give him a proper pyre, I promise," Jordan said. "Come."

Ashaya looked at her father once more. She leaned down and gently pulled the arrow from his chest. She held it up, the remaining sunlight gleaming from the silver tip. She rubbed the arrow with her thumb; it was hot to the touch. She wiped the blood on her breeches and added the arrow to her quiver.

They gathered the remaining horses and rode toward the ruins. Some men remained to collect the dead; others rode to get the supply wagons in the distance. She looked back to her father.

Get up.

They entered the small village of Longleaf again, following their path from earlier. She stopped where a few women were still out in the dirt roads. The same dog growled at her.

When she looked at it, the dog tucked its tail and vanished behind a broken house.

"Your men will not be returning," she said.

"Good," one of the women said, without even looking at her. No one else said a word.

Ashaya, Mitch, Jordan, and the other men continued through the upper gate to the old temple. "This place hasn't changed much," Jordan said.

"You've been here before?" Ashaya asked.

"As I boy, I lived her for a while after I lost my parents. I do not remember much else. I did not stay long. I moved from place to place, trying to find a life. Your father gave me that. He gave me purpose." A tear rolled down his cheek, leaving a trail.

Ashaya tightened her lips and looked down. They came to the front of the temple and dismounted near the crumbled statue.

"Stage our supplies here when the others bring the wagons. We'll go make sure it's clear," Jordan said to the others.

"Yes, my lord," one of the men replied.

"It's clear." Ashaya sat on the stairs and leaned on her knees, looking down. Jordan sat beside her. "I know it's a horrible time, but what was that back there? I would say you would have gotten yourself killed, but you moved like—"

"I can't explain it. I don't know what is happening to me."

"And you look different…"

"So I hear. And the men are scared. Who can blame them? I saw the way they looked at me afterward, like I'm some kind of monster."

Jordan put his arm around her. "Whatever is happening, we are here for you. William would be proud of all you did."

Ashaya shrugged and stood, turning to the entrance. Jordan grabbed a torch and followed.

"Who were those people? The men I…"

"Dragon slayers, of course," a deep voice rumbled from the back of the hall.

Jordan drew his sword. Ashaya could see the man as clear as day even in the dim light. He seemed familiar. His long black ponytail swayed behind his muscular body. His black leather lappets formed a layered skirt of armor that reached for his knees. The sandals he wore had thick lacing that wrapped around his legs. He had what was left of a leather bracer on one shoulder and a tattered half-cloak draping toward the stone floor behind him. A bearded man and a boy stood beside him, their wrists bound. She recognized the boy's faded linen tunic with tattered sleeves, coarse wool breeches, and lack of shoes.

"Welcome to the family," the man said.

"Who are you?" Jordan asked, his sword pointed at the man as they walked closer.

"I was talking to the girl." The tall man looked back to her. "You did well, from what I could see from the shadows. You move like your mother."

"You know my mother?"

"Of course. This was her temple once."

"Why would my mother need a temple?"

"She was a god, before she grew a conscience."

"Who are they?" She motioned to the man and boy beside him.

"The last of the line of the candlemaker. His crusade has lasted long enough."

"I do not understand."

"This is the one responsible for killing your brother," he said, nudging the bound man and smiling.

"How do you know of my brother?"

Jordan stepped closer to her, never taking his eyes from the man. "What is he talking about? What happened to Sirich?"

"No. It's Merek. He's... dead."

Jordan looked over at her. "How?"

"Neph here killed him," the man said. "Mistaken identity. The dagger was meant for another."

Ashaya walked closer. "How do you know?"

"I have tasted his memories."

"Who are you? And what is happening to me?"

"Ash, wait!" Jordan grabbed her arm. "What in the hell is going on here?"

Ash stopped and looked back at him. "It's alright. I must know."

"I was the first made."

Ashaya closed her eyes for a moment, then paced back and forth. She could hear the whispers in her head, in her blood. "Lucian."

He offered a slight bow.

She continued toward the stairs. Lucian's eyes shimmered in the darkness. He walked around the bound man and boy. "I thought I would give you the honor, the newest among us, to avenge your brother," he said with a smile.

She slowly ascended the stairs, her veins burning.

"Why would you kill my brother?" Ashaya's voice grew deeper. Neph said nothing, looking straight ahead.

"Where are your manners? Introduce yourself to the lady." Lucian forced the man to his knees with one hand on his shoulder. He held the squirming boy with the other hand.

"Please don't hurt him," the man finally spoke. He fought back tears. "It's alright, son. The Elder will protect us."

"I *am* the Elder," Lucian snapped.

The kneeling man looked at Ashaya. "I am Neph. I..."

Lucian grabbed him by the top of the head. "He and his boy are the last of a line that has played their game for nearly two millennia. This man killed your brother out of fear for what he was, for what he would become. What he does not know is he and his zealots live their lives based on a lie. His ancestor, who was the reeve of my fields, also wanted to be like us. They even passed down the same stupid name."

Neph tried to look up at him. "Blasphemy!"

"I assure you, candlemaker, he came to me in this very hall and asked for our… gift. He took his own life trying to show his loyalty to me. You kneel where the stone soaked up his cold blood. He wanted to be a god. His wife, Aza, and his son started your pathetic little group." Tears ran down Neph's face, dripping into his unkempt beard. The boy beside him still whimpered. "Your grandfathers never told you?" the man asked, laughing.

Ashaya looked back at Jordan, who stood watching. "Leave us."

"Ash, I won't—"

"Leave! Please, Jordan. I will be alright."

Jordan reluctantly walked backward then turned toward the entrance, sheathing his sword. She stepped in front of the man and kneeled. "Is it true? Did you kill my brother?"

"I did, with my son's blade," he said defiantly. "He would have become a monster like him!" Neph turned and spat toward Lucian.

Ashaya kneeled. "You mean a monster like me?"

Lucian leaned the man's head to the side. "Take your vengeance, girl. You will see the truth in his blood."

Ashaya looked up at Lucian, then back to Neph, his eyes still defiant. Ashaya felt as if her blood was boiling. Her brow lowered; her eyes narrowed. She felt the tightness in her top lip. She jolted forward and bit deep into the man's neck. The man screamed; Lucian held him in place. Ashaya did not stop. She couldn't. *The thirst. The lust.* Ashaya drank deep until she heard the man's heartbeat slow.

"No, please!" the boy said, sobbing. She did not quit until the man stopped struggling. She leaned back as he slid to the floor, closing her eyes and inhaling deeply. A barrage of quick visions came to her like before. A man in this very room, kneeling before Lucian with a bleeding arm. She saw others' entire lives flash before her. She saw her brother sleeping peacefully under the stars, a gleam of silver, and then embers floating to the sky. It all ended with seeing herself, the bloodlust in her own blue eyes, a sudden bite. She slowly opened her eyes.

The boy's screams and Lucian's laughter echoed in the damp hall. Ashaya took a deep breath and stood. She felt the warmth of the blood dripping from her chin. She looked down at the dead man laying beneath her.

She wiped her mouth on her sleeve. "What have I done?"

"You avenged your brother… *our* brother." Lucian walked around the boy. "Did you see, as I said you would?"

"Yes."

Lucian squatted in front of her. "I will leave it to you. What will you do about the boy?" He let the boy rush to his dead father, rocking back and forth over his body.

She looked at him and back at the blood on her sleeve. "It was his blade but his father's hand." She turned and walked away down the stairs. Lucian grabbed her arm. She could not pull away, even with her newfound strength.

"Easy, child. You are not your mother. Not yet."

"Let me go!"

Lucian released her. "I do apologize, my lady. We are on the same side, I assure you. We *are* the same."

Ashaya leaned down and snapped the ropes from the

boy's wrist with her bare hands. "We are nothing alike. Run to your mother. Go! Before I change my mind." The boy ran past her, out of the temple. She started to follow.

"Ashaya," Lucian said behind her. "You are going to leave him alive to continue this eternal game?"

"He is not his father. He can be the last candlemaker."

Chapter Thirty-Nine

Amari

The Middle Sea had been choppy during the entire voyage to Port Kutua. Amari had gone in search of the mysterious woman, leaving Abana at their childhood home with their grandfather. Abana did not understand what was happening or what was wrong with Sirich; neither did he. Amari rode through northern Ethorya. Snow capped the rounded mountains behind him, the remaining leaves shades of red and yellow crunching under the shoes of his horse as he passed. Geese flew overhead in their formations, heading south. Amari saw his breath and occasionally caught a shiver.

He had been to the Fang when he was a child, but he had not been this far north beyond the golden city of Gizani. He had passed the last small village hours ago.

Why would this woman live out here alone?

"I hope I am right about this," he mumbled to his horse. The horse only nickered.

Amari had made the turn west as the sun dropped below the horizon. The moons were bright already, the red moon much farther from the blue moon, a ghostly ring surrounding it. The road had ended a league back, and he continued on little more than an overgrown trail.

I have to be close, he thought. He saw the sea on both sides of him, and very few trees remained in the salty air. Like most Ethoryans, he had heard this tale many times as a boy, of an old warrior who had retired to solitude to meditate for the rest of her days.

"The Lady of the Rock," he mused, shaking his head. "What am I doing up here?"

The anguish in Sirich's eyes flashed in his mind. *Those blue eyes. What has he become? What can I do to help him?*

"You smell that?" He patted the horse's neck. "Smoke." Ahead, the trail vanished into the surrounding terrain. Boulders lay everywhere, and rocky stone cliffs rose on either side of him.

There. A small plume of smoke came from the top of the rockface ahead. He rode to what looked like a natural staircase of stones and dismounted his horse.

One large boulder had faded, red paint in the shape of a flower, perhaps. He ran his hand along the indistinct red glyph as he climbed.

He went up over a huge boulder then back down, a natural hidden opening below. "Hello?" his voice echoed in the entrance of the cavern. The stones here were shades of greys, browns, and greens, each color a small line like the rings of a downed tree.

"Hello? Is anyone here?"

Only his own, echoing voice answered.

He climbed down to the sands below and stopped, looking around the natural courtyard. He saw the flicker of light in the darkness of the cave. *This has to be it.*

Amari slowly walked deeper into the darkness. His hand found the hilt of his sword. "Hello? I mean no harm."

"No harm done," a voice said behind him.

He turned, drawing his sword halfway before stopping. A woman stood, holding a staff, almost silhouetted in the faint light behind her.

Only her eyes gleamed a deep blue.

"*Gonaun Gisg Vehundru, Gon Galmed Ormeddon Gonmevan?*"

"I'm sorry, I do not understand."

She approached. "What can I do for you?"

"Stay back!" He pulled his sword and pointed it at her. "Are you one of—"

"Yes." Her voice was now behind him.

He turned. The sword trembled in his hands.

"Of course, you already knew what I was, otherwise you would not have come here. Do not worry, I have already killed two today. I do not need a third."

"Please, I..."

The woman laughed. "I jest. Besides, it looks as if someone has already taken from you. We are not *all* monsters."

Amari touched the bandages on his neck. He took a deep breath and stepped out of his defensive stance.

The woman turned. "Come on. I thought someone may show up here eventually."

"So, it *is* true?" Amari lowered his sword and slowly followed.

"What may that be?" She approached the fire and sat cross-legged on a woven mat.

"You. The legend, I mean."

"There is always a grain of truth in every legend. What is it they call me again? The Lady of the Cave?"

"The rock. The Lady of the Rock." Amari stood across from her, still looking around.

"Such an original name," she said, smiling. "Please, sit. Now that you've calmed down, after so impolitely drawing your blade… How may I help you?"

"How did you know someone would come?"

"The wolves. They keep us… informed."

"The wolves?"

"Thade and his kind. But that is a story for another time."

Amari slowly sat and studied the woman for a moment. Beauty radiated from her. Long beaded hair lay over one shoulder. She wore traditional Gazi warrior attire—a ringed necklace covered her neck, a golden skull adorned one shoulder like armor, and she did not have much covering her breasts other than the traditional leather wrap that extended around her neck and behind her back. Beads decorated her bracers. She had laid down her staff beside her, a broken skull fitted on its top.

She met his eyes and offered a small smile. "So, who did this to you?"

Amari only sat staring. *I have never seen such…*

"Who did this to you?" she repeated.

"I apologize. I am Amari, by the way."

The woman ate from a bowl of nuts. "Yes, I know. So, Amari, can you answer my question?"

Amari took a deep breath. "Yes. I… that is why I'm here. My friend, Sirich of Vaegomar. He… bit me."

"Ah, the prince."

"You know of him?"

She smiled while chewing. "I told you—the wolves."

"A man with eyes like yours told him that he was born... well, like you."

The woman leaned back on her hands, her legs still crossed. "Nonsense. Only two have been born like me, over two thousand years ago. The rest of us..."

Amari continued, "A man named Ethan told Sirich that he knew his mother. That he would have become like her in time."

"What did this man look like? Let me guess... tall, dark hair, scars up to his neck, always wearing a smile?"

"Yes. You know him?"

"Of course I do. He is my brother. A blood brother, if you will. Always the mischievous one." The woman shook her head. "Promethial."

"Promethial? Named after the fire god of the thirteen?"

"He *is* of the thirteen," the woman laughed. "I told you, there is always a grain of truth, but only a grain. I told Val to kill him the first time. I told her I would gladly wipe that smirk from his face."

"So, if he's the..." Amari's eyes drifted toward the fire. "Who are *you*?"

"The original queen of the Gazi, of Ethorya."

Amari snapped his head back up. "*Gaziael?* The goddess of the earth? But how can this be..." *This is all insanity.* Amari sat there, shaking his head.

The woman laughed. "I told you, just a grain. The rest is merely exaggeration and religion. To this day, an ancient order of priests and priestesses try to serve us, spreading their gospel as if we are to return. We never left."

For a moment, only the small fire crackled through the cave. Amari finally found words. "So, you live here?"

"I choose to live as normal a life as possible. I hate rotting in the ground like the others, waiting to see if I ever wake again."

"I do not understand."

"The Crescent Isle. That's where the others sleep. Only two of us walk Aahsgoth at a time, as part of the covenant."

"Why sleep?"

"To bear immortality without insanity, I suppose. A gift and a curse. Forever is a long time."

"Why are you here, then?"

"I do not like dying." The woman stood. "I choose to face it. I stay here and wander among you. I love and I lose, over and over again."

"I'm sorry, I—"

"For what? Most would bow to Promethial and hope to receive the gift. Undoubtably some have. If he turned your friend, something is afoot." She paused and looked up at the ceiling. "The promise of eternity without sickness, inhuman strength, and all that comes with it. They would throw away the light, their families, the meaning of life… just for a taste."

Amari took in her words, the fire reflecting in her eyes.

"Go to your friend. It's too late to reverse what has happened, but Promethial must want more… Wait! Sirich is the son of William, the original line of Val." The woman stood. "Lucian. Only Val can wake him, unless… she didn't leave Sirich behind. She left…"

"Ash and Merek?" Amari finished her thought. "What in the hell is going on?"

"Go to your friend. Keep in his ear. Do not let Promethial corrupt him."

"What will you do?"

"I will go to Thade. Only he can wake Valkarial. Unless

he already has. Either way, I will kill Promethial myself. His schemes are old, and he will never stop."

Amari stood. "Why are you helping me?"

"I suppose that's what so-called goddesses do."

Amari smiled. "How can you stop him?"

"I am much older. He believes he was the second made, but his belief is misplaced. Now go. I must wait until—"

"Yes, the sun must set." Amari turned toward the entrance. "Amari."

"Yes, my lady?"

"Go to the tip of the Fang. There is a small village there. A man named Abdu will take you and your horse across the sea to Vaegomar. Tell him I sent you. You must get to Wolfpine quickly."

Amari nodded. "Where will I find you?"

"You will not. I will find *you*."

Chapter Forty

Theodor

Aethial had been right. The room under the waterfall held another secret. Another, much larger room behind it had been there the entire time, the small entrance sealed with stone. Once the bookshelf was removed, it was clear that newer stone had been used.

Overlord Aethon had kept his word to open the vaults and reveal the truth, although he'd shown only a select few. Now he walked around as if he were Theodor's age. Every book, scroll, and loose piece of ancient parchment in this room had been written in this Vedician language. And it seemed as if he were eager to read them all. He had told Theo to recruit a few of his trusted friends to copy the texts. Theodor, Ridley, Ian, Sam, and the others had all been busy scribing. The old books were in bad shape, often barely legible.

"Can you believe all this?" Ridley slid closer to him. "If I hadn't seen it with my own eyes, I wouldn't…" She lowered her voice. "Her blood healed him. How?"

"Because she let it cool, according to what your grandfather said. Otherwise, he would have—"

"Would you two please shut up? Go to your quarters already."

Ridley turned and slapped his arm. "Shut up, Sam."

Theodor kept reading. He, along with the others, had figured out some of the phonetics based off the few words the woman had spoken, along with the translations he had made, referencing poetry with rhyming words. He had looked into how the Common Tongue had been influenced by the Old Tongue by identifying what those ancient words had evolved into.

"The language of the gods," he mumbled.

Ridley dipped her quill into the inkwell. "What about it?"

"Now we know why that era is called the Age of Gods. People worshipped them."

"Some still do."

"I suppose the prospect of death is a good motivator."

"What do you mean?"

"It says here that dragon's blood was more valuable than gold. Men hunted them. But all the stories are lies. They were not the terrors of the skies that the singers would have us believe."

Theodor leaned back, rubbing his eyes and suppressing a yawn. "As much as I love this, I need to go."

"Where?"

"Wolfpine. My father should have been—"

"I'm sure he's alright, Theo." Ridley put her quill down and turned to him. "But I understand. Can I come with you?"

"Do you think the overlord would let you?"

"Of course," the overlord said, coming up behind them. "Go, Theodor. Go to your father. I have no doubt Galen would love to hear of this newfound knowledge. Bring him back to Ashbourne. We have much to discuss. The council will decide if all of this should be shared beyond this room."

Theodor stood and slid his chair in, loudly scraping like a horn rubbing across the stone. "Thank you, my lord. I am sorry for what you had to go through, I just—"

"Nonsense," the overlord interrupted. "You did nothing wrong. Besides, it was a blessing from the gods."

Ridley stood and smiled. "Literally."

All three laughed. "All of this is quite unbelievable." Theo looked around the room at the others. "I will go, then. It looks like you have plenty of help."

"And we will have more. Now go." The old man nodded and walked away.

Ridley took his hand and led him up the stairs. "Let's go! I've never seen Wolfpine."

They crossed the yards, heading to Theodor's quarters. "I'll meet you there, then we will go to the docks. I just need to grab some things."

"I will stop by the kitchens and steal us some food," she said with a slight smile. He smiled in return as he watched her run toward the building down from his.

Theodor grabbed his pack from his quarters, quickly stuffing it with supplies. He would not need much; this would be a quick trip by sea. He went to his desk and retrieved the small sack of coins and shook it. By the way it jingled, he figured he only had a few silver pieces among mostly coppers.

On his desk sat the copy of the foretelling. He hoped his father had made sense of it, if it meant anything at all. A smile came to him, picturing his father's face. Theodor was a man grown now, and he hoped his father would be proud.

Ridley leaned into his room. "Ready?"

"I think so. Are you?"

Ridley dropped her bag and walked over to him, looking up into his eyes. His face grew warm, his stomach twisting, his heart suddenly racing, ready to leap from his chest. She put her hands on his arms and stood on her toes to kiss his cheek.

Theodor stood there frozen, looking at her smile. He was finally able to meet her eyes, then her lips. He leaned down.

"Theo!" Sam's voice rang in his ears.

"What, Sam?" His eyes must have rolled into the back of his head. Ridley did not seem to care; she still looked up at him.

"A corvid came, you got a letter."

"From?"

"I don't know. It has the order's seal, but your name on it."

Theodor took the rolled note. Sam was right, it had the wax seal of the Order of Preceptors. His name was written below it. He broke the seal and began to read.

"So, what does it say?" Sam asked.

"Nothing that matters to you, Sam."

Ridley looked back at his sharp words. For a moment there was only silence.

"Theo, are you alright?" Ridley asked. "Theo?"

Theodor dropped the letter to the floor. He slowly stumbled around his desk and almost fell into his chair as tears welled in his eyes.

Chapter Forty-One

Ashaya

Ashaya lay on her bedroll, staring up at the stars through the tops of the trees. She and the others had made it back to Water's Edge. The wounded men had taken all the beds in the inn, and the rest crowded an old barn. She made camp in the woods just behind it. Mitch lay beside her, the wrapping on his side stained red. Jordan lay across from them, lightly snoring. They would take the ships to Capeton at first light.

Has Sirich made it home safely? Has he heard the news of Father? He might be out here looking for me. Tears leaked from her eyes. She could see her father lying there, the silver arrow in his chest. She looked over at Mitch. The wound smelled now, a sweetness through the rot, and his forehead glistened with fever in the firelight.

"Ash…" the familiar whisper came again.

"Leave me alone." She sat up. Jordan moved but did not wake.

"Ashaya, come to me."

She stood and walked deeper into the wood. "Who are you?" She looked around, hoping no one saw her talking to the trees.

"Come."

"Come where? What do you want?"

"The isle…"

Somehow, she knew which one. "The Crescent Isle is far south of here."

"Run."

"Run? Just take a leisurely stroll for a few hundred leagues?"

"Run… like the wind."

Ashaya stopped. She realized she could see as if it were day. Red auras surrounded every living thing near her. She heard every insect that crawled, every snake that slithered. She could even focus and hear the men breathing in the camp behind her. She started to walk again. Then faster. She picked up her pace until she was running.

It happened again. The world around her slowed.

Trees passed her as if they were running the other way. She had time to dodge limbs and avoid holes and jump boulders. She pushed harder and the trees blurred past her. She stopped and stood at the water's edge. She turned and looked behind her—a wake of shadow faded in the breeze.

"How is this…"

She looked ahead. The isle lay right across the water in front of her. She backed up a few steps and ran forward again, leaping over the water and landing with a roll. She saw she had landed some forty yards inland. She stood and looked around.

The weeping trees, the boulders ahead. *I have been here before.* She followed the stone path she had seen in her dreams. She came to the round room where she felt like she had stood in another life.

"Do you see? That was easy," a woman's voice echoed from the entrance.

"Who are you?"

"The darkness, I suppose." The woman appeared. First, Ashaya saw her eyes as she walked from the doorway. She was tall with long black hair and fair skin. She wore strange clothing, her neck covered in bound leather extending over her shoulders. Various straps and buckles joined the thick shoulder piece to the tight bodice, all positioned over a matching leather undershirt. Everything was black, including her leather trousers and high-laced boots. The woman walked toward Ashaya and circled her.

"Do I know you? Are you familiar to me?"

"I should hope so. But first—do you know what you are?" she asked with a smile, looking out of the corners of her eyes.

"What is happening to me?"

"Do you know what you are?" the woman repeated.

"No, but I suppose you are here to tell me." Ashaya caught a scent and sniffed the air.

A loud growl came from behind her. Ashaya turned and reached for her sword. She had left it beside her bedroll. The largest wolf she had ever seen stalked toward them. It stood almost as tall as them on its four legs, all black with a white tip on its tail, its eyes a deep blue.

"A white tip? I thought they were long extinct." Ashaya held her hand out and moved backwards. The woman looked unfazed, standing still.

"It is alright, my child. It's only Thade. It is time you learned the truth. All of it."

Ashaya looked over at the woman. "Thade?"

The woman did not respond. Ashaya turned back to the large beast. It stopped and sat. The wolf started to growl, and chunks of fur fell from its body. Its nose shortened, and its howl was the most violent she had ever heard. If pain had a sound, this was it. Its body reshaped, and she winced at the sound of bones cracking. Its claws fell to the stone floor, its ears lowered and rounded, its large teeth shortened as it took the shape of a man. His growl became a deep grunt. Where the wolf had stood, a naked man kneeled, dripping with sweat and beathing heavily, his hands on the cold stone.

"My brother," the woman said.

Ashaya stood still, her mouth agape. The man looked up and ran his hands through his wet black hair and beard. Ash noticed the tattoos covering both arms. "Can I do that?" she asked.

"No, I'm afraid not," the woman smiled. "Thade is... something else. A story for another time, perhaps."

The naked man stood and looked at Ashaya. "I'm sorry to frighten you, my lady. But the time has come for you to know the truth of what you are. What *we* are."

"You're the man from Carolyn's place. You followed me?"

"I did, and I took your supper once. I do apologize for that. The thirst is sometimes... insatiable. I did not mean to frighten you. You must learn to anticipate it, as well."

"Wait, just wait." Her hand shot out toward him. Ashaya looked between him and the woman as she paced the room. "Alright, what are you? What am *I*?"

The woman turned to her. "We have been called many things. Monsters, gods, bloodkin. I would say 'dragon' is the most accurate term in the Common Tongue."

Ashaya looked up. "Dragons? They died out centuries ago."

"Yes, but their gifts were passed on—and their weaknesses. Two humans acquired these traits through blood magic. Others have been given this gift since."

"Gift?"

"'Curse' would do just as well," the woman continued. "Dragons lived for an eternity, as long as they fed. They ruled the night, carrying the power of the sun in their throats. The ancient ones, our ancestors, the Vedicians... they believed there were two suns in the sky, just as there are two moons. Some say the first dragons ate one, and the sun god cursed them by giving them dominion over the night, never to see the sun again. Hyperbole, I am sure. Men found that they were affected by silver, and eventually hunted them down using sheer numbers. I am sure some were a scourge to humans, but they were not the monsters your history books say they were."

Ashaya stood silent for a moment. "Who were they? The two that you say—"

"You're looking at them. Thade and I," she interrupted, as if she had anticipated the question. "You see, we changed over time—as you have. We came of age. We inherited their gifts... and their curse." She stared at the blue moon. "Our mother was dying. My father found a way to try and save her before she birthed us. The blood of the last dragon."

"How do you know all of this?"

"I remember." The woman looked out into the night. "History, it seems, has mixed accounts of our existence. Angels to some, demons to others."

Ash lowered her head, blowing hair out of her eyes. "What does this have to do with me?"

"You and your brother were the first born with this affliction in over two thousand years." The woman turned back to her. "But it is different this time. *You* are different."

"How am I different?"

"You gained our strengths, but none of our weaknesses. You can walk in the sun, and silver will not harm you."

Ashaya squinted her eyes. "I do not understand."

"You, Ashaya. You are the daughter of the dragon. *My* daughter. When I left Wolfpine and your father almost two decades ago, I left behind you and your brother, Merek."

"Val? *The* Val?" Ash's voice sank to a whisper. "Mother?"

"Yes."

Ashaya shook her head. "Father spoke of you often. He told me stories." Ashaya backed up against the wall and slid down the stone. "Why would you leave him, leave us? Why is this happening to me?" She covered her face with both hands.

The woman kneeled in front of her. "I thought it better at the time that you and your brother not know of me, so that I would not have to watch you grow old and die. I did not know what you were. It turns out the gods have a sense of irony."

Silence fell over the stone room as the woman sat beside her. "I kept watch over you for a few years, until I could no longer bear it. I came here—as I have hundreds of times—to sleep. To forget."

Thade spoke up. "I know it is a bit... overwhelming."

"A bit?" Ashaya snapped.

"Quite a bit," he replied. "We are here to help you with whatever your destiny is. If there is such a thing."

"What could it be? In the last few weeks, I have run from home, killed, lost my brother, my father, and now I am some kind of monster! What else would destiny ask of me?"

Val put her hand on Ashaya's shoulder. "There's more."

"How could there be more?"

"It is your brother, Sirich."

Ashaya snapped her head up. "Is he alright? Tell me he's alright."

"He is, for now, but he's been turned."

"Turned?"

"Yes, made like us by another. A man named Promethial."

"Promethial, the god of fire?" Ashaya could do nothing but laugh. "First you tell me of blood monsters, and now *gods* are walking Aahsgoth?"

Val and Thade exchanged a glance. "Men made us gods, truths were twisted over time, legends were born."

Ashaya rolled her eyes. "So, what about Sirich?"

"Promethial snuck into his room and turned him."

"How do you know? Why?"

"Thade and his pack keep an eye on things, and I confirmed it through Promethial's blood memories."

"Why Sirich?"

"Promethial thought he was my son."

"What does he want?"

"What he has always wanted—chaos, power. He wanted him to wake another I had banished."

Ashaya already knew. "Lucian."

"Yes. You will start to remember. When you taste blood, you see only truth. Promethial promised Sirich the world, only so he could hand it to Lucian. They did not stick to our covenant."

"And what was that?"

"To stay in the shadows, to stay out of human affairs. We once ruled our various clans, but for our own survival, I changed all of that. Lucian and Promethial want to live as they once did, and their own legend went to their heads." Val walked back to her. "Lucian will create a small army like us. He will go to Wolfpine when Promethial tells him of this new king."

Ashaya felt it coming. She leaned over and retched on the stone. She spat and tried to breathe. When she finally caught her breath, she asked, "So, what now?"

"You must go to Sirich. Promethial will corrupt him. He's already started."

Ashaya stood and ran her hands through her hair. "I will go back with the others. We are going home."

Thade stepped forward. "What of your friend? The boy."

"Mitch?"

"Yes. He was wounded. He doesn't look well."

"If we can get home quickly, Galen can help him."

Val looked at Thade. "He cannot, but *you* can, Ashaya."

"How? Wave a wand over his wound?"

"Your blood."

Ashaya rolled her eyes. "Of course. I'll just give him some blood, then."

"Yes, but you must let it cool."

"Or what?"

"He will be turned. The gift is yours to give, but he must have a choice. He must understand the consequences."

"So, let me get this straight. Cool blood will heal him, but straight from the tap, and he turns into a monster?"

"Well, as you so eloquently put it... yes." Val smiled along with Thade.

"I think she's getting it."

Ashaya looked up at the moons, farther apart, the trees that swayed in the breeze around them, the double shadows that crossed and flickered.

"Wait... I could have saved my father?"

"Perhaps, but you can't change the past." Val walked over beside her and put her arm around her.

Ashaya's face grew warm. *Father.* "Why didn't you tell me? With your damn whispering!"

"Ashaya, I—"

"Get off me!" Ashaya threw Val's arm off. "You can't just show up, tell me you're my mother, tell me all of these strange things, and expect me to just... run into your arms and pretend everything will be alright."

"You are right, Ashaya." Val started to walk away. "Come, brother. She has a lot to process."

Thade followed her. He stopped and glanced back at Ashaya. "We are trying to help. This *is* what you are. And none of this has been easy for her." He nodded toward the woman. "Go home. Talk to your brother." He walked toward Val, who waited in the distance.

Ashaya stood quietly and watched them walk away. The breeze whistled through the stone room. She wiped the tears away with her sleeve and called out, "Valkarial!"

The woman stopped and turned. "Yes?"

"What will you do, then?"

"It is time for me to go home as well."

Chapter
Forty-Two

Sirich

The towers of Wolfpine rose over the distant trees. Promethial walked behind him. The moonlight reflected high on the queen's tower.

"Home sweet home," Sirich mumbled. They had stowed away on a small fishing boat before sunrise the day before. He could feel the hunger.

Promethial caught up to him. "What will you do first, my lord?"

"*Lord?*"

"Ah, yes. King, it is. So, what will it be, then?"

"I do not know. First figure out how to become king, perhaps?" Sirich shook his head. "What will I do? Just walk in and proclaim myself the king?"

"Yes, that is exactly what you do. Who would oppose you?"

"My father. I... I will speak with him."

"Your father?"

"Yes, you know, my sire."

"Your sire rode south for your sister, remember?"

Sirich stopped. "No, I do not remember. You only told me that Ashaya rode south."

"Well, then, your father rode south. Which makes it easier for you, I suppose."

Sirich just stared at him. He rolled his eyes, then turned to keep walking through the market. Most of the vendors had left by now, but a few people still wandered. "I need to... eat."

"Take your pick. Look at them and choose." Promethial's usual grin had returned since they had left the isle.

Sirich stopped once again. "I cannot..." He looked around. "I cannot just start... killing people," he whispered.

"Who said you have to kill them? You do not have to bleed them dry. As a matter of fact..." Promethial pointed over his shoulder. "*She* would be willing. To her and the group she represents, it would be an honor."

Sirich turned and saw a woman at the crossroads, standing in the back of a wagon. A long black robe fluttered in the breeze as she spoke to passersby. He noticed the tattoo of the lotus on her wrist and looked over to Promethial. "Who is she?"

"Part of an ancient order of familiars. They used to hide in the shadows, do our bidding, even offer sacrifices in the old days. As of late, they send out these so-called priests and priestesses. I suppose their membership is running low."

They approached the woman. She continued to speak to anyone that passed. "*Gisgnagraph gedmed galfam gonur vehmedtalgraph!*"

Sirich approached her and stopped before her. "*Gon-graphfam gisgnagraphgon gongonur.* Yes... they will."

"Very nice! You are starting to remember!" Promethial patted him on the back. "Such a beautiful tongue, is it not?"

The woman looked down with wide eyes. "Are you..."

"Yes." Sirich reached for her hand. "Please, come with me."

The woman looked around and slowly reached for his hand, stepping down from the wagon. "My lord, I...?"

Sirich leaned in close to look at her, and she stumbled backwards.

"Do you not like his eyes?" Promethial laughed. "You preach of us, yet when you see us, do you not believe?"

"Yes, my lord, I just... they tell me to... but I have never..."

"Please come, my lady. I mean you no harm." Sirich took her arm in his. "Accompany me to my castle." The woman put on a fearful smile and walked with him. Sirich looked over at Promethial. "I could get used to this."

Sirich approached the outer gates; the guards were closing them for the night. "Wait."

"Lord Sirich, my apologies," said one of the guards. "Open the gates!" he yelled back at the others.

"Thank you, Gorban," Sirich said.

"It's Goran, my lord."

"Pardon?"

"My name... it's Goran, my lord."

"I do apologize, Goran. It's been a long... day. I'm sure you will serve me well."

"Yes, my lord." He stepped out of the way as they passed.

They made their way through the outer yards into the main courtyard, the dogs all growling and barking before fleeing as they approached. Sirich led the woman into the great hall. The hall was quiet; only the usual guards were here.

"There she is. A chair fit for a king," Promethial remarked.

Sirich led the woman over to the old stone chair. He let her go and walked around behind it, rubbing his hands along its stone ridges, outlining the sigil of his house. *So many tales. From my father to his father and the one before him.* Galen had told him the story of Edwyn the Bold, who had gone to the large island, that you now call Nahmana, alone after one of its royal sons had thought to proclaim independence. He challenged the would-be king to a duel in front of his palace, and the Nahmen clan leader thought it so daring, he changed his mind. The supposed first Blacksun king, Jameson, who had taken the surname and ruled over the first united clans. *It's all true.*

"A flower?" he mumbled to himself looking at the old stone chair.

He slowly sat, leaned back, and laid his arms on the arm-rests, gripping the ends in the shape of a beast's closed hand.

"So, how does it feel?" Promethial asked.

"Uncomfortable and cold. What do you think, my lady?"

The priestess kneeled. "It fits you well, my lord."

Sirich sat for a moment and looked around the hall. The banners that hung here now had new meaning to him. Heath Promen entered from the back of the hall, and his daughter Elya followed. Their footsteps echoed from the walls until he looked up and slowed down, seeing Sirich.

He hesitated. "My lord... Sirich? You have returned."

"Ah, Heath Promen, Lord of Mudstone, high council member. Why are you still here? The council should have adjourned a fortnight ago or more. You seem a bit surprised to see me?"

Promen shifted his eyes to Promethial, who walked up beside Sirich. "No, my lord. I just thought that—"

"Hello again, Heath," Promethial nodded. "And you, Lady Elya."

"You two know each other?" Sirich turned to Promethial.

Promethial leaned down to whisper in Sirich's ear. "This man conspires against you and your father."

"How so?"

"Ask him." Promethial's eyes shifted up to the man and his daughter, before he stood and walked toward the doors.

Sirich stood. "And where are *you* going?"

"I have business to attend to. As do you." His footsteps echoed in the hall as he left the room.

Sirich sat again, resting his chin on his knuckles. The apprentice to Galen walked into the hall, approaching the chair. "The beautiful... Nivara, is that right?"

"Yes. Thank you, my lord. I heard you had returned."

"Indeed. Are you happy to see me?" Sirich motioned toward Heath. "Lord Promen here seems a bit... uneasy."

"Yes, my lord. I need to speak with you," Nivara said, avoiding Heath's gaze.

Heath stepped forward. "I bid you farewell. I need to prepare my things. I will be returning to Alarya immediately." He took Elya's arm and walked back toward the doors.

"Not so fast, my lord. Be the first to know, and your beautiful daughter, that there will be a few changes in Wolfpine. In all of Aahsgoth, for that matter." Sirich turned back to Nivara. "We will speak in time. Perhaps tonight, in my quarters? For now, I need to speak to Galen. Go get the old man."

"My lord, that's what I wanted to speak with you about. Galen."

Heath Promen turned again to leave. "Come, daughter."

"Just a moment, my lord. I told you to stay," Sirich said, holding his hand up.

"I am a council member, and you are not the prince. I will have my leave."

"Elya, are you so eager to leave?"

She looked down. "Yes, my lord. I must return with my father," she said in a soft voice, avoiding eye contact.

"Really, after all those nights together? Even talk of marriage?" *The lying whore.* She did not respond.

"Come, Elya, we are going home," Heath said.

Sirich moved like the wind, now standing in front of him. "You will stay, as I commanded."

Heath and Elya stopped where they stood, both of them wide-eyed and speechless. Heath raised his hand. "Guards, please escort me and my daughter to the stables. I am not on trial for a crime. I am a member of the council."

Sirich looked over at the guards; they stared at one another but did not respond to the man, the whites of their eyes still wide beneath their helms.

"There will be no more council. Now sit." Sirich pointed to one of the tables in front of the chair. They slowly walked over and sat. Sirich sat once again, eyeing the priestess, who was still on her knees. Nivara was walking backward, reaching for the table behind her. "Now what did you have to say that was so urgent?"

"My lord I... I wanted to tell you of... about Master Galen."

"Yes, speak up."

"Galen is dead."

Sirich leaned back and rubbed his eyes. He took a deep breath. For a few moments, no one said anything. *Old Man Horseshoe.* Sirich stood and paced around the closest table before grabbing it and flipping it. It flew over a few others and landed near the back of the hall. One leg remained; the others dangled like splinters. Heath Promen would not look up.

"How?" Sirich asked in a near whisper.

"I found him at the bottom of the stairs going to his quarters." Nivara looked down and paused. "My lord, may I speak to you alone?" She glanced over at Heath and Elya.

Sirich sighed deeply. No one would look at him. "Guards, escort Lord Promen and his daughter to his quarters and do not let them leave."

Two guards walked to them, spears in hand. Lord Promen and his daughter stood and went with them. Promen cursed under his breath as they were led away.

"Priestess, go to my chambers and wait for me."

"Where are your chambers?"

He nodded at another guard, who came and escorted the priestess away. The woman looked back at him with a slight smile. They waited for the woman to leave.

"What happened to him?" Sirich spoke in a soft voice.

Nivara sat on the edge of the table. "I found him at the bottom of the stairs, as I said, the ones closest to his chambers."

"So, the old man fell?"

"Yes, but I think it was something else."

"What do you mean?"

"He had no head injuries, yet his nose and ears had bled, and his blood was too... thin. In Ashbourne, I have studied such things as he did. Perhaps he had taken something, I don't—"

"Poison?" Sirich interrupted.

"Perhaps. But who would..."

Tears welled in his eyes. "I will get to the truth of this. Whatever I have become, he deserved no such thing. Where is he now?"

"In the cellar. Lord Promen had wanted him laid to a pyre that day, but I wanted to wait for William to return."

"Do the Serwyns burn their dead or bury them?" Sirich asked.

"They typically have a funeral pyre."

"Burn him, then."

"Do you not want to see him first, my lord?"

"No need. I will get the truth."

"Yes, my lord," Nivara said hesitantly. She walked away as Sirich listened to her heartbeat racing.

Sirich walked to the staircase and up to the second floor. He knew where Galen had lain. The area had been scrubbed clean, the stone darker, but he could still smell the blood. He continued to Galen's quarters.

He opened the door and looked around. He could almost imagine the old man sitting there at his desk. Piles of parchment littered it, as usual. The leather bag that lay on the featherbed looked to be full. He walked around to the back of Galen's desk and sat. He put his elbows on the desk and covered his face, trying to fight back tears, clearing his nose repeatedly. They had had many talks here, Galen's voice echoing in his mind. All of the advice and lessons came back to him.

He exhaled and stood, turning to the dusty shelves behind him. Glass bottles of herbs and potions sat unorganized, as usual. He picked up a few and looked at them. *How did Old Man Horseshoe know what was what?* He saw a familiar green bottle. *Oil of hemlock... he always said too much was...* Sirich picked up the bottle. A strong sweetness radiated from it. He set the bottle down and sniffed the air. Another faint sweetness filled the room that he had not noticed through his runny nose.

"Elya."

His face flushed. He turned and walked from the room. He would know the truth. He walked toward the northern staircase to Promen's quarters. He was about to pass his own room.

"My lord? Are you coming?" Seductive eyes peeked out of his doorway. The priestess wore a devilish grin. He stopped when she left the door slightly open.

He paced the hallway, hesitating. He felt his hunger growing. *Promen can wait.* He walked in. The woman lay in his bed, naked and waiting.

He closed the door behind him.

Chapter Forty-Three

Amari

The sun hung low, and Amari could see the towers above the tree line ahead. He had not been to Wolfpine since before his father had died. He missed it there. He could almost see the past, when he and Sirich would jump out and scare the other children. Ash would always chase Sirich down to slap him, but never Amari. She thought he had put Amari up to it, and he had. Most of the time.

Amari would always chase away the boys who picked on Ash; he had been as much of a brother to her as Sirich and Merek. William would come down to the yards and personally train with them. He was a master swordsman, and Amari had never felt out of place. William had looked at him like a third son, and he would, on occasion, call William "uncle."

His ride had been easy, only a little more than a day after

the quick trip from the Fang. Gaziael had been right. Amari had asked the man for passage, and upon hearing her name, he had taken Amari straight to his boat.

Amari rode through the mostly abandoned market. Sweat beaded on his forehead, and butterflies tickled his gut. He let go of his horse's reins for a moment and held his hand out, watching it tremble. His other hand gripped the hilt of his sword. He had not been to Wolfpine since before his father died—and never to confront his friend who had become something from a fairytale.

What will I say? he thought.

Amari approached the southern gates. The sun shone brightly ahead, wrapping around the northern towers as it set. He remembered the lively markets of summer; now that autumn was settling in, he only passed a few farmers and their wagons carrying the last of their grains. He brought his horse down to a trot as he got closer to the gates.

Amari slowed his horse to a stop and dismounted, walking him through the open gates. One of the guards stared at him through his helm and tilted his head.

"Amari?" The man leaned his spear against the wall and took off his helm.

Amari stopped and looked closer. "Yes, and you are?"

"Goran. Do you not remember me?"

"Oh yes, Goran! Hello, my friend!" The man came over and reached for his forearm. Amari smiled politely and returned the gesture, patting him on the shoulder.

"How have you been? Good to see you back in Wolfpine."

"I am doing... alright, I suppose. Good to be back, I think." Amari had played with many people here as a child, but he did not recognize the man. "So, Goran, you are all grown. Guarding the castle now."

"Yes, my lord. Just doing my duty."

"Say, have you seen Sirich, by chance?"

"Yes, my lord. He came in a few nights ago. He's in there somewhere. I haven't seen him since he got back. He stays inside a lot."

"Alright. Well, if you will excuse me, I have business with him and William."

"Oh, William isn't here. He rode south."

"Is that so? Well then, good to see you. I'll be on my way."

"Good to see you, Amari." The man put his helm back on and returned to his post.

Amari led his horse to the stables and handed him off to a stable boy. *Great*, he thought. *I wanted to see William first, to find out if he knew what the hell was going on.* He shook his head.

He stopped in the outer courtyard and looked upon the old castle. He managed a smile, thinking back to his younger days here. Even with all that had happened recently, pleasant memories found a way to reveal themselves. He imagined himself as a child still, running around the courtyard with sticks, the laughter coming back to him immediately. Freshly cut firewood filled the air, and the warmth of the sun through the cool breeze made him momentarily forget why he was here.

When reality came flooding back, he remembered he was in the middle of a nightmare where he had to go confront the monster. He continued toward the great hall.

As he made his way through the inner yards and walked inside, only guards stood around the room. "Excuse me, have you seen Sirich?"

"The king is in the cellars, I believe," one of the guards responded.

"The *king*?"

"Yes, my lord... I think. I saw him go down before dawn."

What has he done? "Am I too late?" Amari mumbled.

He shook his head and walked toward the stairs at the front of the hall. He climbed down the narrow, winding stairway. He had not been down here since he was a boy. He and Sirich would come peek at prisoners in their cells in the dungeons below the cellars. The air was damp down here, and the flames flickered low in the wall sconces.

"Siri?" His own voice echoed back to him. "Are you down here?"

He walked down the dim hallway, barrels of wine and bags of grain filling the alcoves on either side. "Siri?" His hand moved to the hilt of his sword. He grabbed a torch from the wall and entered the dark room at the end of the hallway. He swung the torch around, but the room seemed to be empty.

"Doc?" Sirich sat on the floor against the wall in the darkness, his arms resting on his knees, his head hanging low.

"Siri?" Amari clutched the hilt of his sword and exposed the blade.

"I will not hurt you, Doc. Not again."

"How can I be sure?"

I didn't mean it. I... I could not control it."

Amari stood in the doorway for a moment, unsure.

"I am sorry, old friend," Sirich's voice was laced with genuine pain.

"I know, I know." Amari took a deep breath, a relieving sigh. He kneeled down in front of Sirich. "Can we go speak? Maybe in a place a bit more..."

"I cannot. The sun still shows."

"Right, the sun."

"How do you know?"

"I did not know what to do. So, I looked into it." Amari slid down the stone wall across from Sirich. "And you are no monster, Sirich. *He* may be, but not you."

"How would you know?"

"I've met another like you."

"So you know the truth." Sirich looked up. "There are others, as he said. Gods." Sirich chuckled slightly.

"Where is he? Promethial?"

"Do not worry. He is gone. He left days ago. I am sure he is plotting some chaos. The next time I see him…" His voice trailed off.

"I do not know what I know. It's all a bit much." Amari paused and laid the torch on the floor between them. "I know he's a lying bastard. I know he used you for—"

"The old man is dead." Sirich never lifted his head.

"Who? William?"

"Galen."

Amari sighed and leaned his head back. "How?"

"Heath Promen. Seems a lot of people used me."

"Murdered? *Galen?*"

"Yes, I will find out why soon enough."

"Where is Promen now?"

"He and his daughter are in a cell below us. I had him moved from his quarters. I wanted to wait until Father arrived, but I must accept who I am, what I am."

"A guard called you 'king.'"

"You do not think I deserve it?"

"Siri, we have talked about this. William is trying to better Aahsgoth. You cannot simply call yourself a king. There is a ruling council. Sure, you would have made a good king, but the changes your father is making will, in the long run, be a good thing." Amari watched him before continuing. "You have to let that go."

"Perhaps, perhaps not. I will talk to him when he returns."

"From?"

"He rode south to find Ash and Merek."

"Did you not find her?"

"Promethial assured me she was alright."

"He assured you of a lot of things."

Sirich looked up, running his hands through his hair, his blue eyes glistening in the firelight. For a moment, Amari only heard the dripping of water somewhere in the darkness. "So, what now?"

"I will speak to them when they return. I will try to make Father understand. People need a clear leader, not some local lord—"

"Our father is dead." Ashaya stood in the doorway, her eyes gleaming blue.

Chapter Forty-Four

Ashaya

irich looked up, his mouth popping open. He stood slowly, exchanging a quick look with Amari before focusing on Ashaya.

Amari walked over and hugged her. "Ash, good to see you, even under these circumstances. I'm sorry to hear about William."

She returned the hug and laid her head on his chest. She had always felt safe with Amari nearby. He had always been a voice of strength and reason. "I am glad you are here, Doc." She stepped back and looked to Sirich. "Brother?" He paced around the room, his hands on his head. "Siri?"

Sirich walked over to her and gently grabbed her upper arms. "Ash?"

"Yes, Siri, it's me."

Tears streamed down his face. He leaned down and gently kissed her forehead. "Do you know of our brother, Merek?"

Ashaya looked down at the cold stone. "Yes." Sirich hugged her. They stood there in each other's arms for a moment. Sirich stepped back and gently lifted her chin to look at her. "Your eyes. Your hair."

"Yes, we need to speak."

Ashaya reached for his shoulders to hold him, but this time he pushed back. Within the blink of an eye, he was gone, her hair ruffled in his wake. She looked at Amari, regaining his balance, his dagger in hand. "So, he is a—"

"Yes. And from what I understand, you are, too."

"Yes. But how does Sirich have this affliction? He is my half-brother, but Merek and I..."

"Promethial."

"So she was right."

Amari stepped closer. "Who was right?"

"My mother."

"Your mother? Ash, I thought—"

A voice echoed in the hallway behind them. "I have no reason to lie."

Amari pulled his sword halfway out of the sheath and stepped in front of Ashaya.

"It is alright, Doc. This is Val. She is... my mother." Amari slid his sword back into its place, and Ashaya laughed softly. "Besides, that would do you no justice, I do not think."

"No," Val said. "But no need. I mean you no harm."

"What the hell is going on here? This is a bad dream that I cannot awaken from," Amari said, looking behind Val. Thade followed her. "Let me guess—Thurel, the god of lightning, since every bullshit tale we heard as children seems to be coming true lately."

Val laughed. "Thurel is sleeping. This is my brother, Thade."

"Hello, Amari Docksider, from the line of Gaziael," Thade answered.

"Thade?" Amari asked. "I cannot say I have heard of that one. Which god are you?"

"I am no god."

Val reached out to Amari. "Nice to meet you."

Amari looked down and took her hand slowly. "And you, my lady. I think."

Val smiled and turned to Ashaya. "Go to Sirich. He needs to know everything."

"Even *I* do not know everything," Ashaya replied.

"Go to your brother, Ash. Time is short, and he is on the way, no doubt."

"Promethial?" Amari asked.

Val turned to him. "Lucian."

"Of course." Amari rolled his eyes. "I think it is time for me to go home."

"No, you must help your friend. He needs you, both of you." Val looked between them.

"I'll find him. Wait for us in the main hall, Doc," Ashaya told Amari. She walked past them toward the winding stairs.

She investigated the main hall, but Sirich was not there. She nodded at Jordan, who was taking Mitch up to one of Galen's apprentices to clean his wound. Mitch looked over, pale and with his eyes half-closed.

Ashaya walked to the old stone chair and sniffed the air. She could smell Sirich's scent. She followed it to the back of the hall and into the stairwell. She continued up to the top floor where their quarters were. She walked to her door and put her hand on it. If only she could lay down in her feather bed, go to sleep, and wake up free from this nightmare.

"Ash?"

Ash jumped and turned. "My gods!"

Clara stepped back. "Ash... your eyes, and hair, and..."

Ashaya hugged her. "I'll explain later. For now, just go."

Clara shook her head, confused. "Where would I go?"

"Just go!" Ashaya snapped. Clara turned and vanished down the hallway.

Ashaya walked farther down the hall to Sirich's chambers, stopping at his door. She could hear a low groaning. "Siri? Please, we need to speak." The groaning stopped. "I do not know what he did to you, but I am sorry."

Ashaya knocked again. Finally, she opened the door. Sirich stood over a naked woman, blood running from her neck, following a path down her outstretched arm to the floor. Sirich turned to Ashaya, his mouth dripping with blood. Ashaya ran over to the woman, her eyes open and staring unseeing toward the ceiling. She did not move.

"The priestess from the market?" Ashaya heard no heartbeat. "Sirich, why? Why would you?"

"The hunger, it is... insatiable. I did not mean it." He wiped the blood from his mouth and looked at his red-stained hands.

"You have to control it, you have to—"

"Are you an expert in such things already?" Sirich dropped the woman and stormed across the room. "He did this to me. He snuck in that very window and did this. He gave me no choice!" Sirich turned to her. "Are you so innocent? Have you not killed yet with your newfound gift?"

Ashaya looked away from his piercing eyes. Sirich walked around, keeping his eyes on her. "You have. Who are you to judge me? We are no different."

"I killed the man who killed our brother, and others while trying to save our father on the field. We are *very* different."

Sirich walked over to the vanity. "This is all due to that scheming bastard, Promen."

"What do you mean?"

"Promethial was truthful about one thing. Promen schemed against us. Against our father. He wished to murder us."

"Why?"

"I'm sure he was offered this curse... and Wolfpine. His whore of a daughter betrayed us, too."

"How do you know?"

"Come, let us know the full truth." Sirich walked out and Ashaya followed.

She walked briskly behind him as they made their way back to the main hall. She tried to think of what to say to him. *Where will this end?* Ashaya wanted answers, too.

They came to the great hall. Sirich sat in the chair. "Guards, bring the traitor and his daughter."

Two guards walked toward the stairs that led down to the dungeons.

Amari waited at one of the tables. "What will you do, brother?"

"Get to the truth of this."

Amari stood. "From whom?"

"The traitor, Heath Promen."

"How? Do you expect him to just openly admit to treason?"

Ashaya stood beside Sirich. "Blood memories."

Amari rubbed his eyes. "What the hell does that mean?"

Sirich looked over at him. "I saw yours, Amari. I saw your father on his deathbed. I saw you leave him and run away on your boat. I saw you leave Abana there alone to watch him die."

Amari stepped forward. "Enough! You do not know—"

"You took blood from Doc? Your best friend in this world?" Ashaya stepped down from the platform.

Sirich sat quiet for a moment. "I had no choice," he said, his voice almost a whisper.

The guards returned, pushing Heath Promen and Elya in front of them, their hands bound in iron.

Sirich stood. "Come before me."

The guards brought them in front of the chair and forced them to kneel.

"We hold our first court," Sirich said with a slight smile. "Tell the 'ceptor girl to come scribe. Let us make it official. After all, the king is dead."

"Sirich!" Ashaya stepped in front of him. "How dare you?"

"Enough, sister. You and Merek were his favorites. And your mother. You could do no wrong."

"Nonsense." Ashaya was at a loss for more words. She looked over at Amari. "Sirich! Brother, if you have brought charges against this man, fine. But he must stand trial."

"A trial? There is no need for that any longer. Who needs witnesses and evidence when we have memories?" Ashaya looked over at Amari, unsure. Sirich turned back to the man and his daughter, still on their knees. "Tell us, my lord. Tell us your schemes to take Wolfpine. To have us murdered."

"I know nothing of what you speak!" the man spat back.

"And you, fair Elya? You knew of his deception? You came to my chambers and fucked me, urged me to sit with the council, urged me to leave here... Wait." Sirich stood.

"The village. Valton was all..." The girl remained on her knees, silent, never looking up. "Nothing to say?"

"She had nothing to do with this!" the man said defiantly.

"We shall see. Or rather, taste." Sirich stood and moved like the wind behind Promen.

"Sirich, wait!" Ashaya urged.

With one arm, Sirich lifted the man by his collar and bit deep into his neck, blood pouring from the wound.

Ashaya looked over at Amari. He had stood and backed up, drawing his sword. Sirich yanked his head back, ripping the flesh from the man's neck. He leaned back and closed his eyes, the lower half of his face dripping blood. Heath Promen fell to the stone floor, soaking in his own blood. Elya screamed over him, sobbing. The man reached for her one last time. His arm went limp, and he laid back motionless, his eyes open toward the ceiling. The hall echoed with the girl's screams.

"So, it is true. Promethial murdered that village of people to get me there. He promised these two this... curse. Elya came to me and Merek both. Learned our secrets, only to whisper them to her father. They conspired against us all." Sirich looked at Ashaya. "Even you, sister. All of it for Promethial, the god of fire." A sinister grin came to his face. "What gods shall we be, sister?"

Ashaya did not answer but walked over and pulled Elya up from her knees. She stood there, tears dripping from her face. "I'm sorry, Ash. Please. I just—"

Ashaya slapped her across the face. "I trusted you."

Sirich laughed. "Go ahead, Ash. Take your vengeance."

Ashaya glanced back at him, standing in front of the chair, blood dripping from his chin. Elya stood there, her face a mess. Ashaya heard her heart racing. Her veins almost glowed red, pulsating. Tempting. Ashaya could smell her blood, almost taste it. She turned back to Sirich. "No, brother. This is not the way. We are not gods. We are freaks of nature, nothing more."

"Guards, bring him!" Sirich yelled.

Amari spoke up. "Sirich, please. Stop this madness!"

"Oh, brother, why?"

"This is not you, Sirich. Please think of what you do."

Sirich walked over to Amari.

"Leave him alone, Sirich. Of all people, he is family!" Ash put her hand on the hilt of her dagger.

"Do not worry, Doc. I will not hurt you."

Ashaya watched Amari's face as Sirich walked slowly behind him, a hand on his shoulder. She heard Amari's heart racing, sweat running down his face. Amari's eyes shifted, trying to see Sirich behind him, until they met hers.

"Oh, good," Sirich said. "The rest of the family." Sirich walked back to the chair, and Ashaya could see the relief on Amari's face.

Out of the corner of her eye, she saw the guards approaching with a limping man. She heard him cough. Ashaya finally looked away from Amari.

Mitch stood in front of the guards. "Ash, what is all this? What is going on?"

Sirich stepped down to him. "Just a family reunion, as you can see." Sirich motioned toward Heath Promen's body and Elya, still on her knees beside him.

Mitch hobbled toward him. "Father? Father!"

"Oh, no, Mitchel." Sirich grabbed his arm. "You will stay with me."

Ashaya saw his eyes well with tears. "Why?" Mitch mumbled.

"Your father is—*was*—a traitor. So is your whore sister. Are *you*, Mitchel? Did you ride with my sister, plotting her murder as well?"

Mitch stared at his father, lying in a pool of his own blood. "My father was *what*? I do not—"

"You do not *what*, Mitchel? Do not want to admit it? Did you know of this?"

"No," Ashaya said. "Leave him out of this."

Sirich smirked. "Oh, I see what is going on here."

Ashaya looked at Sirich sternly. "He is not his father."

"Are you on my side, or theirs?"

"Leave him alone. Stop this madness. You are consumed by the darkness."

"Who says what is right and wrong? Men? Kings? Gods, perhaps?" Sirich walked around Mitch. "We are so much more, Ash."

Ashaya's lips tightened. "Do not do it."

"Do what? This?" Sirich leaned Mitch's head to the side and opened his mouth, his fangs gleaming. "I can see you are angry with me, sister. Your eyes burn like sapphires."

The world slowed down again. Ashaya was instantly there, pulling Mitch out of the way. She grabbed Sirich, but he resisted, locking onto her arms in a stalemate.

"You always were my shadow. How dare you cross me, little sister?"

Fire ran in her veins again. She freed one arm and hit Sirich in the chest with an open hand, sending him flying backwards into the wall. She looked over and saw Amari moving slowly toward Mitch, his eyes wide, reaching for his sword. She turned back to Sirich, meeting his clenched fist. It landed square on her nose, and she felt the sharp pain, blood droplets almost floating as she flew backwards. Sirich moved like her, though a bit slower. He pushed Amari and grabbed

Mitch off the floor by the back of his neck. He held out his hand and opened it, the claws extending from his fingers like five small daggers.

Ashaya landed and rolled, sliding backwards, but she quickly found her footing. She realized she was near the back of the hall. She focused hard to stop herself and moved forward. Sirich seemed to move slower, his hand creeping toward Mitch. She pulled her bow from her shoulder and reached for her quiver. She felt the warmth of the arrowhead. For a moment, the image of the dream where she had hesitated to release her bowstring came back to her.

It was clear now.

She nocked the arrow and lined her eye along the shaft, the arrowhead gleaming in the well-lit hall. Sirich's hand approached Mitch's neck. She thought of her father lying in the mud. She pulled back on the bowstring. She heard her own heartbeat. She hesitated. "I'm sorry, brother," she whispered.

The silver arrow flew straight and true, burying itself in Sirich's chest. Mitch fell to the floor, his mouth agape, screaming in slow motion. Amari's sword hung above his head, swinging down to where Sirich had stood. Ashaya ran toward him, catching her brother before he fell backwards. The world around her sped up, the screams returning, Amari's sword clanking against the stone behind her. The guards were gone, a few of their spears and helms still clattering on the floor.

She kneeled with Sirich in her arms, his eyes never leaving hers.

"Ash... I... I am..."

"I'm sorry, Siri, I didn't want to hurt you. I..." She looked to where the arrow had struck him. The silver arrowhead had broken when it clanked against the stone floor under him. Only a hole of glowing embers and the putrid smell of burning flesh remained, spreading outward to the rest of him. Tears ran down her face and evaporated where they hit on what remained of his disintegrating body.

He reached up and put his hand on her cheek, rubbing the tears away. She reached for his hand but found nothing except small floating embers. She looked at her hand, pressing her fingers together. Where she had held him, only embers and ash and smoldering bone fragments remained. The sorrow on his face burned into her mind and his voice echoed in her head.

What have I done?

Chapter
Forty-Five

Amari

Amari looked at Ashaya as he collapsed to the floor, catching his breath. Mitch held his wound, watching Ashaya with a blank stare.

Amari looked down and said nothing. For a time, the only sounds heard were the crackle of flames throughout the hall and Ash's whimpers, still on her knees where Sirich had lain.

Ashaya stood, her face expressionless, and walked toward the back of the hall. Amari leaned his head back and closed his eyes.

He heard the doors open at the back of the hall. Val entered and approached Ashaya. "I'm sorry, Ash."

Ash almost collapsed in her arms. Val held her like a mother would. She walked Ash to one of the tables.

"Oh, a family reunion," came a familiar voice from the doorway.

Promethial walked in, smiling until he saw Val's vicious expression as she turned to him.

"My queen, I—"

"Enough! Enough of your games, Promethial. Where is he?"

He kneeled before her. "*You* are my queen-mother, as always."

Amari did not even see her move. Val seemed to simply appear in front of Promethial from across the hall. Only a cloudy, dark-purple mist dissipated in her wake. Promethial hit her in the face, her head snapping sideways a tiny bit before she looked back at him, smiling.

She backhanded him, throwing him away, shattering the stone column. Before he landed, Val stood where he would fall. She held him by the throat and pulled his arm to her mouth, biting deep. He tried to struggle, but he could not escape her grasp. Amari watched, still seeing Sirich's face in his mind.

Val leaned her head back and closed her eyes. "Your blood never lies. I do not know why you play these games, but I know I made a mistake."

She threw him to the floor. "My queen," Promethial managed, gasping for air. "I am sorry. I have failed you. I—"

"No, I have failed *you*, by giving you a second chance at life after your unfortunate incident all those centuries ago."

She reached down with one hand and picked him up by his jaw.

"Wait!" Gaziael entered through the back of the hall. Amari nodded to her, and she returned a slight smile.

Val looked to her. "Gazi, it is good that you are here. We have a problem."

"So I hear, but I will gladly take care of the one you hold."

"So be it." Val threw him at Gazi's feet.

Promethial grabbed for his jaw as if to adjust it. He stood and faced the woman. "What will you do? You are no match for me. I am your elder by hundreds of years."

"Who told you that?" she asked.

His eyes narrowed, and his smile faded. Promethial looked over at Val. Amari noticed her slight grin.

"But I was the third," Promethial said uncertainly. "Only Lucian and Valkarial herself..." Promethial's eyes widened in realization and denial.

He ran, but Gaziael cut him off. They moved from spot to spot, a blur of black and brown. He pulled a dagger and plunged it toward her neck. She dodged and knocked it out of his hand. Her closed fist connected with his jaw, and he fell backwards, sliding on the coarse stone. She followed him, but as she reached down, he drove his dagger deep into her stomach.

Gaziael staggered back. She looked down, pulled the dagger, flipped it in her hand, and waited. Promethial moved in a blur but stopped quickly. Amari never saw Gaziael throw the blade, but he saw the dagger's handle sticking out from Promethial's chest. Gaziael dashed around the room, leaving what looked to be faint purple shadows in her wake.

Amari felt the breeze as she passed him, as well as a slight nudge. As he caught up to the barely visible blur, she stopped in front of Promethial, still holding his wound. All Amari heard was a quick whoosh, and she stood in front of Promethial holding a sword.

Promethial's eyes were wide, and blood ran from his mouth. His head fell from his shoulders as his body dropped straight down. Amari looked down; his sword was missing from the scabbard.

Silence filled the hall for a time. "Such a shame," Val finally said. "He was a good man once." Amari looked at Ashaya. She and Mitch had not moved.

Gaziael walked over and handed the sword back to Amari. He took it, Promethial's blood still running down the blade, steaming.

Amari slid the sword back in place. "Will he heal from—"

"No," Val answered. "Not from that."

Ashaya stood. "So, what did he... I mean... What did his blood say?"

Val turned. "Lucian is coming. It will take a few days, maybe less."

"Why? He can move like you, correct?" Amari asked.

"But you can easily stop him," Ashaya added.

"Him alone, yes, but he has turned a small army. He is only waiting on them to go through the change. Promethial was to open the gates for him. He was to tell Sirich that he was here to help him. To join his cause."

Ashaya paced back and forth. "What do we do?"

"We fight," Mitch chimed in. He had not spoken since seeing his father's corpse.

"You are in no shape to fight, Mitch," said Ashaya.

"You are already dying." Val turned to him. "I can smell the infection in your blood."

Mitch looked down. His bandage was still stained red in the center. Amari walked over to check. "She is right. You need to get to a 'ceptor." Amari turned back to them. "How do we fight against others like you?"

"You don't," Val replied.

"We have to try." Ashaya walked to the stairwell at the front of the hall. "Nivara!" she yelled into the stairwell. "Come quickly!"

Amari helped Mitch over to a table.

The girl rushed into the room. "Yes, my lady, what is it?"

"Send out corvids to all the local houses. Call all the banners that can get here within a day."

"All of them, my lady?"

"Yes. Death marches our way."

Chapter Forty-Six

Ashaya

Val walked around William's chamber. Ashaya watched her rummage through the shelves and stacks of paper on his desk. Val smiled and pulled a piece of paper from a drawer.

"What is it?" Ashaya asked.

"A note I left for your father. I could not bear to face him."

"You loved him?"

"Very much. I had loved in the past and swore to never do it again. It was not fair to them. Or to me." Val sat in his chair. "But I came through here when I heard there was a new king, and I saw William. A gorgeous man, he was. Tall. A bright smile, but an even brighter wit." She took a deep breath as she ran her fingers over the paper. "I walked the yards of Wolfpine as I had in the past, in the guise of a commoner. He had recently lost his wife, so I thought it best not to pursue him. As fate would have it, he saw me coming through the gates. Only a moment sooner or later, and none of this would have come to be."

"I miss him," Ashaya said. The look on his face on the battlefield still haunted her.

"Ash, *you* must continue what he started."

"Me?"

"Yes, you are the only one who can." Val paused. "I am sorry about your brother. It took courage to do what you did. I wish Promethial had not gotten to him. He was a good man."

"Then we must kill Lucian and his minions."

Val leaned forward. "These people cannot fight our kind. They will all be slaughtered. Besides, there will always be another Lucian, or another Promethial. I tried to only pick those I thought worthy, but who was I to choose? Power, real power, eventually corrupts us all."

"I will not allow the death of my father and siblings to be for naught." Ashaya sat on the edge of her father's desk. "So, what then? Shall we just kneel to him?"

"No, but I cannot let it come to this unholy war. There are too many now. The covenant was broken. He will attack tomorrow night. By then, his followers will have turned." Val stood and walked to the doors. "Come, it is almost dawn."

They walked from William's quarters down the hallway and stopped in front of the old queen's quarters.

"This was my favorite place during my time here." Val put her hand on the door. "It was built over a thousand years ago by Marcus Blacksun the Fourth. Your great-great... however many grandfathers ago."

"My father used to bring me here when I was little, when I would ask about you," Ash said. Val smiled and opened the old double doors. Ashaya followed her in and looked around. "He said he never changed anything."

Ashaya ran her hand down the drapes while Val picked up an unfinished fabric doll from the vanity and smiled. "This was to be for you. I used to make them when I was a girl, except they were only sticks back then." She walked around the room, smiling. "Exactly how I remember it. I tried to be a queen again. To be normal. It was hard to hide what I was. I never had the chance to ride with your father during the day, always finding an excuse to go outside at night. I am sure it wasn't easy for him either."

Val walked to the balcony doors and pulled them open. Ashaya walked out with her, and they both put their hands on the railing. Ashaya looked down at the old river below. She could hear the trickle of water as if she stood next to it. The sky was a dark purple, getting lighter by the moment. Fireflies blinked in the darkness below, leafhoppers sang their song. She looked over at Val, standing quietly.

"I would stand out here every night and have to run back in before dawn. No light other than firelight ever lit this room while I was here."

"You better get inside. The sun is rising." Ashaya turned to walk back in.

"Not this time." Val stood staring into the distance.

"What do you mean? Come inside."

"I haven't watched a sunrise in over two thousand years. I think it is time I saw one."

"What are you saying? You know what happens if you—"

"This cycle will never end, Ashaya. I could kill Lucian easily, but some of his minions will undoubtably turn more. Even Thade and I could not keep up. We are the past, Ashaya. You are the future."

"You cannot just abandon me. I have lost everything! You show up and come to Wolfpine only to—"

"I'm tired, Ashaya, and I will not let Aahsgoth turn to ruins. It is time."

"I do not understand."

"It is the only way. I can undo all of this, but only me."

"How do you know this?"

"It has happened before. Not all of the thirteen remain. When some of the others perished, anyone they turned was destroyed." Val pointed down to the courtyard below. Ashaya walked back over and looked. Thade, Gaziael, and a red-headed woman stood in the yard below looking up to them.

"Who is the red-headed woman?" Ashaya asked.

Val smiled. "Aethial. Promethial killed her sister, Serphial, and her clan died with her." Ashaya stared down to them without responding. "Aethial has helped the preceptors of Ashbourne discover your true history. It will be up to you, Ash, whether to share it or not."

Val looked down to them once again and nodded. They all turned and walked away into the darkness. "This is why I came back here. This was a special place for me. I knew this day would come, and I welcome it." She put her hand on Ashaya's.

"What will happen to me?"

"You were born this way, as Thade and I were. There is nothing to undo." Val looked at the brighter sky and turned to Ashaya, taking Ash's hands in hers. "Now go. Finish what your father started. Besides, Thade will be here for you."

"You planned this? I cannot do it alone. I don't even know who I am, *what* I am."

"You are a dragon, Ashaya. Follow your heart and do

what is right. Everything you need to know is in you, in your blood. Now go."

Ashaya stood quietly for a moment. "No. I will stay with you."

"You know what the sun will do to me. It will not be... pretty."

"I will not leave you." Ashaya hugged her, tears rolling down her cheeks. Val held her and stroked the back of her head.

"I do apologize, Ash. This was all thrust upon your shoulders. I do love you. I always have."

Val let go and turned toward the east. The sky was turning a light purple, and yellow lined the horizon. Ashaya watched her close her eyes for a moment. Ashaya stood beside her and reached for her hand.

Val looked over at her and smiled, then turned her gaze back toward the sky. Ashaya watched the sunrise with a new perspective, studying the intricacies of its beauty while also watching her mother.

The sky lightened. Feathered clouds were now highlighted across the vista. Sunrays trickled through the distant trees. The purple became a light blue and a bright yellow, bleeding over the tree line as shadows crawled across the yard below. Ashaya turned to her mother. A single tear rolled down Val's cheek before it evaporated in the light upon her face.

"Beautiful," she said in a whisper.

The sun reflected in Val's blue eyes for a fleeting moment before her body started to disintegrate. The sun shone brightly, wrapping the queen's tower in light. Ash felt the warmth of her mother's hand grow hotter. Her body crumbled to embers, her skin turned grey then faded to ash as it floated away in the breeze. Ashaya looked down. Where her mother's hand had been, only grey dust remained. Ashaya rubbed her fingers together, remembering that Val had never lost her smile.

Goodbye.

Ashaya stood alone on the balcony for some time. She leaned on the railing, tears welling in her eyes. She stood in the light, the sun warming her face. Birds whistled in the distance, and the sounds of a regular day started to fill the courtyards below. In the distance, she heard the lone howling of a wolf.

Thade.

The hint of a smile came to her face knowing that she would not be alone.

A New Day

Ashaya

Ashaya stood in her quarters. After washing her face, she looked down at the maroon-red velvet dress with a matching corset Clara had once again laid out for her. Gold and blue floral trim wrapped around the neck and upper sleeves. She glanced over at her usual riding leathers, still in a bundle where she had thrown them last night.

A smile came to her face.

It had been a little over a moon since Ashaya had called for the council. She walked around her father's old stone chair, rubbing her hand over the smooth carved lotus. Her dress swept the floor behind her. She turned to all the lords and ladies that stood behind her. Twelve banners now hung in the great hall, six on each side. The thirteenth was a new banner that hung behind her. In the center, the Blacksun sigil, surrounded by twelve smaller versions of the others.

The lords and ladies all talked amongst themselves and exchanged pleasantries. Ashaya cleared her throat and silence fell across the hall. "My lords and ladies. Thank you all for coming back to Wolfpine. We have a few new members whom I would like to welcome."

Ashaya stepped down and sat at the long table, the others following suit. "Welcome, Lord Marcus Lucian of Castle Lochlan."

Marcus stood and bowed.

"Also, please welcome a good friend to my family: Amari Docksider, originally of Ethorya. Since we are learning—or I should say, *relearning*—our history, it has come to light that his late father was of the original Gazi bloodline of Ethorya and would have been the rightful king in a different time. I asked Amari, and the Ethoryan royal family agreed that he should represent Ethorya on this council. I am pleased that he has accepted."

Amari stood and raised his hand, nodding to the others. "I am happy to be here, my lords and ladies."

Ashaya smiled at her old friend. "In light of the recent death of Galen, Master Preceptor of Ashbourne, please welcome his son, Theodor Serwyn. He will take Galen's place here at Wolfpine and represent Ashbourne and the original kingdom of Serwyn, now considered part of Alarya."

Theodor stood up and smiled at the others. "Thank you, Lady Ashaya."

Ashaya looked over at the two young women standing off to the side, both scribing. "I would like to recognize Galen's apprentice, Nivara, as well as her sister, Ridley Aethon. They are the daughters of the overlord of the Order of Preceptors. They will both be helping Theodor here in Wolfpine and keeping this council on track. I have no doubt they will be granted the rank of Master of the Order once they complete their studies and if they so choose. Thank you, my ladies."

The other members clapped for the girls, who looked at one another and smiled.

"That leaves only one seat remaining. Heath Promen, who sat on this council, will be replaced by his son Mitchel, once he has fully healed."

"My lady." One of the lords stood. "The son of a traitor?"

"He is not his father. Treachery is not passed down through blood, my lord."

"Yes, my lady." The man took his seat.

Ashaya took a deep breath. "My lords, this will not be easy. We have much to learn and unlearn. As we discover our true history out of the vaults in Ashbourne, we can reevaluate as needed. Please, my lords, take the night and enjoy your stay here. We shall start on the morrow, with much to do."

Amari stood and walked over to her. "Ash, your father would be proud."

"Thank you, Doc. Your father would be, as well."

Amari turned to the others. "I urge you all to put Aahsgoth first. If you do, there is nothing we cannot accomplish." The others stood and clapped.

Ashaya nodded to the council before her and turned, walking toward the stairwell at the front of the hall.

Ashaya knocked on the door of Galen's old chambers.

"Come!" Mitch called through the door.

She walked in. Mitch sat on the edge of his feather bed.

"You look much better already. Not so pale as before."

"I drank it, as you said. I didn't have much choice."

Ashaya looked on the nightstand. The pewter cup she had filled stood empty, only a few crimson droplets remaining. She looked back to him and smiled.

"So how did you take it? Warm or cold?"

ACKNOWLEDGMENTS

Writing a book starts as a daunting task. As you creep ever so slowly toward a bigger pile of words, they become paragraphs, and those paragraphs become chapters. From there, it gets easier to notice the proverbial light at the end of the tunnel. This has been over a two-year journey, and although for the most part, I sat alone in the dark of night hacking away at my keyboard, this book is the result of many others and their efforts to both directly and indirectly push me. Here, I would like to take the opportunity to thank them.

First, I would like to thank my daughter, Kamdyn. Although I have become a bit older and a lot more cynical, you still push me to set an example. Since you came into my life, you have driven me to be a better person. From the long nights of rocking you back to sleep, to being your personal coach and catcher as you grew. Once you were grown up, I felt as though I had lost my purpose in life. I have learned that I do not have to change diapers or show you how to throw a rise ball to still help you grow. I hope this testament to determination and sacrifice can be an example to you and others that everything is a choice. I love you more than you will ever know.

To my long-time friend and critique partner, James Wright. Just hearing your words of encouragement and answering the questions you had during those many late-night conversations drove me to continue. At points, I almost let the demons talk me out of finishing this damn thing. I could always hear the genuine excitement in your voice, and I know that if you are remotely excited by anything fantasy, I might be on to something. A genuine thank you for being one of the few to really see what a smattering of paragraphs could become. Keep dreaming, my friend.

I want to thank my parents next. I know that sometimes you did not agree with my choices, but I hope that you both can at least understand. To my mom—you are my rock. You are the very definition of strength, and to this day, I feel better just hearing your voice. Your example is what keeps me going through the dark times. I did not take the normal path after all, but that seed was planted a long time ago. Movies made me dream, and once I started dreaming, the rest is history. To my dad—technically this is all your fault ;) You took me to see that galaxy far, far away in 1977, and I never came back. I did not choose the safe route, but the core values and decency that you both instilled in me allowed me to remain grounded and to navigate an uncertain world. Once I became a parent, I gained a greater appreciation for your sacrifices, and I am eternally grateful. I can only hope that you are both proud.

To my small dysfunctional family, I thank all of you. Specifically, my cousins Chad and Eric, whom I consider my brothers in every way. We have always been a trio of trouble, and I am proud to have been the provocateur in most cases. I sincerely appreciate the support through this self-employment roller coaster when most just told me to "get a real job." To Chad specifically, I am proud that you have never—and *will never*—beat me in basketball. I will have to literally die before that happens, but you still better bring your A-game. To Eric, I am proud to say I can still outdraw you even after years of being out of practice. But you are pretty damn good for a lefty. ;) On a serious note, competition is a wonderful thing, and it brings out the best from all of us. I hope I have inspired both of you in some way over the years, as you have done for me.

I also want to take the time to thank my extended virtual family over the last six years (at the time of this printing). YouTube, specifically my channel SmokeScreen, has changed my life. I have been honored to help grow and be a part of a community of fantasy lovers from all backgrounds. Thank you to all who have watched videos, chatted in live streams, commented, liked, and subscribed. It means the world to me. You all allowed me to work toward a dream. Thank you to my friend Val (Valu) Carias—you have kept me partially sane for the past six years. I appreciate you being my online partner in many ways and being there for me both personally and professionally. You always encouraged me and cheered this project on. A special thanks to my friend Ertaç Altınöz for the amazing artwork that helped bring Aahsgoth to life.

Specifically, thank you to my patrons on Patreon. You all have given your own hard-earned money to support this venture, and you've literally kept food on my table at times. I have made some lifelong friends through this project, and I love every one of you. A special thanks to Corey "Doc" Clendenen for the long conversations and allowing me to vent my frustrations. (Also, for being my teammate and still-undefeated cornhole co-champion!) A special thank you to the DC Diva, Carole Brown, for the advice, suggestions, and being my coordinator over the years (and for the awesome food when you visited). Thank you to Dee Brown for the moral support, well wishes, and the huge financial donations over the years that have at times kept this ship afloat. I know your accountant hates me. ;)

A special thanks to my "Hands of the King" and "Small Council" for joining calls and listening to me ramble. Thank you for making suggestions and sticking with me when everything went to hell. This includes Lala Gig, Lo Horton, Desert Dragon, Mark Clark, Bryan P. Austin, Aaron Bridgers, Legal Jedi, Hoonjive (and Mr. Shoon), Lauren Wagstaff, Peach, Monica Nakamuru, Neph, my brother from another mother, Mizuma, and so many others in the past. Thank you to Carrie C. for always emailing me those writing contests, her constant advice, and sharing her world with me.

A special thank you to all of my Patreon supporters:

Joshua Kluender	Sneaky McCheese
Kyle Marlow	Michele Dominguez
Voodoo Darlin	Linda Guerrero
Mikael Karlsson	Kieran Geoghegan
Wade Davey	Lord Kev
Jessica Shook	Craig Boone
Kellie W.	John Witt
Cesar E. Lopez El II	Richard Hough
Justin Forrest	Melissa Blackwood
Nicole Wardin	Terry Tiemann
Haily	Alan Garcia
Barry Sellers	Slope
Tina Bojan	Karen Gates
Jack Wimberly	Sharon Pollitt
Zara Sawi	Elisa Banks
Nathaly Sanchez	Ellen
Patti Wicksteed	Marisa V.
Cornelius Contreras	Living My Rhapsody
Shelia Buchanan	Angie Delehanty
Mark Clark	Capthegoat
Amira Hamzar	Linda Blowey
Fractured Empiricist	Felichia

Thomas-McCormick
Nancy Tockstein
Helen Ledwith
SensibleCPA
Omar Ortega
Michael Smith
Lisa Phillips
Nick Capuano
Karen Richmond
Jared Caldwell
John Kelly
Karen Wennerlind
Meemee Keykat
Shirley Flagler
Nicole Stewart
Tonya Gonzalez
Angel
Pre4scifi
Jovita Loeri
House Vinyl

Skolvikings73
Brooke Geer Person
Oliver Witt
Grace-Keira
Lori Claire
Vicki Jack
James Greene
Josh Friend
BRIC23
Matt Shields
Bolo7678
Brock Thaemlitz
Jessy C.
Lydia Quinn
Goska Biczysko
The Sennett
Amanda Bohn
KSoze1024
Michele Everly

And to all former supporters, thank you as well.

And finally, a thank you to the many authors out there who have inspired me, and not just the famous ones. The YouTubers, indie authors, vloggers, etc. I have learned so much from everyone who has put themselves out there to be criticized, and I could not have done this without you. Any of you.

I would be remiss if I did not thank Diane Callahan from Quotidian Writer for the advice and both Natalia Leigh and Meredith Allison from Enchanted Ink Publishing as well. You all gave me my invaluable first taste of the indie process.

COMING SOON

"The wolves, they keep us enlightened."
"The wolves?"
"Thade and his kind, but that is a story for another time."
-Gaziael to Amari, Chapter 39 of *The Crimson Gods*

The Crimson Gods Book 2 TBA

Thade TBA

The Crimson Gods: Origins TBA

Riddick Lost His Ball (A Children's Book)
Illustrated by Eric Melton TBA

Visit https://chrismchristian.com/newsletter for updates!

NOTE FROM THE AUTHOR

Thank you so much for reading *The Crimson Gods*! There is much more to come in Aahsgoth.

I would really appreciate it if you could:

Review this book. Reviews, even if brief, are a huge help to authors. If you enjoyed this story and do not mind sharing your opinion, please consider leaving a review on Amazon and Goodreads.

Share this book. When you share this book on social media, more people will discover this story. Word of mouth is the best tool for a new author.

Connect with me. I would love to hear from you! Subscribe to my YouTube channel at https://youtube.com/smokescreenvids1 and join me for live streams, writing and publishing advice, and more. Also visit my website at https://chrismchristian.com to subscribe to my latest updates and find my links to social media.

Thank you in advance!
~Chris

Chris Christian was born and raised in a small town in the piedmont of North Carolina. He left the information technology industry to become a full-time content creator, podcaster and author, who co-authored the nonfiction book The Thrones Effect: How HBO's Game of Thrones Conquered Pop Culture. Chris is a single father and when he isn't spending time with friends and family, you can almost always find him outdoors with his best buddy, Riddick the German Shepherd dog.

CPSIA information can be obtained
at www.ICGtesting.com
Printed in the USA
BVHW071255181021
619201BV00007B/361